Return of the High Fae

A Vegas Fae story

By

Tom Keller

Copyright

The moral right of the author has been asserted. No part of this publication may be reproduced, stored in a retrieval system, or transmitted, in any form or by any means, without the prior permission in writing of the publisher, nor be otherwise circulated in any form of binding or cover other than that in which it is published and without a similar condition including this condition being imposed on the subsequent purchaser.

This book is a work of fiction. Names, characters, places and incidents are either products of the author's imagination or used fictitiously. Any resemblance to actual events, locales, or persons, living or dead, is entirely coincidental.

First Print Edition

Acknowledgements

I'd like to thank everyone that helped make this book possible, especially my incredible wife, Karen, without her support this book would never have been written.

I doubt any project is ever completed without help and support from a lot of folks, but as always, a few names stand out in the crowd; Paula Ludwig, my most vocal test reader, my best friend Ray Flynn, for his comments and expertise, and Al Tobin, who pushed me to start writing again.

Special thanks to Abby Goldman and Greg George for help with editing, Meg Varhalmi, my critique partner, and Cara Michaels for help in writing the short description.

Cover Design by Cory Clubb

http://www.coryclubb.com

Dedication

In memory of Maria Hofstetter
1895 – 1985

Chapter 1

I really hate process serving, it pays lousy and people tend to get all righteous and indignant when you lay papers on them. Like it's my fault they got themselves involved in some legal mess. But a local lawyer who had referred me a lot of business asked me to do this one, so I took the job.

I knew the target, an old time casino boss by the name of Carmine Pontedra. Several others had tried but he'd slipped by them each time. But I had something they didn't, access to the private lot at the Neptune where he parked. You needed an entry card and code, something not easy to get, but I still had a few contacts from my police days.

I'd come in from the rear, off of Dean Martin Drive. The Neptune's Landing is a posh hotel and casino located just off the center strip. From the front, it's a beautiful property, with its statue of King Neptune holding his trident in the middle of the dancing fountains in a saltwater lagoon. His arm is outstretched, his webbed hand beckoning all to come inside.

Like most hotels, however, the rear is all parking lots and delivery bays. It takes a lot of products and people to keep a big property like this going. Vegas is like a magic show. The audience sees the end performance but all the real work happens behind the curtain.

I waded through the maze of structures and entrance ways and accessed the executive level parking garage. I lucked out and found a spot just across the bay from his Mercedes. My car was hidden nicely behind one of the hotel's executive limos. Now it was a waiting game. It was getting close to 8:00 p.m. I knew he worked the day shift but I also knew he seldom left the property before this time of night. Then I saw the elevator doors open.

I slipped out of my car and stood in the shadows by a pillar, hoping it would be Carmine. Instead it was Eddy Milagre who came out. Damn! Milagre was Carmine's boss and part owner of the place. He'd gotten his start running numbers for the mob and worked his way up the ladder before he became legitimate when corporations took over the Vegas scene. I didn't think he knew who I was and I wanted to keep it that way. I eased around the pillar and hugged the shadows as I watched Milagre walk toward his car. Suddenly he stopped and looked around. I thought for sure he'd seen me, and then it happened.

Out of nowhere three men appeared and grabbed him. He started to fight back but these guys were armed. I wasn't sure what they were carrying but I could see them pointing something at him. At first I thought they might be billy clubs or maybe some kind of short baton. When I heard the crackling sound, I figured they were some kind of modified stun gun or cattle prod. I saw a flash of blue light and he was down.

I drew my gun as soon as I heard the sound and jumped from behind the pillar. Before I knew what I was doing I reverted back to my police days yelling, "Freeze, drop your weapons!"

The guy who had first shocked Milagre stood up and turned toward me, firing. I didn't know what the hell he was carrying but it damn sure wasn't a stun gun.

I was a good twenty feet away when blue lightning struck me. As it hit me I felt the electricity, or whatever it was, surge through me. What the hell, since when do bad guys carry lasers? Ignoring the pain I fired back and he dropped like a stone. Then I grimaced; I had expected some type of electrical shock feeling. Instead, it felt like someone was trying to claw their way through me. I took a deep breath to block out the pain and then it suddenly stopped.

Whatever it was hadn't been enough to kill me or knock me out like it had Milagre, but it did make me drop to one knee. Based on how fast Milagre had gone down I figured the shooter had just grazed me but it still hurt like hell. I didn't let down my guard. I ducked behind a parked car and peeked over the hood.

The second guy had started to move his weapon towards me as I had taken cover. After the first near miss, and the pain, I knew these things could probably kill me so I wasn't going to give this one a chance to do better than the other guy. I popped up and fired. I watched him go down as my bullet hit his chest.

I started to run parallel to his direction to get to better cover when I saw the third guy move to square off with me. He was holding his weapon and just as I thought he was going to take the shot he suddenly turned and ran around the parked cars and disappeared. I would have gone after him but not knowing how bad Milagre was injured I stopped to render aid.

When I knelt down I was relieved to see he was still breathing. I rose and quickly checked the two shooters. My shots had been center of mass and these two weren't getting up again. Out of instinct I knocked the rods away from their hands. I scanned the area in case the third guy decided to come back.

The next thing I knew the elevator doors opened and the posse arrived.

Five black clad figures carrying M-4s and other weapons surrounded me as two others went to check on Milagre. I knew the drill. I put my gun down on the ground and my hands behind my head. There was no way I was going to argue with military grade weapons. Two of them cuffed me and yanked me up, not too gently I might add. I started to yell out that there was still a third guy out there. I never finished.

I felt a blow to the back of the head and my vision started to fade. Then I heard someone's voice saying, "No, he isn't one of them." Then the blackness seemed to swirl around me and I didn't hear anything at all.

When I woke up I tried to determine where I was. The last thing I remembered was being hit in the back of the head. Damn, it still hurt. I opened my eyes slowly and tried to compose myself. I was half afraid I'd been tied to a chair like a scene out of a bad movie; I mean, this is Vegas. But instead, my hands were free and I was on a couch. I knew there were people around but I couldn't tell who they were. It might have been because I was squinting.

It was a nice office, there were pictures on the wall and the place had an expensive look. I started to sit up but I was still groggy. At least I could move, even if it did hurt like hell. I took the pain as a good sign, I was still alive. I pushed myself up into a sitting position and leaned over and rested my head in my hands. "I have the mother of all headaches," I exclaimed." Would someone please tell me what the hell is going on?"

"Glad you're still with us," I heard a voice say. I felt a glass being pushed into my hands. I took a sip of what turned out to be ice water and looked around the rest of the room wondering how long I'd been out.

Then I heard the voice again. "Now, please tell me what you are."

My eyes rested on none other than Eddy Milagre. For someone who I thought had been gravely wounded, he looked damned good. There were two other people in the room. One was a lady I'd never seen before and the other had to be one of the guys who had knocked me out. Dressed in black camo, he was a tall blonde man with a Special Forces physique and that military air about him. "I'm Robert Hoskins, a P.I. I'm also an ex-cop. I was working a case."

Milagre leaned back against what I assumed was his desk. A mix of exotic woods, it looked expensive. The lady and the other guy didn't move.

Taking a good look at him I saw that he had an abrasion on his face and his eyes were red. But he still looked better than he had when I'd last seen him lying on the floor of the parking garage.

"Look, kid," he continued, "I appreciate you saving my ass back there but I need to know what you are." He stared at me as if he expected me to say something profound.

I had no idea what he wanted to hear. Calling me kid was something I hadn't heard in a while either. I was pushing fifty, but then again, I knew he was older than I was. He'd made a name for himself when I was still in high school. I still remembered my grandmother talking about the way he ran his casinos. Hell, even with the puffy eye and scratches on his face I could see the power the man commanded. Eddy Milagre wasn't just old Vegas, he personified it.

"Mr. Milagre, I was waiting to serve a subpoena on Carmine Pontedra when you came out of the elevator. Before I knew what was happening those three guys jumped you. I figured they were going to kill you when you went down, so I did what I had to do. I'm sorry the last guy got away but I was more worried about you at the time. They had some kind of weird weapons so when the first one fired at me I responded as I'd been trained, same with the second guy. Your SWAT guys got there after that and, well, here we are." I took a deep breath. "I know those two are dead. Where are the police? Where's my gun?"

"That's all you want to say?" Milagre asked dubiously, looking down at me from the desk.

"What else is there, Mr. Milagre?" I caught myself before I sounded angry. This was one man who I probably didn't want to piss off. What was I missing here? "I'm glad you're alright, even if it does surprise me a bit. To be honest, I thought you were in worse shape than you seem to be. So are the cops coming, or what?" I was starting to get a little worried. I mean, come on, I was sitting here chatting with an old Vegas mob boss and I had just shot two people, even if it was in his defense.

He looked like he didn't believe a thing I had just said and then he shrugged. "Ok, Mr. Hoskins, I'm being a terrible host. Let me offer you something stronger than what you have there. You did just save my life after all." He stood up and walked over to the bar behind the desk and opened a cabinet. "What will it be?"

"Tequila," I said, setting down the glass of water on the table in front of me. "Anejo if you have it," I chuckled, trying not to act like I was worried.

"Tequila it is then," he said, removing a bottle from the cabinet.

I watched him pour what looked to be at least a triple of Herradura Suprema into a tumbler. No shot glass for me. It was good liquor, too, around $300.00 a bottle at any liquor store, if you could find it. He walked over to me and set the glass down.

"Thank you, sir," I said, taking a drink.

"Let's take a minute here, shall we? There's someone I'd like you to meet," he said, turning to the lady who was still standing next to the desk. "Please bring Meredith down; I'd like her to tend to our guest."

The woman looked like he'd just asked her to jump out the window. "Meredith? Yes sir, but she may be busy."

Milagre cut her off. "Just get her," he barked.

She spun around and left the room.

I was starting to get concerned. How bad could this Meredith be? I looked over at the SWAT guy to gauge his reaction but he was a blank. Since my options were limited I kept my mouth shut. I decided to enjoy my tequila and let things play out.

Milagre turned to the SWAT guy. "Siegfried, where is our guest's weapon?"

Now I was a guest. I wondered what that meant.

"The tech unit has it sir. Do you wish me to see if they are finished?" the man asked. His accent was Swiss, or maybe Norwegian. This was starting to feel like a bad movie. Tech guys, since when do casinos have a CSI unit, or for that matter, a SWAT team?"

"Yes, Mr. Hoskins and I will be fine until you return," he said as he waved an arm at Siegfried, dismissing him.

Siegfried replied with a "Yes sir," and then turned and left the room.

It was just me and Eddy Milagre now.

"So, Mr. Hoskins, things must be a little confusing right now. Let me have one of my girls look at you and then we'll see if we can get things straightened out." He walked back to the bar and poured himself some cognac. Then he walked around his desk and eased into the oversized leather chair.

"Sure," I answered, taking a few sips of tequila. "Very smooth," I said as I put my glass down.

I needed a few seconds to compose myself. I had to think of this from both a legal and a "cover my ass" standpoint. I'd shot two people while trespassing at a major hotel and casino. Sure, it was in defense of someone's life, or at least I think it was. I was in a guy's office that used to run with the mob and had access to the guys in black. They not only have bigger guns than me, but they have my gun. To top it off, I didn't think anyone had called the cops. Not my best day if I say so myself.

"So, Mr. Milagre, who are the guys in black, are they the hotel's?"

"Siegfried and his men are part of my security team. They also serve as my bodyguards when necessary," Milagre explained, "and before you ask, they answer only to me."

"I see," I replied, catching the subtle hint. I figured it was time to lay some cards of my own on the table. If I was in trouble there were very few options. "So where do we stand, Mr. Milagre? You and me, do we have a problem?"

"A problem?" Milagre answered with a chuckle. "Mr. Hoskins, you saved my life back there. So if you mean our little incident in the parking lot, then no, we don't have a problem where that's concerned," he replied, putting down his cup and leaning toward me. "What we do have a problem with is what you are."

I looked up at him blankly. "I told you, sir, I'm a P.I. ...."

He put his hand up. "Stop, stop, that's not what I'm talking about, I just can't figure out why you are hiding..."

I cut him off in mid-sentence. "Okay, maybe I'm just dense. I don't understand your question." He continued to look at me skeptically, so I asked, "What do you think I am?"

He stood up from the chair and walked around the desk but before he could get around there was a knock at the door.

The door opened and a stylishly dressed woman in a dark pant suit and white blouse entered the room. Her hair was completely gray yet it shined like silver. I thought she might be Milagre's mother or aunt, as there was a slight resemblance, but that was silly, she'd have to be over 100 years old.

"Meredith, my dear, thank you for coming," he said, taking her hand. "You have been informed of what has transpired?"

Informed? Transpired? They were a little too formal for my taste, especially since two people were dead. Granted, they were bad guys, but they made it sound like it was a regular occurrence for them.

"I have already been working on it," she answered, closing the door and walking over to him "I was with Siegfried's people when I was asked to come down." She gave Milagre a hug and then turned toward me. "So this is the gentleman who came to your rescue. I must thank you. Edward is very special to me. I would have been very upset if he'd been hurt," she proclaimed, matter-of-factly.

Just doing my duty, ma'am, I thought to myself as I stood up to shake her hand. She gave me a hug instead. "My pleasure, ma'am, I was just lucky to be there."

"Please sit young man. I am sure you are still tired from the incident," she said in a pleasant voice as we sat down on the couch. "Edward, I am guessing that you feel there is still something missing and you'd like me to talk to our new friend?"

Milagre went back over to his chair and also sat down. "Please," he agreed, with a wave of his hand toward us. "We were just getting ready to have that discussion."

I thought to myself that the office must have been bugged because Meredith obviously knew beforehand what Milagre had wanted. Well, at least I had graduated from a guest to a friend. I think that was a good thing.

She turned to me and took my hands in hers. "Mr. Hoskins, will you humor me a moment?"

"Umm, ok, sure, why not." I turned towards her as she grasped my hands. This was not exactly what I had expected.

"Edward, I sense no deception, mmm, interesting." She looked at Milagre. "I must ask you not to interfere."

Well, that was a weird thing to say. What the hell was going on? Maybe I was still unconscious and this was just a dream.

"Mr. Hoskins is it? May I call you by your first name?"

I nodded my head. "Sure, it's Robert." This was surreal. I'd gone from being a trespasser and knocked out, to a guest, and now we were friends on a first name basis.

"Robert it is then, thank you. Tell me, Robert, do you believe in the supernatural world?"

"Supernatural? Like Witches and Vampires or what are you talking about?" That one came out of left field, just where was this going?

"Yes, and myths," she answered.

At this point I figured I was dreaming or maybe these folks were just plain loony. But Eddy Milagre was real and had a lot of juice in town. Still, I couldn't resist. "Myths, like in Faeries? Well, my grandmother told me Faeries were real and she would never lie," I answered with a laugh. Ok, so I was being a little sarcastic, but things were definitely not right.

"Ahem, yes, humor," Meredith rebuked gently. "What if she was telling you the truth after all? What if such things do exist? What would you think then?"

"To be honest, I'd probably think I was still out of it on this couch. But what are you saying?"

"Just bear with me for a moment, Robert."

She pointed at Milagre. "You have heard of Mr. Milagre before tonight, is that not so?"

"Of course, who hasn't?"

"So you know that Edward has been involved in the casino business for many years?"

"I'd heard that."

"What you may not have heard is exactly what Edward does. Edward uses his supernatural abilities to make sure that this casino keeps as much of the winnings as possible."

"Ok, how does he do that?" I asked, playing along.

"There are many ways; spells, incantations, alchemy, and the use of symbols and images of various deities that are enchanted."

I couldn't believe it, she was serious.

"No one is hurt. They merely want to play, but in the long run, they lose. It's very simple, the idea anyway. The actual application is very complex. There are few that rival Edward in the use of such magic."

"Ok, this is interesting. Not that I am saying I believe any of it, but what's that got to do with what happened tonight?" I was really starting to get anxious now. This was getting crazier by the minute.

"As to tonight, it appears that you killed two Mages before they could kill Edward, and that is why he asked you what you are. To be perfectly honest, any normal human would be dead. So I am here to determine why you are not."

I would have thought she was crazy but something about her made me feel like she believed what she was saying. What the hell, I'll play along. What choice do I have? "Ok, let's just assume that that's true. I'm not dead, at least as far as I can tell. So what happened?"

Meredith looked over at Siegfried who was standing by the door. I hadn't heard him come back into the office. "Siegfried, have they finished with Robert's gun?

"Yes, I have the report here," he replied, handing some paperwork to her.

Meredith looked down at the paper for a moment and then looked back to me. "Robert, where did you get the weapon you used tonight?"

"It was a gift. It's a Walther PPK manufactured in the early 30's. It belonged to my uncle from Germany who had been in the military and then later, the State Police. Why?"

"This is an unusual weapon," she said, turning the pages to a picture of my gun. "What does this oak leaf symbolize?"

I'll admit it; I was getting interested now, although I was still not a believer. "That's my mother's family crest. The inscription below reads Beschützer der Eiche in German." I was describing the etching on the grip. It meant protector of the oak.

"Ah, the oak," Meredith said as she turned to Milagre. "Edward, I believe you will find this interesting." She looked back at me. "And your uncle, why did he bequeath it to you?"

"My mother's family estate is in the middle of a grove of hundreds, maybe thousands, of trees. That's where the crest comes from. My aunt told me he wanted me to have it since I was a police officer as he had been. She came to the States after he passed and brought it to me." I wasn't sure why I was getting into such detail. There were few people I had shared the story with and although things were really strange, for some reason, I felt myself getting comfortable with this woman.

"The cartridges, she gave you those as well?

"They came with the gun. I had to promise her that I would use only them when I carried it, although I could use any other to practice. I had them checked just to be safe. The examiner indicated they were a mixture of common metals, some expensive, some not, but nothing illegal."

"I would not call them common. As a matter of fact this weapon is enchanted. The cartridges are made of minerals that are used in magic. That is why the Mages were killed. Their spells were useless."

"Ok, so you're telling me I have a magic gun." I hoped I hadn't sounded too sarcastic.

"Don't be so surprised, a gun is a weapon, just like a sword or dagger, or even a wand. This one was crafted by experts." She grasped my hands again. "I sense no deception in you, how is it that you do not know this?" She moved her hands up to my face. "Look at me, Robert." She gazed into my eyes as she held my face.

I wasn't sure how long we sat there like that. Hell, maybe she was trying to hypnotize me, then suddenly she let go.

She stood up and looked at Milagre. "The magic is old. Like nothing I have seen here in the new world. As I would have expected, it is not of ours. I sense the wood, not the sea, and the oak confirms it. Strange to find it in a male of that line, but the Dryad were always unpredictable." She looked back down at me for a moment and then returned her gaze to Milagre.

"There has been a spell placed on him that protects him. One I cannot break or see clearly through, but it is no longer as solid as it once was. Perhaps the spell was damaged during the attack by the Mage. Although it could not kill him it affected his shield of protection. Edward, we must take care." She walked over to the bar and poured herself a drink.

Milagre looked deep in thought and was still as a statue.

Had she hypnotized me? I was still groggy so I reached down and took another drink. "What, exactly, just happened?"

"You are protected by a very potent spell. I can only tell you that it was, and still is, protecting you. It appears to have prevented you from using any of your supernatural abilities but also prevented others from harming you with theirs. It may also have suppressed your memory. The only other thing I can tell you is that whoever crafted it was very powerful. I doubt there are many left in the world that have such ability. Be that as it may, the Mage you confronted was powerful as well. His attack has damaged the spell."

Milagre became agitated. "Can you remember anything about this? When it happened? Who placed it on you?"

"Whoa," I said. "Give me a minute," I replied, and then I leaned back and rubbed my face. I was still groggy, and these folks were absolutely out of it. Protection spells, Dryads, what the hell was going on? This was not what I expected from a casino owner and ex-mobster. Was everyone here crazy?

I decided quickly I would have to play along. Crazy or not, they still had my gun and I'd seen what Siegfried's people had carried. Besides, this was Eddy Milagre for God's sake. This guy had a reputation that made Hollywood movies read like kid's books. I was going to have to be careful if I didn't want to end up on a slab like the other two.

Meredith jumped in. "Edward, do not push too hard. The enchantment is strong. The little power that the attack has allowed to escape will take time for him to understand."

I thought Milagre was going to have a coronary but he quickly regained his composure. "You're right, I am sorry. Perhaps it would be better to discuss other issues first. Mr. Hoskins, let me introduce my head of corporate security, Siegfried Dorvaror." He gestured toward the tall man with the military bearing.

"Siegfried, what have you learned about tonight's incident?"

Siegfried took a few steps toward us and responded. "Based on our analysis the three Mages entered the garage via the employee entrance on the ground floor. They then made their way to the executive level. Two guards were immobilized in the process and a spell was used to deceive the monitors. We do not know how they gained access to the employee area as of yet."

He paused a moment to see if any questions were going to be asked. When no one said anything, he continued. "Surveillance picked up on them as soon as you exited the elevator, but my team, although already en route, failed to reach you in time."

"That much is obvious," Milagre remarked, a slight frown on his face. Siegfried's face remained blank.

"Mr. Hoskins' vehicle was noted, of course, but had the proper credentials to enter the lot. It is unusual that surveillance did not pick up on him as he entered but the spell he is under may account for it. As to the three, they were cloaked, but surveillance was able to pick up on them just moments before the attack. We responded as quickly as possible. Mr. Hoskins prior actions were not noted by my team so he was taken into custody upon our arrival. We were not informed that he had assisted you until after we immobilized him."

He looked over at me. "My apology for the harsh treatment, our concern was for Mr. Milagre."

"Noted, I would have done the same." Yeah right, but what else could I say, at least they hadn't shot me.

"The two dead Mages have not been identified," Siegfried continued. "They may be followers of Circe as they carried a similar mark. That clan is known to seek dark magic and what we have pieced together about them indicates that they are well versed. As to the third Mage, we are still searching for him. I will inform you when he is captured and have the team report to you when they return."

"Circe, that would seem to make sense, they do want it all for themselves. But still, this is brazen, even for them. Meredith, your thoughts?" he asked, looking as if he had just swallowed something distasteful.

"Her followers are indeed becoming bold if they attempt such actions in our own territory." She responded, a look of unease on her face. "Notify me immediately when you have discovered any further information. Edward, please take care of our guest." She turned and walked towards the door.

She started to exit, but turned back, looking directly at me. "I look forward to discussing this further. I would be curious to hear how your gift emerges but now is not the time."

"Whoa," I said, looking over at Milagre. "What about the fact that I shot two guys? How do we explain this? What about the bodies...I mean...what are the cops going to think?"

"Don't worry about the police, Mr. Hoskins. Siegfried, explain it to him," he replied, stifling a laugh.

"Mr. Hoskins," he said, handing me a small USB thumb drive. "This contains a copy of the surveillance tapes that did record the attackers. Also within it is the complete log and images of the attackers as well as their weapons." Then he pulled a small baggie out of his coat and gave it to me as well. "These are the fragments from your weapon. I will return your Walther to you before you leave the property. I should also mention that you may only view the contents once. After that it will be erased. Be sure to study it carefully and commit it to memory. As to the bodies, it is as if they never existed."

Erased, never existed, ok, you ever hear of computer forensics, tough guy? Wait a minute; did he say the bodies never existed? "I'm not sure I understand."

Milagre looked over at me and smiled. "We have lived side by side with mortal men for a very long time. There is no evidence of anything that you saw today, except what is in your hands, and that will not last. We follow our own ways and with very few exceptions, make every effort not to let the mortal world know what we are."

To say I was comfortable with any of this would be an understatement of epic proportions. Yet here I was, surrounded by crazies telling me that I just stepped into the pages of a fantasy novel. But what could I do, it was take the trinkets and leave by the back door or possibly never leave.

"Okay," I said. "It is what it is. I suppose I have to trust someone. So what happens next?"

"I believe we should let you get some rest. It has been a trying evening."

The lady who had been in the office when I first woke up took that moment to return. She handed a package to Siegfried and then she turned to Milagre. "Will there be anything else, sir?"

"No, you may return to your regular duties."

I heard her say "thank you," and then she left the office.

Milagre walked over to the table in front of the couch. He took my empty glass and walked to the bar to refill it and then returned and handed it to me. "After tonight, you may want to consider coming to work for me. I could use someone with your skills. I am also concerned that our adversaries won't be happy with you dispatching two of their agents. They may want revenge. I can offer some protection if you are here."

Yeah right, that's all I need to finish this day off, a job in the mental health field. But I did want to make it out of here in one piece, so I stayed nice. "I'll consider it, Mr. Milagre. But I have to tell you that I like working for myself. A lot has happened tonight and I'd like to move slowly. Maybe we can do some contract work until I've figured this all out. Would that be ok?"

"As you wish, but we will discuss it further. I will help you if I can. Siegfried, will you escort Mr. Hoskins to his vehicle? I believe there's been enough excitement and discussion for tonight. Wait a moment, tell me about Carmine."

"That's why I was here. I was going to serve Mr. Pontedra a subpoena. It's in reference a civil case he is involved in."

"He would have left by now. He's on his way to our Atlantic City property. He should be back in a few days. I'll arrange for him to contact you when he returns, will that be acceptable?"

"That would be fine." God, I hope he's not part of this madness.

I reached in my pocket and removed a card from my wallet. I laid it on the table and looked back up at him. "My contact info is on there, including my cell number, just have him call me."

"I'll make sure he gets in touch with you," he said, returning to his desk. "Siegfried, take care of our new friend."

"Of course, Mr. Hoskins, will you follow me please?"

I downed the rest of my freshly poured drink and got up to follow him out of the office. As we entered the elevator down the hallway Siegfried handed me the package he had received.

"Your weapon as promised, Mr. Hoskins.

"Thank you, Siegfried."

"If I may be frank, I do wish you would consider Mr. Milagre's offer of employment. Our opponents are dangerous, and there is strength in numbers."

The elevator door opened and we walked toward my car. There was nothing to indicate that anything out of the ordinary had happened. No bodies, no yellow tape, nothing. As for me, I just wanted to get the hell out of there, but I stayed cool.

"Perhaps I will, but for now, I still have to digest all this." We paused as we reached my car, a newer Lexus hybrid. I wasn't rich but I did ok.

"Mr. Hoskins, thank you for saving Mr. Milagre," he said as I opened the driver door. He reached over to shake my hand. We shook and I got into the car.

"Look, don't worry about it, I'm just glad we're both ok."

"Still, you did save him, and for that I am in debt to you," he replied, pushing the door closed.

I rolled the window down deciding I didn't want him to think I was being rude. Crazy or not, these folks had a lot of juice in this town. "Look, maybe we can meet again under better circumstances," I said as I started the car.

Siegfried didn't say anything else, but I thought I saw the beginning of a smile. Niceties done, I didn't lose another minute getting out of there. As I left the property I kept an eye on my rear view mirror just to make sure I wasn't being followed.

What the hell just happened? Alright, I'll admit it; I once spent a year working cases involving black magic and witchcraft. Hell, I even had a few contacts still out there in that community. But that was nothing like this, this was insane. I needed a drink and a place to lay low for a while so I could think. With nowhere else to go I headed toward the freeway and home.

Chapter 2

It may be the desert but Vegas really is a beautiful place, especially early in the morning, or late at night, depending on your perspective. The city lights engulf you and it can be crystal clear. On some nights you can see the entire valley.

I turned on to Craig off the 95, and then went west, turning right onto one of the side streets toward Lone Mountain. You may not know it, but this is as close to a rural area as the city proper has.

They call it the Lone Mountain corridor. Before the city had grown to the two million plus it has become, this had been horse property. Some of it still is. The rest is studded with pockets of the rich, famous, and business owners who want the good life. Unlike most places in the city, where your neighbor's house is so close you can spit on their wall, here, there was nothing less than 1/3 an acre. Many homes had a half, if not a full acre, many even more.

As for me, I had an acre in a section that had once housed a dude ranch and stables. The original property had been parceled up and sold off bit by bit but I had been able to buy the ranch house. It was an old fashioned two story with a covered front porch. It even had a hitching rail in the front. Just in case anyone ever came over by horse. This is Vegas, after all, and where I lived you just never knew.

Before my wife and I divorced we'd purchased it from the old couple that had owned the ranch. I had modernized and upgraded the house but left the trees that were fed by an underground spring alone. It was nice to have a well with water being so precious in the desert. The property was fenced and gated, which wasn't at all unusual in this city, and I liked my privacy. But the best thing about it was that the property was surrounded by trees. Once inside the gates, you would never know you were in the desert.

I pulled up to the front and pushed the transmitter, waited for the gate to open, and drove in. As I got out of the car Charlie came running up and almost knocked me over. Charlie is a two year old Great Dane mix. Black and white, he weighs in at somewhere around 180 pounds. Of course he thinks he's a lap dog. We had the obligatory few minutes of petting, hugging, and licking. Well, the licking was mostly on Charlie's part, and then he calmed down and walked with me to the front porch.

I unlocked the door and went into the house, emptying my pockets and putting my keys and cell phone down on the counter. Opening the refrigerator I grabbed a beer and went into the back yard to sit on the patio. It had been a long, strange night. I still didn't know what to think. So I sat in my rocking chair on the patio and stared at the stars

Charlie walked over and dropped a ball in my lap. I could have sworn he said "play" as he stared at me, his tail wagging back and forth.

Start with an Oreo colored Astro from the *Jetson's* and that's Charlie. Now, throw in a dog who thinks the pool was built for him and loves to play ball and you're getting close. I would have been smart to own stock in a tennis ball factory, as many as he went through in a week. He doesn't care where you've been or what your day was like; when you walk into the backyard it was play time and that meant throw the ball. So when he dropped the ball in my lap I did what every good pet owner knows to do, I threw the ball across the yard and watched him take off after it.

While I tossed the ball I was trying to make sense of the supernatural thing. Not to mention having shot and killed two alleged Witches, Warlocks, Mages, or whatever they were supposed to have been. The whole thing made no sense. Was I being played? But that didn't figure right either. Milagre and his folks had no reason to act that way with me. They could have taken me out like I had the two thugs and no one would have been the wiser. Could they really believe all this magic nonsense?

My grandmother had told me stories about Faeries and the Dryad who lived in the tree in her yard. I remembered those stories well. But Milagre and Meredith would have me believe it was all true. I was missing something here. I'll be damned if I knew what it was. Maybe it was their way to cover up the attack on him and my actions against the attackers.

I should have called the police the second I had gotten out of there. Hell, I was an ex-cop myself and now I was part of a conspiracy as well. Yeah, I should have called the cops. But here's the honest truth: I may be dumb at times but I'm not stupid. Calling the police wouldn't do me any good. Eddy Milagre had way too many connections for a guy like me to get in his way. Besides, there was no trace of those bodies when I left the place. I didn't like it but I was just going to have to wait and see what was next. I took another drink and sat back to think.

I opened my eyes to the bright sun beating down on my face and a very large dog licking it. I pushed Charlie away and took a moment to figure out where I was. Still in the backyard, I sat up from the lounger and checked my watch, 9:30. Well, at least it was still morning. I spied the half empty tequila bottle and several 'dead soldiers' of my favorite beer on the table. Expecting a hangover, I stood up slowly. You can imagine my surprise when my head was clear. Well, clear was a relative term. I needed coffee, now.

I went into the house and pressed the button on the coffee pot. I lived on the stuff so I was always careful to clean the pot and have it ready for the next time. Nothing is more irritating to a coffee drinker then having to empty the dregs of a forgotten pot and add those tortured minutes to the time one has to wait till that magical elixir begins to fill the house with its aroma. Be prepared, as the scouts say. Although I actually prefer the Coast Guard motto better, Semper Paratus, always ready.

As the coffee began to drip, I looked over my collection of cups and chose one that said *Frak Me*. Considering the events of last night, that one seemed to sum up my current state of being. With nothing to do now but wait I peeked out my front window to make sure the cops weren't already looking for me. With the coast clear and the coffee brewing I headed upstairs for a quick shower.

As I let the hot water wash over me I was starting to feel normal again, normal being a relative term. I don't know if anyone could feel that way after last night's events. Where the hell had all that magic shit come from? I had even dreamt about it last night.

I don't remember much of it, which was how I could recognize the difference between the dream and reality. I remembered everything that had happened at the Neptune but the dream was already fading. My grandmother and I were walking in the woods. She was telling me something about magic. Damn, that pissed me off. Bad enough I had to go through last night's debacle but now it had to invade my memories of the woman who had raised me.

I suppose I should mention that my parents died when I was seven. My father had been a pilot and my mother, who'd worked in the casinos, often flew with him on the weekends. One Sunday they just didn't come home. They'd sent me to my grandmother in Germany but she decided to bring me back to the States. She moved me back to Vegas and stayed to raise me. Telling me that this was where my mother had wanted me to be.

I stepped out of the shower and dried off. Finishing my morning rituals I put on a pair of jeans and headed downstairs for my long awaited cup of java. Feeling almost human again I filled my cup and sat down at the table. Ah, the aroma of fresh brewed coffee filled my nostrils as I took a sip. Wonderful, I thought to myself, and then I damn near dropped my cup. There on the counter next to my keys was the memory stick. I had forgotten about the thumb drive Siegfried had given me!

Grabbing the drive I went into my office and booted up my basic laptop. It's basic because I can put anything on it and I don't care what happens to it. If it's got a virus or something nasty I can just wipe it and reinstall it. Having some familiarity with computer systems and forensics I never attached anything unknown to my primary desktop. Once it had booted up, I inserted the thumb drive and burned a copy of it to a CD, then opened the files on the laptop.

Damn if it didn't look like everything was there. Images of the two guys I had killed still lying on the parking garage floor, surveillance video of 3 figures moving through the grounds and some docs of logs indicating when things happened. I slowly went through the files and stopped at the images of the rods that the bad guys had been carrying. Looking over the pics I saw what looked like miniature versions of something out of a bad imitation of *Lord of the Rings* or *Harry Potter*.

What the...? Was this some kind of a joke? These things were only about one inch in diameter and maybe 14 or 16 inches long. Just fancy sticks, they sure didn't look like something that fired a bolt of electricity. The tips had some sort of red crystal attached to them. One had been broken and thick red goo had oozed from it. I threw up my arms in amazement. These folks were taking this magic thing to the limit! What were these things supposed to be, magic wands?

I'd had enough; I started to pull the thumb drive out of the slot when the damn thing bit me. Then a light flashed. It started as a bright spot in the center of the screen and then burst out in all directions all at once and was gone. What the hell?

I reached over and gave the now removed thumb drive a quick touch and pulled back, nothing. I picked it up carefully but it was cold. My laptop was cold as well, the screen blank although the power was still on. I quickly pulled the battery out of the back to preserve it. Lesson one in saving damaged data, kill the power.

Although I had never seen a computer act like this before I had spent some time in the forensic lab when I was a cop. Whatever had happened to the thumb drive and laptop could hopefully be reconstructed and I wanted to prevent it from doing anything else until it could be examined. I grabbed the laptop, thumb drive and the CD I had made and put them all in my briefcase. Then I went back into the kitchen to make a call.

Malcolm Smitt had first worked for me when I was a rookie sergeant on the force. Then we had worked together again when I did a stint in the computer forensics lab. He had gone on to become the Department's leading expert in computer forensics and hacking until he'd retired last year to start his own business. We'd actually talked about working together for a while but I was tired of computers and he didn't want to do regular P.I. work so we settled on just being friends and referred business to one another. If I had ever known anyone who I believed had possessed real magic before this, it was Mal. He had a way with computers that was uncanny.

I poured myself another cup of coffee, the first one was cold, then grabbed my cell and dialed Mal's number.

"Bobby! Where the hell you been hiding? Got any new movies out?"

He knew I hated that name. Not that I had anything against Bob Hoskins, the actor. But ever since the Roger Rabbit movie he'd called me Bob or Bobby whenever he had the chance. It was all in fun of course.

"Malware, written any crappy programs lately?" I countered, using my nickname for him.

"As a matter of fact..." Then he just laughed.

"What's up, Rob, I thought you forgot about me."

"Never, my friend, never, just been busy. Hey, you gonna be at the office in a while? I just had the weirdest thing happen to my laptop while I was viewing some data. I pulled the battery and have a copy of the file I was running when it died."

"System crash?"

"Honestly, Mal, I'm not sure, never seen anything like it."

"Bring it on then. I'll be here all day."

"Great, see you in an hour or so."

I disconnected the phone and headed back upstairs to finish dressing. I threw on a collarless button down shirt and a pair of shoes and then went downstairs and filled a travel mug before I dumped the coffee and got the pot ready for next time.

Standing in my kitchen I thought about what I should do. If no one outside the Neptune knew about last night then I was just gonna have to see what played out. But just to be sure I grabbed my cell and dialed another old police friend. This one would confirm it, one way or the other.

Lieutenant Ray O'Malley was the man in charge of Metro's Homicide Bureau. He looked the part, too. A good looking Irishman with a full head of silver hair, tall and well built. He was also a whiskey drinking, cigar smoking old school cop. The kind you might expect to see on the screen of a classic film noir title.

With thirty-four years on the job he didn't worry about the brass, officials or the city's elite. If it involved a murder you were either the victim, a suspect or a witness. If you didn't fit into one of those categories then you'd best just get out of his way. I'd first met him when I was still a cook working my way through college. I probably would never have been a cop if it wasn't for him. Later he'd been my training officer and then my sergeant when I first made detective. If anything about what happened at the Neptune had hit the light of day, he'd know about it.

"O'Malley, Homicide," he said as the phone connected.

"Ray, it's Hoskins, got time for a cup?"

"Friggin' lovely! Here I was gonna take the morning off to play a few holes and all you got to offer me is coffee?"

"Yeah right," I said with a laugh. "No seriously, you got some time?"

"Ah, I wish, but some rich bastard got himself fried. I'm heading out to the scene as we speak. Hell if I know why CSI wants me out there, hold on..." There was a short pause, and I could hear him pounding the keys on the car's MDT, the Mobile Data Terminal. That was the official name for the laptop computer in his undercover car.

"Yep, that girl of yours is the crime scene tech. She called it in by phone. This better be good or you're gonna owe me a lot more than a coffee. I was going three whole days without a body. You could almost see my desk."

My daughter, Nikki, was a CSI at Metro and Ray had been there the day she was born. I wondered why she'd called it in that way and not on the radio. It had to be something out of the ordinary. Most calls didn't rate the lieutenant from the get-go, either.

"I'm sure I will...fried?" I asked, quizzically.

"E-lec-tro-cu-ted," he said, emphasizing each syllable.

"Better you than me," I offered, laughing again. "But you ain't got balls if you don't check out at a BBQ chicken place for lunch." It was a joke from our old uniform days. If you went on a particularly gruesome murder you had to go to lunch at a restaurant that served food that matched the crime. Call it a macho thing, or a coping mechanism, whatever you want.

"Chicken and waffles, my boy, chicken and waffles," he joked. "I'm almost arrived. I'll get back to you later."

"You got it," I said as the phone disconnected. Three days without a body? That answered that. I strapped on my gun, grabbed my keys and started for the door.

"The big one, sure," I answered without thinking.

This was it, it was official, I was losing my grip on reality. I could have sworn Charlie had just told me he wanted me to bring him back a bone, and not just any bone. I had distinctly had the impression of one of those big roast beef bones that you see at the buffets and, I might add, that they just happen to sell at the corner market.

I stopped and looked back at him. He was just sitting there next to the sofa where he always was when I left the house. He was watching me with his tongue hanging out and his tail wagging. It wasn't just answering out loud that was nerve wracking. When you live with a dog it's easy to think of them as a person. Hell, who doesn't talk to their dog? No, what scared me was that it was so specific

"You say something, boy?" I asked, half joking and praying that he didn't answer.

He stared at me for a moment, like dogs sometimes do when you talk to them. It's almost like you can see their brain trying to figure out what you said. Then, without a bark, or a word, thank God, he came over to me and jumped up, licking my face. Pushing him down, I gave his head a good rubbing and then headed out the door.

Aw shit, I thought to myself, I'd better stop at the store on the way home, just in case.

Chapter 3

The drive to downtown was short; the early rush hour traffic long since subsided. I pulled into the alley off of Ninth Street, accessing Mal's office by the rear entrance. The offices in this part of downtown are mostly comprised of converted homes from Vegas' early days. While the buildings weren't necessarily small, some even had basements, they didn't have a lot of property so street side parking was always at a premium. I was being polite, as he would have been; my office was just a two blocks away.

Malcolm was bent down over a 32 inch flat screen monitor gazing at lines of binary code as I walked in. He was one of the few people I knew that could read it instantly. He drove me nuts when he sent birthday cards written in it, they took forever for me to translate.

"Ah! About time," he said, stretching as he stood up. "I need a break from this one. It's putting me to sleep. Whatcha got?"

I put the laptop down on one of the tables and held up the CD and thumb drive. "Here's the little beastie and a copy of the file I took off of it."

"What exactly happened?" Mal asked, taking them from me while twiddling the thumb drive between his fingers. Moving to another workstation, he plopped down in a chair in front of another monitor.

"It was weird, man, let me tell you. First, I inserted the thumb drive in the laptop and burned a copy," I answered, knowing he would want a blow by blow description. "Then I reviewed the files on the thumb drive. There was nothing special, (Ok, I wasn't gonna tell him everything, at least not yet) just a folder, some spreadsheets, movies and pics. No hidden files present that I noticed. Anyway, I took a look at the files and everything was fine. Then, I go to pull the drive from the PC, and WHAM, it shocks me."

"Shocks you? What do you mean...shocks you?"

"I mean like an electrical shock. What'd you think I meant?"

"You know better, Robert, USB only pulls 5 volts and there isn't enough amperage for you to even notice. Must have been static electricity."

"Mal," I retorted, "I know what a USB's voltage is and it wasn't static. I was sitting at the desk and had already touched it several times. I'm telling you that the damn drive had a live current. That or the PC went haywire."

Mal looked at me like I was a kid who just told his teacher the dog had eaten his homework assignment. "Ok, ok, let me take a look, go on," he finally conceded, inserting the thumb drive in the computer. He tapped the keyboard but nothing happened. The thumb drive didn't register.

"Well, it's dead now. I'll have to pull it apart to see what's up." Mal looked around the desk for a moment. Locating the CD I had given him, he reached over and picked it up and then inserted it into the computer as well. Once again, nothing registered. The CD appeared to be blank. "Are you sure this is the right CD?" he asked, looking over his shoulder at me.

"Yes, I'm sure," I answered, getting irritated. "Let me see that a minute."

Mal ejected the CD from the computer and handed it to me.

I looked at the back carefully. I could tell that the disk had been written to, the telltale coloration was clear around the center. "Do I look like an idiot? Look here," I said, pointing to an area on the disk, "you can see that it's been written to."

Taking the disk, he put it under a light on the table and examined it. "Okay, you're right, I forgive you. I'll have to play with this one as well. Hand me the laptop. Maybe we can find something there.

I picked up the laptop and handed it to Mal.

He flipped it upside down and located the hard drive slot. After rummaging around in a drawer he took out a small screwdriver and within seconds he had removed the computer's hard drive.

I watched as he attached the drive to a hardware blocker he had hooked up to the PC. This was a device that would allow him to see the contents of the hard drive but not let his computer do anything to it. Once hooked up, he could examine the drive and make an exact duplicate or just look at it without worrying about modifying anything. In this way he could perform any further examinations on the copy, rather than on the original drive, which could be used as evidence. In my case it didn't really matter and I watched as he fired up his forensic software and began looking at the data on the drive.

"What the...?" I heard him say as he looked at the data on the screen. "These files are all shredded; nothing is in a logical manner. Chunks are just...missing...what happened to this thing?"

I looked closer at the screen. The forensic software projected a graphical representation of the data on the hard drive. One thing to remember is that unless you use special software, just because you delete something doesn't mean it actually gets erased. The computer's operating system merely flags the area that that file is located as writable but leaves most of the data intact. Assuming something else hadn't written over it, the right person, or the right software for that matter, can easily recover it under most circumstances. That wasn't going to happen this time. It had been a while since I'd worked in the forensic lab but the data left behind was mangled.

Mal shook his head before continuing. "Some kind of advanced wiping program, maybe? Where did you say you got the thumb drive you were looking at from?"

"I didn't, but it's from a client," I offered, not wanting to explain further. I wasn't ready to tell him that I got it from someone claiming to be supernatural. "Can you tell anything else?"

"Not with this machine. But let me play with this stuff a while. If a program did this, I want to know how, and I want a copy!" He declared, pushing back his chair. He ran his fingers through his hair, his eyes never leaving the screen. "Let me pull this stuff apart in the clean room. Maybe I can find something it left behind." He turned to me with a suspicious look.

"I don't suppose you can tell me anything else about these files?"

I paused for a moment, wanting him to at least think I was considering it. "Not yet," I replied. "Can you live with that for now?"

"Yeah, sure, but you're gonna owe me," he snickered as he reached over and disconnected the drive. Then he picked up the laptop and drives and carried them into another examination room as I followed. "I gotta finish this other case but I'll look at these when I get a chance and give you a call if I find anything."

"Thanks, Mal." I said, smacking him on the shoulder in a friendly way. "I need to get back to work anyway." We walked to the door together. I paused before I went out. "One more thing, let's keep this between us, ok."

"Keep what between us?" he joked. "Don't I always?"

I didn't say anything else as I exited and headed for my car. The truth was we'd shared plenty of secrets over the years and we trusted one another. I'd probably end up telling him most of what happened last night eventually, except maybe for the magic part. I didn't need to burden him with all of it.

As I pulled into my parking spot in the back of my office, I reflected on what had been happening to me. Magic beings, cursed computers, talking dogs, bad dreams, you name it. It was turning into a helluva week. You'd never know it from the way things were going, but most of the time my life was boring. You read these stories about P.I.s and the dangerous and glamorous work they do, but up to now, the reality had been somewhat different altogether.

I'm not saying there isn't the occasional exciting moment, but a lot my work is done on the phone and on the computer. When I usually do get out of the office, it's to talk to a witness in some civil suit or deal with a criminal matter that the cops are too busy, or too lazy, to deal with. That, believe it or not, was my bread and butter. Sure, that wasn't the way things were going, but it was the way they were supposed to be!

I know I used to be a cop and all, and sure, I've had my fair share of the glamorous side of this business, like catching robbers and murderers and being on the evening news. Hell, I've even proven the cops wrong and gotten folks out of jail. But civil and criminal work doesn't usually include Wizards and magic wands. I just shook my head and hoped this wasn't an omen of things to come. I stepped out of the car and walked over to the doorway and waved hello to Hailey as I entered. She was on the phone, but I saw her wave back as she continued her phone conversation.

Hailey owned a legal services business. Paralegal work, document filing, subpoena services, that kind of stuff. She'd been in the business longer than I had and had known me when I was still a young rookie on the beat. It was a small business, and although she did have a staff, she usually acted as the receptionist and answered the phones herself. I rented office space from her so that I had a downtown business address and a place to hold meetings. More importantly, she was a good friend and treated me like family. I spent a minute chatting with her after she hung up the phone and then retrieved my mail and messages.

Once that was done I poured myself a fresh cup of coffee from the kitchen and headed into the back. Before you even ask, the cup is black and says "*I want to believe*". I plopped down at my desk and booted up the computer. Most of the mail was junk but there were a few checks and letters. The messages were return calls or calls from other business acquaintances. The checks were a nice bonus; it was always a good sign when clients actually paid on time.

The P.I. community in Vegas isn't small and, although the large firms like to think they are the big shots, at the core of it all are a group of folks just like me that I've known for years. These guys are ex-cops, ex-agents or security professionals that cut their teeth on the Vegas streets. Many as far back as when the mob ran the town. Although I wasn't old enough to have been there for all of it, I'd known most of these guys and gals when I was still a rookie on the force and the others from my childhood days growing up.

I called back a few of them and spent twenty minutes just bullshitting, or as we say in the business, keeping up with my contacts, and then reviewed my to-do list on my computer. Aside from my regular client caseload, I had to do a few backgrounds; some phone interviews and one witness locate for a girl from a wealthy family that was now a stripper. There you go. Here's something that sounds like it would be out of the ordinary: Head out to the night clubs, find a stripper and let her know daddy's sick and mommy wants her to call.

I love it when some guy asks me what I did interesting this week and I tell them I spent an evening hitting the bars and the strip clubs. "Wow", they'll say, "I wish I had a job like that, wink, wink."

Sure you do buddy. Hell, unless I set it up in advance, I usually don't even bother going past the check-in booth where you pay unless I have to. Most of the time, I just drop a dime.

Of course I don't tell them that. Let them think what they want. It lends an air of mystery which can be good for business. The reality is I've spent so much time in those places and too many hours close up with the girls. Hard bodies or not, I see way past the makeup and poor me stories.

Don't get me wrong, I don't dislike strippers, or exotic dancers, as the profession is called. I get along fine with them and they're usually good sources. I do run across a few of them in my line of work. Most of these girls are professionals and believe me when I tell you, it's just business.

If you think some hot-bodied gal is gonna risk her $1000 bucks in nightly tips for a roll in the hay you've got another thing coming. I'm not saying some of them don't do that but it's a quick way to get blacklisted or arrested if they meet up with an undercover vice cop. The clubs do not look fondly on a girl if that happens.

I picked up my phone and called a vice cop that owed me a favor or two. Within minutes, I knew my girl was a dancer at *Darlings*, one of the more popular Vegas strip clubs. I got up from my desk and walked back to the reception area and refilled my cup.

Hailey was doing paperwork but she looked up at me and gave me a smile. "Hey sugar! Any luck with that subpoena last night?" she asked, taking a sip from her own cup.

"Sort of," I groaned. I eyed her as I decided what to say. I couldn't exactly explain what really happened, could I? "I got hooked up in some drama and ended up getting a promise from the folks to have him call me. He was already on a plane to Jersey before I could catch up to him."

"Drama? You slippin' darling?" Hailey was from Texas, and even in her 60's she could still turn on that southern belle drawl. It didn't fool me though; she could make a truck driver blush if she wanted to.

"Actually, no, I wound up stopping some bozo trying to mug Milagre, if you can believe that." Sometimes it's best to just tell the truth, even if it is a slightly altered version.

"You're shittin me?" she sputtered, almost dropping her cup. "I didn't hear anything about it. Did you get him?"

"Nah, he got away, I had to check on Milagre as he'd had been knocked to the ground. But corporate's handling it so no press."

"I'll be damned, he all right?"

"Yeah, he's fine. He promised me he'd have Pontedra call me when he got back into town."

She shook her head and sipped her coffee. "That seems like it'll be worth a few favors." That was Hailey; a favor was money in the bank.

"We'll see. Hey, you still have Alicia's number?"

Alicia was the house mother at *Darlings*. A house mother was the girls anchor, not management, but not just an employee either. She, or he, acted as the go-to person for all their needs, clothing, food, personal items such as shampoo or perfume or just someone to listen to. Although I had dealt with her a few times I knew she was one of Hailey's regular sources.

"Alicia DeVries at *Darlings*? You bet, hold on a minute." She reached down and opened a drawer and pulled out her rolodex. Hailey was as computer literate as anyone but some things would never change. The rolodex was one of them. If you were important to her, or ever had been, you were in there. The names in her list were priceless. She started going through the cards. "Yeah, here you go," she replied, writing the number down on a card and handing it to me. "What you got, or are you just going for the show?"

"Don't you wish," I chortled. "It's just a locate, rich kid's dad is sick and mom wants her to call."

"Boringgg, just make sure you let her know first, you know how she can be about her girls."

"Yes, mom, I know, she's just like you," I quipped.

Hailey just gave me a good bye wave. "Go back to work, I got things to do!" She'd acted gruff but I could tell by her smile she approved of my use of the word mom.

With my evenings' locate planned out, I spent the rest of what was left of the workday running computer searches and talking to people on the phone. The immediate cases were filed and the reports written. Those that could be sent electronically went by email. The others went into envelopes for the morning's mail. Invoices printed out and accompanying the reports, my office workday was over. I looked up at my retirement clock on the wall; it was 5:30 p.m. Wow, I thought to myself, nothing weird had happened to me in a good 6 hours. That was a good sign.

Before I left for the day I called Alicia and set up an appointment to see her. I told her what I had and she confirmed that the girl was working tonight. Then she told me to be there at 10:15 p.m. and to call her when I was on my way. I hung up the phone and headed home, stopping at the market for Charlie's bone. I mean, you never know, right?

Chapter 4

I pulled into the driveway and tried to get out of the car but Charlie beat me to it. He was in my lap as soon as the door opened. After a minute or two I was able to get out. They say you shouldn't let your dog jump on you, but let's be real. He knows who the boss is, and besides, it'd break his heart. I grabbed the bone, still wrapped in butcher paper out of the trunk, and he froze. He eyed the package, his tail wagging at 90 miles a minute.

"This what you want?" I asked, holding up the giant bone.

With a bark he rushed to my feet and sat, remaining perfectly still.

Believe it or not, he did have some training when he wanted to remember it. I unwrapped it and gave it to him and then breathed a sigh of relief as he took it and headed towards the backyard. That was a load off of my mind. I hadn't heard a word, only a bark, maybe I wasn't going crazy after all.

Placing my keys and wallet on the counter I kicked off my shoes and started the coffee. As I reached for a cup from the cupboard, my stomach reminded me that I hadn't eaten all day. Settling on a *Piedmont Airlines* cup, I fixed a sandwich and waited for the coffee to brew. When it was done, and with food and drink in hand, I sat down at the kitchen table and thought about the day.

It hadn't started great, shocking computer files and all, but at least the remainder had been quiet. I still hadn't figured out Milagre's "what are you" act but there had to be a reason for it. Maybe I just hadn't seen it yet. For just a moment I tried to convince myself that it was just the ramblings of eccentric rich folks but I didn't buy that one either.

I finished my sandwich and refilled my cup, then plopped down on the sofa to see what was on. I'd missed the local news, so I surfed for a few minutes but like the song says, 57 channels and nothin' on. Of course I had 4 times that many, but it still applied. Giving up, I set the timer on my phone and took a short nap. I still had to go out tonight and who knew how late I would be.

It was 9:30 p.m. when the alarm sounded so I cleaned up my dishes and set the pot for the morning. I grabbed a clean shirt and then headed out the door, telling Charlie to guard the house. I waited a moment at the doorway and then relaxed when all he did was sit at his spot by the sofa. No requests, a good sign.

I was halfway to downtown when I remembered to call Alicia. "Alicia, Rob Hoskins here. I'm on my way."

"Thanks for the heads up, baby. Where are you, by the way?"

"Just on the freeway, I should be there on time."

"Great. Oh, Robert, can you do me a favor?" Oh, oh, Robert wasn't a good sign but what was I gonna say, no?

"Sure, Alicia, what do you need?"

"Can you stop at Walgreens and pick me up a box of tampons?"

"Tampons?" I asked reluctantly. "You're kidding, right?" I hadn't bought tampons since before my kids were born. I had to move the phone from my ear, her response louder by several decibels.

"No, I'm not kidding. Some dumbass took my last box out of my storage locker and now the vending machine is empty. I'll never hear the end of it if I don't have some available."

"Ok, ok, I'll pick them up. You need me to investigate the theft as well?" I asked, sarcastically.

"No, but thank you for offering, that one I can handle myself." She countered with a hint of anger in her voice.

Not wanting to get her riled up, she was doing me a bigger favor after all, I simply asked, "any particular kind?"

"Just get a box of regular." I heard her say and then she hung up.

Like I said, house mothers take care of the girl's needs.

15 or 20 minutes later I pulled into the *Darlings* parking lot and threaded my way through the throng of cars to the side alley and then navigated my way to the back. Pulling my car into an empty space I cut the ignition and dialed Alicia. "I'm in the back," I announced when she answered.

"I'll open the door."

Picking up my recent purchase from the passenger seat, I got out of the car and walked towards the back of the building. Like most businesses, the back was utilitarian and ugly. Just what one would expect in an industrial area where city zoning allowed the clubs to be. Unlike the front of the club, here there were no fancy statues, no full size photos of scantily clad women, no neon signs beckoning all to enter, just steel doors and loading docks and naked bulbs to break up the darkness.

A light appeared, and a door on my left opened. The shadow of a woman's figure, framed by the light, called out my name. "Rob, over here baby!"

"Here," I answered, and walked towards her, the box, still in its plastic bag, held up before me.

"You're a doll," she whispered, as she took the bag and motioned me in.

As I strode through the doorway I found myself in what can only be called a large dressing room. There were two long rows of countertop, back to back, with mirrors and the tools of the trade on top. A variety of make-up, panties, G-strings, tops, the occasional corset and other accoutrements of the profession dotted the landscape. Several scantily clad women were vigorously applying lipstick, eye shadow, and various other powders to their faces. One was doing the same to her nipples. No one bothered to look up as I entered the room.

"This way," I heard Alicia say as she grabbed my arm and led me into a small office down the hallway from the room. A slim, attractive woman in her late 30's, Alicia was dressed in blue jeans and a pink silk top. "Thanks," she said, holding up the shopping bag as she gracefully slid into the chair behind her desk.

"No problem," I answered, taking a seat in front of the desk.

"Give me just a minute." she muttered and I watched as she opened the box of tampons and grabbed a handful. Then she opened the top drawer of her desk with her other hand. "I'll be right back, gotta fill the vending machine," she said, taking out a ring of keys and walking around me out of the office. "Tiffany!" I heard her yell.

Then I could hear her talking to someone in the hallway and then there was silence as the voices faded.

I changed my focus to her office. It was small, the desk half the size of mine. The walls were covered in glossy photos. People she'd met, celebrities, porn stars maybe, judging from the outfits. I didn't recognize half of them but I wouldn't expect to. There were also several of her when she'd been younger. She'd been beautiful, not that she still wasn't, just older. But in this game, youth is everything.

Her office made me sad. It wasn't her profession, we all have to survive and make money. It just seemed as if I was surrounded by faded dreams. It was as if one could see time ticking by, its force reducing the dreams to nothing but what was left on the walls and small desk, only memories. Alicia's voice brought me back to the here and now. Damn, I'm getting morose.

She sat back down behind the desk and gave me a smile. "Essence is on the floor at the moment, she should be done in a few."

"Essence?"

"Shit, Robert, wake up baby. Essence is the girl you're looking for."

"Oh, sorry," I laughed, feeling silly. Of course she would use a fantasy name.

"She knows why you're here. She isn't happy about it but I told her you were only the delivery boy *and* that you weren't here to take her back. That's still true, right?" she asked, eyeing me warily for a moment.

"Yeah, of course." I pulled the letter the girl's mother had given me out of my shirt pocket and unfolded it. I held it up and waved it at her. "I told her momma I would find her and deliver the message, that's it. I'm not here to kidnap her."

That said, she relaxed and we shot the breeze for a few, she, asking me how Hailey had been doing and I, asking her how business was. About 10 minutes later, a young woman, blonde, robed, and wearing altogether too much makeup peeked into the doorway. She pointed at me.

"This him?" she asked.

"Essence, this is Robert Hoskins. Robert, this is Essence, also known as Victoria Reynolds," Alicia responded, introducing me.

I started to stand up but the girl held her hand out and waved me to sit.

"Just tell me what she wants."

I started to hand her the envelope but she snatched it out of my hand.

"Your dad's sick. Your mom wants you to..." She never let me finish.

"Fine, anything else?"

Alicia looked at me, I shook my head. "No, Essence, thank you," she said.

The girl turned around and left without saying another word.

"Well," I mused, "I take it I won't be on her Christmas card list."

Alicia broke out in a giggle. "Fraid not, baby, she's a tough one. Hates the world and despises her parents." She rolled her eyes, her grin fading. "I'm not sure why. Never could get her to discuss it, you know how it is." She shrugged her shoulders. "I'll talk to her later, maybe I can at least get her to make a call."

"Thanks for that, and getting her to see me."

"Sure, gotta take care of my friends, never know, I might need you myself one day." Her smile returned and she stood as I readied to leave.

One more task completed on my to-do list, I thought to myself as I stepped out of her office doorway.

I saw the Faerie, or Elf, or whatever she was made up as walking down the hallway. Talk about special effects! She was maybe 5' 2", with long straight blond hair that hung down below her waist. Totally nude, she embodied perfection. Exquisite breasts and a perfectly proportioned body that moved with a grace I would not have believed possible. She looked up at me for an instant, her blue eyes sparkling, and my body froze as I watched her go by.

But it wasn't her beauty that stopped me, or even her nudity, it was her wings. I'd never seen anything that looked so real. They sprouted out of her back and flowed upward a foot above her head and then downward to her feet. Light, wispy, gossamer wings attached I do not know how. I watched, breathless, as she continued down the hallway. I turned around to look at Alicia still in her office.

"Holy shit!" I stuttered. "*That* is the most realistic costume I have ever seen! How did she do that? The wings, they're incredible."

She gave me a funny look. "Wings, we don't have anyone wearing wings. What are you talking about?"

"That girl," I pointed, "the one that just went down the hallway."

Alicia stepped around me and walked down the hallway. Following her to the end she pulled the curtain aside to look. We were behind the stage. She let go of the curtain and turned towards me. "She doesn't have any wings, what have you been smoking?"

"What? No, no, no. Here... let me take a look."

Walking closer, I slid against the wall next to her and pulled the curtain aside. I stared for a moment, dumbfounded, and took in all in. There on the stage was the girl I had seen. Only it wasn't her. Gone were the ears, the wings, and that vision of perfection I had just gazed upon. I'm not saying she wasn't beautiful, she was, and she was still graceful. But it was like I had glimpsed her true self a moment ago and now I was looking at her through glasses that weren't in focus. Not wanting to let Alicia think I was nuts I let go of the curtain and turned to her.

"Sorry, you're right, I... uh... must be seeing things." I stuttered, suddenly feeling foolish. "Who is that?"

"Oh, that's Trixie." Alicia peeked through the curtain again. "She has quite the following." She turned and gazed at me.

"She got you in her spell, too?"

"What do you mean?"

"I don't know what she's got but she's got something. The guys go nuts over her. She only has to dance a couple sets a night and she still makes more money than any of the others."

I opened the curtain again. Trixie was still on stage. There *was* something special about her. Even if she wasn't the Nymph I had envisioned she was still something more. I moved my eyes to the audience. I could tell they were enthralled with her performance. Then I realized something wasn't right. They were way too interested.

The other dancers were moving about the crowded club and everyone had stopped paying attention to them. The men in the audience were all watching the stage, or to put it better, they were all watching Trixie, enthralled. I could see the girls eyeing each other, some of them shrugging, one rolling her eyes, they did not look happy. I had no idea what this girl had that they didn't, but Alicia was right, she had something.

"You see it too," she declared. It wasn't a question.

"Yeah, I'm guessing she isn't so popular with the other girls."

"No, she isn't. But management fired a few that said something a ways back and now days everyone keeps their mouth shut," she said as she turned and walked back down the hallway.

With a last look I let go of the curtain and followed her into her office. "What do you know about her?" I asked as I parked myself back in the chair in front of her desk.

"Oh, Honey she is outta your league," she replied with a shrug.

I might have blushed. "No, sorry, I didn't mean it that way."

She laughed, and then continued. "Not much, she comes in, does her sets and then she leaves. Never says too much. Only thing she's ever asked for is some special bottled water so I keep that in stock. As a matter of fact, there she goes now." Alicia tilted her head up as if pointing out the doorway.

I turned to look, but she had already gone. "Well, that's my cue," I said. "Thanks Alicia, I appreciate your help today."

As she stood I extended my hand to shake hers but she came around the desk instead. She reached for me and gave me a hug.

"Don't be a stranger, baby," she whispered in my ear. She took my hand and led me out of her office and back to the exit, which she opened. "And tell Hailey hi for me."

I went through the doorway and waved goodbye and then headed back into the dimly lit alley. As the door closed, I looked around, wondering where the girl had gone. Except for the cars there was nothing visible. I shook my head as I walked to the car. First it was talking dogs and now there were Faeries. Or was it Elves? Hell, did it really matter?

I sat in my car with the engine running for a minute or two just watching the lot. I couldn't figure it out. It had looked so real. I knew she couldn't really have had wings, but, damn, I saw them. What was happening to me? But I had seen the audience's reaction. She *had* done something to them and it was clear the other girls saw it, too.

So I was seeing and hearing things, but as for the girls at *Darlings*, ouch, that had to hurt. Just imagine what has to be going through their minds as they do a seductive lap dance and suddenly their customer forgets they exist. Talk about a blow to your self-esteem. Not to mention the bottom line if he doesn't tip her. Hell with it, I gave up trying to figure any of it out. This wasn't the place.

I put my car into gear and made my way out on to Highland. Making a left at the light, I headed towards Las Vegas Boulevard and the freeway. Eyeing a 7-11, I changed my mind and cut across several lanes of traffic and pulled into a parking space. I needed coffee.

Chapter 5

It must be my night for pretty women. As I went through the doorway I saw the clerk ringing up something for a nice looking gal. She was in her mid to late 30's with light brown hair to the middle of her back. Not magazine pretty, more a wholesome-type look. The kind of girl your mother would probably like. But there also was a subtle hint of sexy about her, just barely peeking out. She was well-dressed, casual style, in pressed black jeans and a black shirt that sparkled when she moved and showed just a hint of bosom. But it was her eyes that grabbed me and they grabbed my soul. They were as green as emeralds.

At first glance I had thought she might be wearing contacts, but when I took a second look, they were all hers. I was a sucker for green eyes. I gave a smile and a hello as I walked by. She just nodded and continued towards the exit, barely noticing me. Oh well, what did I expect, this was 7-11 for God's sake, not a pick up joint.

I grabbed a coffee, paid the clerk, and went back to the car. The Oakey exit was blocked by a limo. I'd seen that they sold hard liquor inside so I guessed a customer needed to make a purchase. I turned to exit on to a side street when I heard a commotion.

Barely illuminated by the street lights, the woman I had just seen in the store was being taunted by two twenty-something's in a red Corvette, their lights dimmed. This was an industrial area so there really wasn't any place for her to go. I rolled the passenger side window down and heard them arguing. I could hear them calling her "Lilly" and making lewd remarks.

Some people say you shouldn't get involved but that was never my style. Besides, I was armed and knew a few tricks. Still, it would have been better if someone else knew I was here. In the police world backup is never far away. When you're a P.I. you're usually on your own but that's the breaks. Maybe I should have dialed 911 but I just didn't think about it. I gunned my car and drove towards them. Stopping behind the Corvette, I switched on the brights and stepped out of the car.

By now one of the guys had the woman by the arm against the storefront. He was reaching for her breast with his other hand and she was struggling. The other was still taunting her, rhyming words with Lilly. I couldn't make it all out, something like "Little Lilly needs my willy," or some silly nonsense like that. I had a sudden vision of a scene from *A Clockwork Orange*, and then I intervened.

"I think that's enough, boys. Fun's over," I declared, just loud enough for them to hear.

They both looked at me, then the one holding her arm sneered. "Back off, twat, this is not your affair."

Say what? I don't think I'd ever been called a twat before. The other guy walked towards me. Normally, I'd have known better than to let someone get that close but it was too late.

"Beat it," he threatened, shoving me in the chest.

He snarled, he actually snarled, and I could have sworn his eyes shifted somehow.

Without warning something inside me snapped and I saw red. I'm not talking about anger although, that was certainly part of it. I mean literally. My perception of my surroundings had changed. I don't know what it was; call it adrenalin mixed with some unknown hormone, call it a shattering of the spell Meredith told me about. It doesn't matter, because suddenly everything was different. There was a red tinge and the world was no longer in darkness. It wasn't infrared, it was something else. Things slowed down and I could see...and hear...almost everything. I'd swear I could even hear the beating of their hearts.

I had no clue what was happening but everything was in perfect clarity. I could hear the sounds of cars, animals, and people, even those blocks away. I could tell you the exact height and weight of each attacker. Hell, I could tell you what they had in their pockets just by the sounds the coins made. One was 6' 1", 203 pounds, and there were 2 quarters, a dime and 3 pennies as well as a coin I didn't recognize in his left pocket.

The other, well it doesn't matter, he had a rod of some kind in his pocket and I saw him reaching for it. From I don't know where, power surged through me. I lunged forward and grabbed Mr. Beat It by the throat and lifted him into the air. I twisted around and slammed him into the trunk area of the Corvette. He groaned loudly and I could feel the metal yield with the force.

The other one pushed the woman down hard and ran towards me, his face and body starting to contort into something not quite human.

Before he could reach me I shot my arm forward and did the same to him. Smashing him into his partner, I watched as he changed back to normal. While they were stunned I pulled the rod from the second one's pocket.

"Let me go!" Mr. Beat It cried out.

I squeezed, and then caught myself before I went too far. Don't ask me how. Whatever was surging through my body was difficult to control. Hell, I didn't even know if I could control it. Holding them down with my arm, I examined the rod I had taken from him. It was not like the ones I had seen in the pictures. This one reminded me of a scepter. It was about 18" long with a handle that was hand carved of hard wood, it looked like oak. One end held a blue jewel which looked as if the wood itself had grown around it to hold it in place.

"You two weren't planning on using this, were you?" I asked, pointing the tip just inches from Mr. Beat It's face.

"No, really, I wasn't...I, I'm sorry...she's just a Lil, man!"

I didn't know what a Lil was but it didn't matter. I rolled the scepter in my palm and it became an extension of my hand. The tip burst into a bright blue flame. His eyes widened as he tried to back away but there was nowhere for him to go. I watched as he grimaced, the bright flame of the rod now just inches from his eyes.

What the hell! I was freaking out and liking it at the same time. I wasn't sure what I was doing but events were out of my control. I slowly pulled the scepter away and grabbed both of them by the throat again. Although they looked human I sensed there was more to them. I'd seen the one boy try to change into something else. Could it have been a wolf? I wasn't sure but I was so hyped up it didn't seem to matter.

"This is my town," I declared. Oh God, did I really just utter that cliché? "If you come here again or go anywhere near this woman you will not find me so merciful." Merciful? Where did that come from? Then I relaxed my grip enough for them to speak.

"I promise...we're going," Mr. Beat It sputtered, gasping for breath. The other one nodding frantically, his head moving up and down so fast I thought it was going to fall off.

"Go," I commanded as I lifted them up and pushed them down off the trunk of the car.

They scampered towards the side of the Corvette, never looking back, and scrambled into their seats without even opening the doors. I heard the tires squealing as they drove off, the burned rubber smell permeating the air. As they turned down a side street towards Main, I heard the roar of the engine fade.

I stepped back and leaned against my car, my vision slowly returning to normal. I felt...drained. What the hell was going on? Was I was having a dream? Maybe I was still in the *Darlings* lot sleeping in my car. But it didn't feel like a dream. I looked at the scepter again; the tip dark, cold, no fire burning within it. Could all this magical crap be real? I was too tired and confused to think. I just wanted to sleep but then I remembered the woman.

She was on the ground, her back up against the storefront, a look of total astonishment on her face. Gathering myself up as best I could I stuck the scepter in my belt and covered it with my shirt. I walked over to her and knelt down. "Are you ok?"

"What are you?" she asked.

That was the second time someone asked me that in as many days. Once again, I didn't have an answer. But at least this time the question made sense.

"Doesn't matter, are you ok?" I asked again.

She started to get up and I reached to help. She grasped her hand in mine and I wearily pulled her to her feet. When she was up, she didn't let go. She just held onto my hand for a moment and then she slowly released her grip. "Why did you help me?"

"Why did I help you?" I repeated, my other problems forgotten for a moment. What kind of a question was that? What do I even say to that? "I'm sorry, maybe I missed it, but you looked like you could use some help."

"Most of your kind wouldn't have gotten involved," she replied, abruptly, as she brushed off her clothes.

My kind? Maybe she'd have some answers. "What does that mean? What kind wouldn't have gotten involved?"

She looked at me with a quizzical expression on her face. "I may not know who you are but even an idiot could tell you are Fae."

"Even if I am Fae why shouldn't I have stopped them?"

"The Were are creatures of the Fae, your realm. Why would you defend me to spite them? Am I not but a Lil to you?" Her face became angry but I could tell she was puzzled. "There is no love lost between our kind, or have the rules changed after all these years?"

She was definitely not acting like a damsel who'd been in distress. But crap, if we weren't supposed to like each other, why did I think she was she so damned hot?

Wait? Did she say Were? As in Were-wolf or maybe, Were-something-even-worse? And what the hell was a Lil? Shit, what was going on here? I was back in the fantasy novel. Maybe I was in a coma somewhere like on that British TV show. Damn, I didn't even know the characters, let alone what part I was playing. Now there were rules as well. But I needed answers and she might be my best hope. I could go to Milagre, but could I trust him? Hell, could I trust her?

Suddenly I remembered why I had intervened, as it were, and no "your realm" or forest bullshit changed that. Damsel in distress or not, I was getting pissed.

"Listen, lady...what is your name, anyway?" My change in tone surprised her.

"Delia, but..."

"Listen, Delia," I interrupted, folding my arms in front of my chest. "I don't know what you think I am or for that matter, what rules you think I should follow." I wasn't being exactly truthful, so what else was new? "I don't give a damn who those punks were. Where I come from we don't let strangers paw a pretty gal and we don't ignore a woman in distress."

Well, maybe I did care if they were Werewolves but why bother her with trivia?

Her features softened, and what might have been a smile began to appear but she caught it before it could emerge. "I'm sorry, it, you just surprised me." She looked down at the ground for a moment as if I might have embarrassed her. "It's just...never mind, thank you."

"You're welcome. Now, why don't you let me give you a ride home or to wherever you're going? That way, I won't have to worry if you make it safely or not."

"No, I'm just going to work, it's not far," she replied but I could see she was unsure.

I needed answers, but to be truthful, I also wanted to spend more time with her. There was just something different about her.

"Please, I insist," I said, trying to smile. "I promise I won't bite."

She giggled and it felt wonderful to watch. I walked her to my car and opened the door for her. She paused a moment, then got in. "I wouldn't have let them go too far, you know. It is not forbidden to protect oneself from harm," she commented, placing her hand on my leg as if to reassure me. Forbidden, what the hell did that mean?

"Right, well," I pointed out, "it looked like they were harming you from where I was standing."

"My life was not in danger, there are rules, you know."

Who makes up these rules? What the hell was that about? I threw my hands in the air. None of this was making sense. "So let me get this straight. They can paw you and maybe rape you, but that's ok. I mean, as long as they don't try to kill you." It was my turn to look at her like she was crazy.

"What kind of screwed up rule is that?"

"You really don't know, do you?"

I just looked back at her without saying anything. I was tired, frustrated, and almost didn't care anymore. Maybe it was the fight; maybe it was just irritability at being thrust into a world that had so many screwed up rules. Hell, I wasn't even sure if it was still the same world I had gone to bed in two nights ago. At the moment, though, I just didn't have an answer, but I was tired of saying no.

"Where to?" I asked as I put the car in gear and pulled out into the street.

"Make a left at the next street, I work at Danu's."

"Danu's, what's that?" I asked, turning down the street she pointed out.

"You've never heard of it?" She was looking at me like the mere mention of the name was all I'd need.

Here we go again. "Sorry, what is it?"

"It's a bar, second building from the end, turn there," she instructed, pointing between two buildings.

Cliché or not, Vegas really is my town. I was born and raised here. I went to school here. Hell, I worked the streets for 25 years here. I knew this part of town like the back of my hand and there was no way that place was supposed to be there.

The front was just an antechamber with a heavy door. There was a wooden sign hanging outside like an old English Pub. Carved into the wood was the name, Danu's, and above it a caricature of a female holding a sword while sitting on a crescent moon that shone over a sea. The letters were white, the name and image appeared hand painted. It was between the old Las Vegas Fire Station #4 and a machine shop.

I'd been down here hundreds of times over the years and I'd never noticed this place. But then, nothing made sense anymore so why should I be surprised.

Delia got out of the car and looked over at me. "You coming in?"

"Let me park the car. I'll be there in a minute."

She closed the door and I pulled around next to the machine shop, still trying to figure out where the building had come from. I couldn't get all the way into the back, so I parked next to the fence and walked back to the entrance.

I opened the heavy wooden door and walked into a small hallway. There was another set of doors about 5 feet into the place. I went through this doorway and took a look around. The place did look like an old English Pub. It was all wood and brick with a fireplace in the far corner that had lion's feet legs and a hardwood mantle. The hearth was raised and made of an antique brick. The bar was U shaped and looked like it came out of a museum. The stools and tables were of heavy wood and all appeared hand crafted. It was definitely unique.

It was also quiet. There were only a few people in the place, assuming that they were people. I didn't recognize any of them. There was a young couple in a booth and a few others sitting in tables in groups of two and three. Delia was behind the bar talking to a blond haired guy. He reminded me of Siegfried in a way, but not as hardened. She waited till I was almost at the bar.

"What'll you have?"

"What do you recommend?"

"Well," she announced, "we brew our own ale here."

"That'll be fine." I responded, taking a seat in front of her.

As she poured the beer from a tap, the blonde guy leaned over the bar and stuck out his hand. "I'm Bart."

"Robert," I replied. "Nice to meet you."

As he let go of my hand his expression started to change but before I could tell what it was he caught himself. It almost seemed like he had expected something more when he touched me and was surprised when he didn't get it. "I don't recall seeing you in here before."

Well, at least he hadn't asked me what I was. "Nope, first time," I remarked as Delia placed a frozen mug down in front of me.

"A new customer," he beamed. "Well then, allow me to buy the first round."

Delia told me that she would be right back and the two of them went to the other end of the bar and began fiddling with some bottles. I couldn't hear what they were saying but by the way they glanced over from time to time, I assumed they were talking about me.

The beer was marvelous; it reminded me of a Belgian beer called Chimay that's brewed by Trappist monks. But somehow I doubted that monks were involved in the brewing process here. As I savored my beer I went over the events of the last two days in my mind. I was just at the part where the naked Faerie, or Elf, or whatever she was had come in when I heard the door open and I saw Bart rush to the other end of the bar.

"You're not welcome here," he said, loudly.

Delia stood right behind him. She started to say something but never got a word out.

"Back off, bitch!" A male voice yelled out. Oh great, another asshole. I started to turn to see who it was.

"That's him, Dad. There's the guy."

Damn, that's all I needed. As I looked towards the door I saw Mr. Beat It standing next to a tall, well-built man with dark hair and a beard. Shit, he was big.

He took one look at me and started coming. "How dare you side with her kind over my boy," he yelled.

I was just getting to my feet when the world slowed down again. I watched as he came towards me. With every step his body changed, his clothes ripping away as a large wolf replaced his human form. I don't know what I had expected, but this wasn't it.

I should have been scared but the power that overtook me earlier once again surged through me at the moment that he began to shift. My vision turned red again and I saw and felt everything that was happening around me. At first, it seemed as if someone else was controlling me but then I knew it was coming from within. I was accessing some part of me that had lain dormant. Something when he shifted had awoken it and information and power flooded my being. Damn, if only I could control it.

I shouldn't have been able to do it. As he leapt towards me I raised my right hand and caught him by the neck before his jaws could snap at me. His momentum and weight forced me back a few steps but I pushed him forward and down. He yelped and blood splattered onto me as the force of my movement slammed him to the ground.

I bent down over him, holding him down like a raptor examining his prey in his talons. I could sense the others in the room, frozen, watching us. Their faces registering shock, not believing what was happening. It felt like I was hearing their thoughts, how did he do that, what is he? The smell of his blood surrounded me and memories flooded in with it. Suddenly, I knew more about him then he probably knew himself.

"Loup-garou," I heard my voice say. "Alsace, 300 B.C., Gaul, yours was once a mighty bloodline." Then I felt myself willing the wolf away and watched as he shifted back to human form, a look of utter surprise and defeat on his face. He was gasping for breath so I released my hold a bit.

"How did you...," he choked.

"You vex me," I hissed. Damn, I was using those old words again.

"I warned your whelp," I said slowly, as I turned my head and nodded toward his son who by now was cowering against the wall by the door. "This female and this place are under my protection. If you or your kind comes near here again, you will die. Do you understand?"

He struggled a bit before answering. "Yes," he said, weakly.

"Do not think to confuse my compassion for weakness. Leave this place, now." As I said the word "now," I flung him toward the door.

When he was done sliding he got to his knees, his naked human form bruised and bloodied. He looked over at me briefly, rubbed his neck, then he jumped up and grabbed the boy, pulling him through the doorway.

As soon as they scampered out the door I felt the power withdraw. Damn, it had been such a rush, yet now I felt only exhaustion. It took me a moment to reorient myself. I stood up and went back to the bar, dropping into the stool. I heard shuffling behind me and I turned to see the other patrons leaving quickly, but quietly, whispering among one another as they made their way through the doorway. They looked afraid.

I grabbed my mug and gulped what was left. Maybe they should be afraid, I know I was. I had no idea what was happening to me. Sure, it had saved me twice but I had no clue about how the hell to control it. Who knows what could happen the next time.

Bart appeared across the bar from me, glaring. "I don't know how you did that but if I'd known Weres were after you I would never have let you stay."

"Yeah, well, live and learn," I said as I pushed my mug towards him. I was too tired to care what he thought.

"You shouldn't have brought them here," he persisted.

"Bjartr, stop," Delia appealed. "It was my fault. I never got to explain. He was involved because of me."

"You? By the Gods, Delia, are you trying to start a war? What did you do?" He looked horrified.

"Hey, back off, it wasn't her fault. If you want to blame someone, blame me. The two of them were pawing her, I couldn't let that continue," I said, angrily. Damn...these people, creatures, whatever they were. They were as bad as regular people, if not worse. "I've had enough. If that's the way you treat each other maybe you need a war!" I reached into my wallet and pulled out a twenty and threw it on the bar. "I'm outta here." I exclaimed, heading for the exit.

When I got outside, I paused, making sure no one was waiting for me. I didn't have the increased senses that the rage had given me but everything looked quiet. I started to walk back to my car when I heard the bar's door open.

"Wait," Delia begged, grabbing my arm. I stopped and turned towards her. "I'm sorry, Bart worries, it's just the way he is."

"Yeah, well. With assholes like those guys, I can see why. But that doesn't excuse their behavior. Why do you put up with it?"

"It's complicated, and difficult to explain. I can't understand how you don't know. Where have you been?"

How do I answer that one? I couldn't tell her I didn't know about this world till yesterday. Shit, I still didn't even know what world I was in. "I don't get out much," was the best I could do. I started to walk away, but turned back. "Look, I'm sorry, it's kind of complicated for me as well. Listen, would it be alright if I came back, so we could talk?"

"I don't know. It's probably not a good idea."

I just tried to look innocent as she stood there.

"Alright, but it'll have to be a night that Bart isn't here or if I can get away. Can I call you?" she finally said.

That didn't sound too promising but I pulled my card out of my wallet anyway and handed it to her anyway. "I look forward to hearing from you."

"I'll try," she whispered. Her face brightened and I might have seen her smile before she turned back towards the door, "and thank you."

Chapter 6

Word of advice: Just because you kick a Werewolf or two's ass when you switch into a superman or you can figure out how much change someone has in their pocket, don't get cocky. I still didn't know how this shit worked. On the way home last night I tried my luck at slots and lost $100.00 bucks for my effort. I couldn't wish my way into a pair, or even a cherry. Well, I should have known better than stop when I had been so tired, so much for my knowledge of magic.

I sat there sipping coffee out of my *terrifying space monkeys* cup trying to wake up while I tried to plan my next move. I didn't have one yet, but I could hope. Up until last night I'd had a nice life. My kids were grown and doing well. Sure, I was divorced, but we still got along. Business had been steady and the money was good. I owned my house and my investments were paying enough to keep me happy. But it's one thing to have fantasies; it's another to wake up living in them.

Ok, I'll admit it; some of it was pretty cool. I got to kick some ass and save the pretty gal. Of course, the pretty girl was a Lil, whatever that was. And I was pretty sure my name was mud in the Werewolf community, assuming they even had a community. But I knew enough about real wolves and read enough books to be able to guess they ran in packs and that did not comfort me. For someone who hadn't believed in magic until last night, I was knee deep in it.

I needed answers. I figured Siegfried from the *Neptune* owed me something for saving Milagre's life. It would have been bad for business if his boss got whacked on his shift, so I started with him. I gave him a call and made arrangements to meet him at the coffee shop a little after noon.

Milagre must know what he was doing. The place was way too busy for a week day. I parked in the garage, the public one this time, and hiked what seemed like a city block to the elevators. Once inside the casino I dodged the horde and made my way to the coffee shop, dropping Siegfried's name to the hostess.

If there was one thing I liked about the place it was that it was old school Vegas. The second I mentioned Siegfried's name the hostess grabbed a menu and led me to an oversized booth in the back calling me sir several times on the way. In the old days they would have called this the executive area. Siegfried, wearing a suit, was talking into a house phone. He nodded as I sat down. Cups and glasses were set down in front of me and Siegfried's glass was refilled. Another pretty waitress took our order and Siegfried took another call.

"My apologies for the interruptions, duty calls as it were. So, Robert, how may I be of service?" Siegfried asked as he hung up the phone.

"I just had a few questions. Things have been a little chaotic since the other night."

"How so?"

"Let me lay some cards on the table, Siegfried. Maybe you can give me some advice or at least help me make some sense of it." I didn't want to get into too much detail, as I still wasn't sure where he fit in into all this but I had to start somewhere.

"Certainly, how can I help?"

A weird sensation pinged in my head as he answered. I turned around and saw Meredith coming out of a side door with another woman in tow. She looked surprised to see me. I could tell Siegfried noticed it also, but he hid it well.

"Hello, ma'am," I said, rising as she approached.

"Please sit," she replied, motioning at the two of us. "How nice to see you again so soon, Robert. Is everything alright?"

"Yes, I just asked Siegfried to meet for lunch."

"Wonderful, and how are you doing since we last spoke?"

I wasn't sure how to answer. I certainly wasn't going to tell her everything. Once again, the truth was best. "Actually I've started seeing a few strange things. That's why I'm here. Thought I'd try and get some hints as to what to expect," I answered, hoping that that would satisfy her.

She gave me a skeptical look, but she didn't inquire further. "Well, please let me know if I can help. Bill this to my account," she said to Siegfried, and then turned and walked away.

Siegfried took a drink and watched her make her way through the restaurant. When she exited to the casino, he returned his gaze me. "Interesting, she did not know you were here."

"...and your point is?" I asked, wondering what that meant. I knew they had cameras everywhere but I doubted surveillance knew everyone that came into the place.

He looked around cautiously before leaning over the table. "Perhaps we should continue this conversation later. Some things are best not spoken aloud," he whispered.

Now that comment *was* interesting. I had thought he was Milagre's boy. Had I had missed something?

Straightening up, he gestured to the waitress. She returned with our food and refills and we ate while we talked.

"So tell me, what exactly have you been seeing?" he asked.

I told him about the winged Faerie girl at *Darlings*.

"Hmm, winged Faeries are not uncommon. Nymphs and Faeries are known to be attractive to humans, though they cannot see their true form as you did unless they wish them too. Still, they are easily influenced. Did you notice the crowd after her performance?"

"No, why, what would I have seen?"

"It depends, if she was just using her magic to seduce, then nothing. But some beings feed on the desire of others. If the crowd appeared weak or confused, she may have been a Succubus. They can appear as anything. But since it was only because of your magic that you could see her true form I doubt that is the case."

"I never know such things existed. What else is out there?

"Ha, the world of the Fae has many beings. Even I do not know them all," he told me as he chuckled. I must have looked dejected because Siegfried stopped laughing. "I am sorry, Robert. It is easy to forget that this is so new to you. I have been of both worlds since I was born. Let me give you an overview. We can discuss more when we meet again."

"That would be great," I admitted.

"First, there are humans and then there are the Fae. Just as humans are different shapes and colors, so are the Fae. All magical creatures, with the exception of Demons and a few others, such as the Lil, are said to be of the Fae."

"There are Demons...and what's a Lil?" I interrupted; here was something I could at least relate to. Well, not the demon part, but I did want to know what a Lil was.

"Yes, there are Demons. But do not think of them as humans do. They are not minions of the devil, although some are indeed evil. Think of them as a separate race of beings."

Well, that helps, not!

"Ok...and the Lil?"

"The Lilin are another separate branch. They are related to both human and demon kind. They are the descendants of an ancient being, Lilith. You have heard of Vampires?"

"Of course, who hasn't?" I answered, trying not to look excited. Was she a Vampire? Wait, I hadn't seen any fangs. Besides, aren't Vampires supposed to be stronger than Werewolves?

"The Lilin are the beings behind the legends," he continued, "but they are not dead nor do they bite their victims with fangs. It is said that the Lilin and the Fae once battled one another for dominion of the Earth. I am not familiar with the entire tale, but eventually the Lilin were defeated. Most of the Fae still regard them with disdain," he explained. "There are actually several in the area, but you need not fear them. It is forbidden of them to drink of the Fae."

"That's a good thing." I think...it also explained something about the rules, but a bloodsucker?

"Indeed," he agreed, glancing at his watch. "As I said, there are many creatures in the world of the Fae." He began using his fingers to keep track. "The Were are shape shifters, Faeries, Dryads like you from the oak, Meliai from the ash, Nereids from water, like the Milagre's." He stopped and laughed again. "There are just too many clans to count."

"I can see that," I said with a smile. Ok, so he thinks I'm a Dryad, whatever that entailed.

"Here in the new world the Fae are sparse, but in this area there are a few clans that have made their presence known. Due to this there is significantly more activity between the Fae than would be normal. It is the magic that attracts them here. I do not know if that helps but suffice it to say that I will help you on your journey if I can." He got that serious look again and leaned forwards a bit again. "Others will offer the same," he whispered, scanning the room with his eyes. "Be careful who you trust."

With that said he put down his napkin and stood up. Taking a card out of his jacket, he wrote something on it and handed it to me. "I must go. It was good to meet with you. I put my direct line on the card, please do not hesitate to call," he said, reaching to shake my hand.

I followed him into the casino where we parted ways. Then I walked back to the garage to my car. Once I closed the door and started the engine I glanced down at the card. On it was the message," *meet"* and an address and time: *8:00 p.m.*, so much for an early day.

So she's like a Vampire, I thought. Bummer. I put the car in gear and headed for my office.

The office was a madhouse. Hailey had half her runners out serving subpoenas on some big civil case while the other half was running paper between lawyer's offices. I had to make a dash for the coffee pot when I got there and then wade through the bodies just to get to my office. I took it as a sign that it would be a good day to get some paperwork done so I locked the door and finished a stack of online research requests and billing.

I spent the rest of my time researching Dryads and other so-called myths. It was interesting but I wasn't sure how helpful it was going to be. I really didn't know how much was real and how much was bullshit but at least it was a start.

The Lilith history did interest me. There are stories about Lilith that date back to ancient Sumerian writings. There were some references to the drinking of blood as well as her seductive nature. But there are so many different legends it's hard to figure out just what Delia could really be. I must have gotten carried away. I was reading up on Vampires when I looked down at my watch, it was already 7:30 p.m. I shut everything off and headed out for my rendezvous with Siegfried.

I punched the address into my nav and followed the car's directions. I wound up at a diner on North Jones Road, an old section of town. I'd seen the place before but it was buried in the back of an old strip mall so I'd never been inside. To be honest, I'd thought the place was closed.

The place appeared to be new inside, if you disregarded the fact that it looked like it had been transported here from the 40's or 50's. The place reminded me of a restaurant in an old drug store picture. The bar was long and had stools. The booths were red leather. The ceiling had old style fans and aluminum tiles; the floor was red and white checkerboard. There was even a jukebox and glass displays for the pies. It must have cost a fortune to recreate.

I saw Siegfried in one of the back booths waving at me. I walked over and joined him, sliding into the booth.

"Nice place, I thought it was closed."

"The owners prefer it that way, as do the patrons," he replied with a grin.

The waitress took that moment to come over. "Hey, Sig, who's your friend?" she asked, giving me the once over.

"Shayla, this is Robert, Robert, meet Shayla," he answered, introducing us.

"Pleasure to meet you," I said, leaning over and doing my best to stand.

"Well, isn't he the polite one?" she snickered, winking at Siegfried. "What'll you have?"

We both ordered coffee, and she swiftly returned with a carafe and cups.

"So, Siegfried, why are we here?" I asked, deciding to make the first move.

It was Siegfried's turn to give me the once over. He took a moment before he spoke. "First, you must understand that my loyalty to the Milagre's is not in question. I am in their employ, and as such, I will not do anything that betrays that duty." He looked serious.

"I understand."

"I asked you here because we have a kinship and I also have a duty to that."

"A kinship, what kind of kinship" I asked, interrupting him. This was definitely interesting, even if I had no clue what he was talking about.

He pulled out his cell phone and showed it to me. On the screen was a picture of the oak leaf symbol from my gun. Then he startled me by putting a knife, almost a short sword, on the table. He pushed it towards me.

It was long, maybe 18 or 20 inches in length. The blade was highly polished and single edged, tapered to a sharp point. Below the guard a symbol was etched into the blade, an oak leaf almost identical to the one on my gun. The blade itself appeared to be made of a number of layered metals and had a pattern of leaves on the top. Siegfried watched me as I examined it.

"That is a seax. This particular seax has been in my family for many generations. The symbols you see are my family's."

I inspected the blade, surprised at the similarities between the crests. Sure, a leaf is a leaf, but these were almost identical in design. "So what does this mean?"

"The oak was a sacred tree to the Gods. Thor's chariot and the handle of his hammer, Mollinir, were crafted of it. It is said that Thor once visited Jotunheim, the land of the giants, to recover Mollinir which had been stolen. To aid him, the oak's offered a score of their kind to be transformed by the dark Elves into warriors. They became his personal guards. I am descended of that line. While my line is not of the Dryad, I am still of the Fae, we are kin." He reached over and removed the weapon from the table.

"Why are you telling me this, Siegfried? I have no quarrel with Milagre," I asked, not sure what he was getting at, especially after the loyalty speech.

"I did not mean to imply that you did," he said matter-of-factly. "But you know little of the Fae. You will need a guide, and possibly a friend."

"Why?" Should I trust him, hell, could I trust him?

"Robert, you know nothing of the Fae," he said with a grin." This is not the human world with its laws and rules. Nor are the Fae here in the new world like the Fae of the old. The lines between clans blur here. Here, the Fae live as they always have. It is a world where alliances are formed through strength, the strength of magic. Have you not read your history? The Greek and Roman Gods were not benevolent. They were vain and jealous. They fought one another continuously. My Gods were no better. Thor, Loki, Odin...always battling one another, pitting one against the other. Even magic is not always enough as the Gods themselves found out. You must not only know when to wield it, but when not too. Such is the world of the Fae."

This did not bode well. I'd already seen some of that battling the Werewolves. Sure, I was able to defeat them. But I had no idea how I did it or if I could tap into that power again. He was right, I would need some help.

"Thank you for the offer, Siegfried. I will consider it."

"That is all I ask."

"I'm still confused though. What was the deal with Meredith?"

"Magic knows magic," he answered. I must have had a blank look on my face. "You sensed her, did you not? I saw it on your face."

"I suppose I did."

"She is eldest of her clan, a powerful Fae, yet she did not know you were there. I have never heard of that happening before. It is most unusual."

"But what does it mean?" I asked, still not sure of the significance.

"It means that you are dangerous," he answered, again watching my reaction.

Just frigging great, now I had more problems.

"Magic is what binds all Fae," he continued. "Most Fae can feel magic in the air, or the lack of it. In most creatures, the sense is limited. But Meredith is a very powerful Fae, she should have sensed you. That she could not means that you are different. Do not confuse what I say. Meredith would not seek to harm you, but she would want to use you for her own benefit. As kin, I needed you to know that your power is unusual. You can choose how that information should be used. Be careful who you trust with this knowledge. Others will want to use that power and not all will be for good."

It seemed like the more he said the less I understood.

"What about you, Siegfried? Can you sense me?"

"No, but I am not like you. My gifts lend themselves to doing battle and I have never been bested." He pulled out the seax again and I watched as he twirled it around several times in an elaborate display. It danced in his hand before he thrust it into the table. It was pretty slick for a guy sitting down.

Note to file: Don't get into a knife fight with Siegfried.

"Hey, hey, watch the table boys!" the waitress, Shayla, commented as she walked up. The mood lightened as she replaced the carafe and filled our mugs. Maybe this was normal behavior in a place like this.

"Nice knife work," I commented as she left.

We talked for several more hours and not all of it was about magic. But get this, the most interesting part was how the Fae took over the mob in this town, but that's a story for another day.

Chapter 7

The noise of the alarm clock was only part of the reason I was awake. The big dog licking my face was the other.

"Charlie, down," I said, pushing him away.

Waking up to dog slobber isn't pleasant but you have to admit it's effective. Reaching over to focus on the time I saw that it was 8:32 a.m. Why would I set the alarm for then? There was another ring. It wasn't the alarm, it was my cell phone.

"Hello," I said, trying not to sound like I just woke up.

"Rob, it's Hailey," said the voice on the other end. "Did I wake you?"

"No, Charlie did that for you," I said. "What's up?"

"Oh, that lug, give him a hug for me." She had a soft spot for Charlie and always brought him a treat when she visited.

"I will Hail, so why the early call?"

"Well, I have Mr. Carmine Pontedra on the other line. I thought it would be a call you'd want to take."

"Oh thanks, can you transfer him?" I got out of bed and headed downstairs to the kitchen for coffee.

"Of course," Hailey responded. "By the way, are you coming in today?"

"I plan to, unless this call changes things. Probably around 10:30 – 11:00. Why, anything up?"

"No, just wondering. Alright, see you in a bit, here's Mr. Pontedra." I heard the click as the call transferred.

"This is Robert Hoskins, is this Mr. Pontedra?" I said as I pushed the button to start the coffee brewing.

"Yes, Mr. Hoskins, I believe you have something for me."

"Yes I do, I have a subpoena for you. I was wondering if you would be available sometime later today. I can bring it by the property." I hadn't expected him to be so pleasant. His reputation had made me think he was going to be difficult despite my new found friendship with his boss.

"That won't be necessary. I have some business in the downtown area. I have your address from the card that Mr. Milagre gave me. Will you be available around 11:00?"

"11:00 would be fine, Mr. Pontedra, I'll see you then."

"Please, call me Carmine. I'll see you at 11:00 then. Oh, and Mr. Hoskins, Mr. Milagre told me about what happened the other night. Please allow me to express my thanks for your intervention. Mr. Milagre means a great deal to me. I would like to return the favor. If there is ever anything I can ever do for you, please let me know."

"Thank you, Carmine; I'll keep it in mind. I'll see you soon."

"Goodbye," I heard him say as the phone disconnected. Well that was interesting, now I've got more folks that wouldn't give me the time of day a week ago offering me favors. What's next?

I poured myself a cup of coffee in a *General Dynamics* mug as I watched Charlie push his bowl around the tile floor. I distinctly heard the word "food" in my mind. He looked up at me and the word was repeated.

Great, I actually could hear him. I guess I had found out what was next. I filled his bowl from the bag in the pantry and set it down in front of him.

"What, no thank you?" I asked, watching as he gulped down his food.

He stopped and raised his head, his eyes watching me. I heard a bark and the words "thank you" as he went back to eating. Well, at least he could be polite.

I went upstairs and showered and then dressed in my standard business casual attire. Tan pants and a long sleeve collarless shirt. Heading back downstairs I refilled my mug, dumping what was left and got the pot ready for the next time.

I told Charlie to guard the house and waited to see if he was going to say anything else. I guess not, as he just headed out the doggie door without a glance back. I wondered if any of my days would ever be normal again.

I got in my car and headed toward the 95 to downtown. Aside from talking dogs, it was a nice day. Although the morning weather report had said it was going to rain today. It sure didn't look like it yet, but that's the desert for you.

It was almost 10:00 a.m. by the time I pulled into the back lot of the building where my office was. Once inside, I spent a minute chatting with Hailey and then retrieved my mail and messages. With that done I poured myself a fresh cup of coffee and sat down at my desk.

As I looked over my mail and caseload I got the paperwork ready for my meeting with Carmine. Looking over my messages, I saw that I had one from the attorney who had asked me to serve him. I figured that one could wait. The rest were return calls or calls from other business acquaintances. I was trying to decide who to call back first when Hailey came in to tell me that Carmine was here.

I grabbed my file and went into the small conference room we had in the building. Placing it down on the table I went out to greet Carmine. As I entered the front office area I was a little caught off guard when I realized that Carmine wasn't alone. He was with another well-dressed man carrying a flap over leather briefcase. He turned and introduced himself.

"Mr. Hoskins, Gerry Cornwall, I'm Mr. Pontedra's attorney, I hope you don't mind that I've tagged along," he responded, giving me a business-like smile.

"No, not at all," I replied, finding this meeting even more interesting.

Gerry Cornwall was perhaps the leading civil attorney in the Las Vegas area. His client list represented most of Vegas' movers and shakers, including the mayor who was his old business partner. He probably also represented over half the other casino owners as well. Frankly, I'd never been able to get any of his business, I just didn't move in his circles.

He was wearing an impeccably tailored business suit. Custom tailored, I might add. Probably a *Gary Franzen*, he was Las Vegas' most sought after tailor. I knew that because I had one myself. Of course, I only had the one, and I was guessing Cornwall had a bigger wardrobe than me. There was one other thing. I felt it the minute they walked into the office. Although I couldn't detect anything from Carmine, Gerry Cornwall smelled like magic! I knew he was Fae. I was a little startled by my ability to detect it but I figured it was best to act as if I wasn't aware of it.

"Let's move on into the conference room, shall we?" I said, gesturing to the hallway that led to the rest of the office. We all sat down at the table and I removed the subpoena from my file, handing it to Mr. Cornwall.

"You may consider Mr. Pontedra served, Mr. Hoskins," he said, handing the paperwork to Carmine who glanced over it and placed it down in front of him.

"Thank you, I appreciate you taking the time to come to my office with your client."

"Not a problem. Carmine and I had other business this morning so this was not out of our way," he said, giving me one of those smiles that always made me think of a used car salesman. "Actually, since I am here, why don't we call Mr. Lagisto and try to resolve this right now?"

"Ok, although to be honest, I didn't work this investigation. I merely handled the subpoena for him." I was surprised at this turn of events. This wasn't the usual way things like this worked.

"Of course, but since we are here and I know Andrew would like to get this resolved, let's get him on the phone."

Andrew was of course, Andrew Lagisto, a local attorney who I did a lot of work for. He had offered me a considerable fee for this service so I figured he'd really be amazed at this turn of events. Since I had nothing to lose I grabbed the phone on the table and dialed his private number.

"Andy," was all he said when he picked up the line.

"Hey, it's Robert Hoskins, how are you?" I asked, looking over at Carmine and his attorney.

"Rob, I'm fine, what's up, any problem getting that subpoena served?"

"Actually, that's why I am calling. I have Mr. Pontedra and his attorney, Gerry Cornwall, in my office. Do you mind if we go on speaker?"

"You're kidding. You have Cornwall in your office. What the hell did you do?" He sounded more surprised than I was.

"Go ahead, this should be interesting."

"We can go over it later. I'm going to put you on speaker now," I said as I reached over and switched the phone to the conference speakers.

"Andy, can you hear me, we're on conference now?"

"Yes, Mr. Cornwall, Mr. Pontedra, thank you for contacting me, what can I do for you?"

"Andrew, it's Gerald. Carmine and I received your subpoena today. Do you have a moment to discuss?" He said "discuss" like it was an event and it probably was, a billable event.

"Absolutely, Gerald," he replied.

"Well, Carmine and I were aware that you were going to subpoena him in this case." Cornwall looked over at me and winked.

I almost fell to the floor.

"After some discussion with Mr. Hoskins, it is Carmine's wish to try and resolve this. Have you given any thought to where you stand on this issue?"

"Well, Gerald, put simply, my client feels that he was unfairly treated by Mr. Pontedra in his employment ratings and at the termination hearing. There's also the fact that he feels that he has been blacklisted. I'd like to see him get reinstated if that is a possibility. As you may be aware, he had a stellar reputation prior to the Neptune and this matter has severely damaged that in the industry."

I saw Pontedra shake his head and start to say something when Andy was talking. Cornwall put his hand on his arm to stop him. Carmine didn't look happy, but he didn't say anything either. All I knew about the case was that it involved a long time Vegas host that used to work for the Neptune.

"Andrew, you know that is impossible. However, in an effort to be fair, we are willing to allow your client to resign. We can offer him a considerable severance for that action. That should remove the stigma of the termination and allow him some breathing room until he can secure employment. Would that be agreeable?" Cornwall asked, keeping his hand on Pontedra's arm.

"That might work," Andy replied. "What type of severance are you thinking?"

"Well, since there wasn't a contract, I'd say a year's base salary would be sufficient, but rather than argue the matter we'd be willing to go two."

"Two year's salary at 250k a year, is that your offer?"

"That's the best I can do, Andrew, and you know as well as I do that it is more than fair. That assumes, of course, that your client provide us with the letter of resignation immediately so we can get this matter resolved." There was a moment of silence on the speaker. Cornwall looked over at me and I almost broke out laughing when he winked again.

"I believe I can convince my client to accept that offer. When can I get that in writing?"

"I'll have my office run the papers over this afternoon." Cornwall replied, sifting through some paperwork in his briefcase. "I can have a check ready when they are signed and we are in receipt."

"I'll get a hold of my client this afternoon and see if we can get this resolved then," Andy said. "Thank you for contacting me."

Cornwall started to get up so I took the phone off speaker and told Andy I would call him back. He leaned over and said something quietly to Carmine that I couldn't hear, but I could clearly read Carmine's lips when he said "bullshit."

"Attorneys," he remarked, shaking his head. "It's days like this when I miss the old Vegas." He was clearly not too happy with the negotiations.

"Times change," Cornwall replied. "And I did have clear instructions from Mr. Milagre."

Carmine still didn't look happy, but he didn't seem to want to argue, either.

"Carmine, can you give me a moment with Mr. Hoskins?"

"Sure, I'll be in the car." Carmine said as he stood up. "It was a pleasure meeting you, Robert. Remember what I said, if I can ever be of service, don't hesitate to call."

"I won't, Carmine, and thank you again for your cooperation today."

I got up as well and walked him out of the conference room. When I saw him head toward the front door, I turned and walked back to Cornwall.

"Is there something else?"

"Robert, may I ask if you have any other interests in this case?" he asked as he put the papers back in his briefcase.

"No, as I said, I merely handled the subpoena, why do you ask?" Hmm, now we appeared to be on a first name basis. I wondered what was coming next.

"I wanted to see what you had to say about what you just witnessed but I wanted to make sure there wasn't a conflict before we talked"

"Well, Mr. Cornwall, I guess I am a little surprised. I know Carmine's reputation and it doesn't quite add up that you would give up so much. Then again, I've met Mr. Milagre and I am sure he has his reasons. I'll also admit to curiosity as why you handled this from my office."

"Consider it an act of good faith on Mr. Milagre's part. I am not completely sure why, but as you said, he has his reasons.

"Good faith?" I commented. "How would giving 500k to someone else's client show me good faith?"

"Come now, Robert, you can't tell me that this doesn't put Andrew in your debt. Besides, his client will never work in this town again, not without an endorsement from Carmine. The money, well, the money will keep him from being an inconvenience. Our kind must show other's that we have influence. Wouldn't you agree?"

"I guess that's true." Our kind, now I saw where he was coming from. I could see that the world was changing for me. I just wasn't sure if it was for the better.

"I wish I had known of your lineage before," he commented as he picked his briefcase up. "It was silly of you to hide it. We could have sent a lot of business your way. We will of course attempt to remedy that in the future," he said as he walked out of the conference room and headed toward the front door.

"I also had my reasons," I remarked, walking along side of him.

"Of course, but now that we are acquainted, let's hope they won't get in the way of business in the future." He turned to shake my hand. "I look forward to seeing you again."

"As do I," I replied.

Hailey was pointing at the phone as I walked back toward my office. "It's Mr. Lagisto, where do you want it?"

"In my office," I answered and headed through my doorway and then plopped down in my chair and picked up the phone.

"Andy that was quick."

"Quick! No shit! I want to know where that came from. I can't get that prick to return my calls half the time and he walks into your office and hands me a deal on a silver platter Why didn't you tell me you knew Cornwall?"

"It never came up, and Andy, you know I keep my business dealings confidential. I figured it was better to play the part but I was hesitant about mentioning Milagre. Still, Andy was a good client. I might not be thrilled about the "our kind" mentality but I'm not an idiot.

"Honestly, Andy, I think I caught Pontedra off guard with the subpoena. You know how good he is at ducking folks. Plus, your client has been around a long time so I'm guessing the negative publicity of a civil suit wouldn't sit well with his boss."

"Yeah, maybe," Andy muttered. "Either way, that's one off the books. I guess I owe you a bonus as well."

"Always appreciated."

"Send me an invoice, and thanks."

"Anytime, Andy, talk to you soon," I said as I hung up the phone.

Fortunately, computers make owning a small business a lot simpler than the old typewriter and carbon paper days. I accessed my accounting program and whipped up an invoice for the subpoena service and the meeting. I have to admit, I toyed with adding hazardous duty pay for battling wizards and getting butt stroked by security, but of course I left that part out. Putting the invoice in an envelope I grabbed my coffee cup and walked out to the front to face the inevitable questions from Hailey.

"Well," she asked, as I dropped the envelope in the outgoing mail slot. "I'm waiting?" There was, of course, no way to get out of it, so leaning against the counter and gave her an abbreviated version of the meeting and outcome.

"That's amazing," she said, after listening to my story. "How did you pull that off? That's the first time I've ever seen Cornwall come to a meeting at someone else's office unless it was one of his high and mighty clients. Us common folk usually have to go to the towers. That's if he'll see us lower life forms at all." She meant his offices at the Hughes complex, which was where a lot of the big attorneys in town called home. She put down her cup and leaned toward me, giving me that look my grandmother used to when she wanted information out of me. "What aren't you telling me?"

"That's it Hail. Look, it's got to be because of Milagre. Hell, maybe he figured he owed me a favor. Whatever the reason, I'm not complaining." I poured myself another cup of coffee.

"You know, I have a few more hours of paperwork and then I think I'll call it a day. How's your workload, do you need anything?"

"No, I'm good, just some motions to finish and file. There's a few subpoenas to get out but I'll use the runners for those. Besides, it sounds like you've already had a productive day," Hailey replied as she shuffled some papers and files on her desk.

"Looks like I can make the rent this month, that's for sure. OK, back to work I go." I headed to my office.

Even with today's interesting start, the rest of the day was just plain boring. It's like back when I was a cop, mad dashes of adrenalin laced excitement separated by long periods of monotony.

One other thing, and this is the most important. I may have just stepped into a world of magic and mystical beings but the rent really did still have to get paid. I had tried using magic to win a few bucks on the slots but that hadn't worked so I figured I was stuck with being a P.I. So in that spirit, I returned my calls and did what was left of my paperwork.

Finishing up a bit after 4:00, I said goodbye to Hailey and headed for my car. I left the office and headed off to the freeway. I guess the weather report had been right after all. By the time I got halfway home it was pouring. The sun had already replaced the clouds by the time I pulled onto my street. Welcome to the Las Vegas rainy season.

Chapter 8

I unlocked the door and went into the house, putting my keys and cell phone down on the counter. Opening the refrigerator, I grabbed a Diet Coke and went into the back yard to sit on the patio. It had been a long, strange week. I still didn't know what to think about it all. So I sat in my rocking chair on the patio and watched as the last of the clouds parted.

Charlie, of course, took this as a sign and walked over and dropped a ball in my lap. This time I wasn't surprised when I heard "play" as he sat there wagging his tail. I looked at him in his usual playtime stance, eyes wide, tail wagging like clockwork. I held the ball up high and watched his eyes follow it.

"Do you want me to throw the ball?"

His eyes never left it, but I heard him say "ball" again.

Well, I don't know if what I heard is the right way to put it. It's more like a wisp of something that appears in my head when he barks. I tried some other words and ideas out on him. When I was finished, I had clearly gotten some responses, "ball, play," and "happy," to name a few. He wasn't a great conversationalist, but we could communicate. Things seemed to get clearer the more we interacted.

Let me clarify something. Apparently, dogs don't think like humans. I didn't get full sentences in my mind from him. I got concepts and images that somehow became words. But who knows, maybe the longer I worked with him we could even have a conversation. That made me laugh, I know I'll be in trouble when I come home and he asks how my day was.

We played ball for an hour or so. Let's face it, with a dog like Charlie, we could do this all day and he'd never get bored. The few times I made a bad throw the look he gave me was interesting. Everyone's a critic and now my dog is too. Yep, life was definitely getting weird.

I sat back down in my chair and threw the ball in the pool. I knew this would give me a few minutes while he swam. Whatever had happened to me had opened up senses I had not been able to access before. I still didn't know how to go into full mode, like I'd done with the Werewolves, but maybe that would come.

Charlie came back and dropped the now wet ball in my lap.

I looked over at him and said, "I don't know what to think anymore buddy." I ran my hands through my hair. I had to get a handle on what was happening to me.

Charlie laid his wet head in my lap and looked up at me. "Sad?"

"No." I said, patting his head. "Just confused. I'm not sure you can help me with this one but I'm glad you're my friend." I rubbed his head and tried to just relax.

Suddenly, Charlie lifted his head up and walked a few feet. I heard him say, "Friend?" I could swear it was a question.

"Yes, Charlie, you're my friend." I said as I watched him.

He came toward me, getting excited, and then trotted to the area behind the pool. "Friend," he said again, and then went to the oak tree I'd planted in the yard when we'd first moved in.

The oak was one of two saplings I'd gotten from my Aunt Cacilia. I had planted one in the front and this one in the backyard. They had been saplings from my family's home in Bavaria and I had planted them in memory of my grandmother. Oaks don't grow that fast, so they weren't huge, but they were healthy and I loved the way they made the yard look.

I watched as Charlie started barking and wagging his tail at the tree. Suddenly it began to shimmer. A golden glow surrounded the bottom part of the tree and someone materialized. Well, it was more like they popped into existence. It was a woman in late middle age. She had dark hair with streaks of white. She was dressed in a white top with a shawl draped around her shoulders and a pleated dress. It took me a moment to realize who she was. It was my Aunt Cacilia.

"What the hell?" I stuttered as she walked toward me.

I looked at Charlie, his tail started to droop but then it sprang back up. He gave me a look, one that almost said danger, but I didn't hear anything in my head. Maybe he was smarter than I thought.

"Robert," she said, her eyes meeting mine. "Robert, I do not know how this could happen. I will have to explain some things to you now." She walked over to me and sat down. "We were only trying to keep you safe, you must believe this." She leaned forward and put her hand on my arm. "But first, I must know what occurred, tell me."

"Aunt Cacilia? What the hell is going on? How did you get here?"

"Relax, Robert, all will be explained. But please, tell me what has happened so far."

"Relax...damn it!" I started to get up and then thought better of it. I mean I did need some answers. "Fine...I'm sorry...it's just been an insane week and now this! Whatever? What do you want to know?" My mind was in a thousand places at once.

"You must start at the beginning."

So I told her the story, almost. After what could only be a warning from Charlie, I left out the fights with the Werewolves. Something didn't seem right here so I held back a bit. I told her about the attack at the Neptune and some of the rest, including being able to hear some animals. When I was finished, she stood up.

"This is troubling. We had hoped to spare you from such things."

"Spare me?" I repeated. "Spare me from what. What the hell is going on? Wizards, wands, magic spells and potions, I feel like I've stepped into a bad story, or is it some alternate reality?" I walked over to the BBQ island and grabbed a beer from the refrigerator, popped the top and sat back down. Taking a large gulp, I continued. "I've got people shooting at me with wands that I ended up having to kill. Now I've got family popping out of trees. I would really like an explanation."

"It is a long story," she said.

"Well, I've got some time. Let's hear it." I took another drink and waited.

"I will have to start with some history," she began. "You've heard a bit of it from what you've told me but I will tell you more, especially as it relates to you and your situation." She leaned forward and looked directly at me. "In the beginning, the world was a different place. Many creatures of the Fae roamed the earth. Nymphs, Trolls, Sprites, Dryads, fair creatures and beasts such as you have heard only in myth. They were all here when the world was young.

"It was a wonderful place. Creatures of the land, sea, and sky moved over the Earth. For the most part, life was good, the Earth provided for them and they protected it. Oh, I don't mean to say that all was perfect. There were minor squabbles here and there. There always are, you see. But for the most part, it was peaceful. We even got along with mortals in the beginning. I suppose it was too good to last."

"What do you mean?" I asked. "What happened?"

"It is difficult to explain, but when man came, we changed. He saw us as Gods and began to worship us and although we were no better than he was, some of us began to believe they were better. As they were more powerful, they placed themselves above the others. That led to wars and battles for dominion over others. Dark creatures began to challenge us. This was *The Fall* and it was a bad time for us. Many of us perished or just faded away. Earth's history is full of these stories. They call them myths and legends, but believe me, they are based in fact. It couldn't last, although we did not learn the truth until much later.

"It was the arrogance, you see. Many used magic as if it was the air itself, never realizing that it would not last forever. As they fought they used up much of the magic and destroyed many of the things that could replace it. So, the magic waned, and most of us had less and less power. When *The Fall* occurred we were no match, even for the humans, who always outnumbered us. Then even man forgot about us for a time and the magic dwindled even more." She lowered her head.

"Wait a minute now, there is obviously still magic, or how did all of his happen? I am not sure I understand."

"Hand me that bottle," she said as she stood up.

I did as she asked.

She took it and held it up in front of me. "This bottle contains liquid."

I watched as she emptied what was left in the bottle, pouring the beer onto the deck.

"Now it does not. The bottle, once full, was like the earth when it was young, full of magic that we could use and access in our daily lives. As we fought, we drained the earth of its magic, just as you drank the liquid that once filled this bottle."

"Okay," I said. If the bottle was empty, it must have been filled again, or none of what has occurred could have happened."

She put the bottle down on the table. "Exactly, but it takes a very long time to replenish what was lost. Magic comes from all around us, the trees, the water, and especially the belief of man. It has taken many years for a semblance of our past abilities to manifest itself. That is why we have been so cautious. Never revealing ourselves unless it was necessary, for fear of further losses, and that brings us to you and your situation."

"What exactly is my situation then?" I asked, hoping to finally discover what was going on.

"When the magic dwindled we distanced ourselves from others that would threaten us. I suppose we did it to hide as well. We had to do this, as well as take other measures to protect ourselves." Cacilia sat back down, continuing to talk.

"We seldom get involved in the mortal world since *The Fall* but it and our world are intertwined. The forests near our home have sheltered us since those times and always have we strived to protect them. We are daughters of those trees and we must protect them to protect ourselves."

"One moment," I said. "I thought you said the magic came from other places, not just the trees?"

"Indeed it does, but the primary source of our family's magic is the trees. Just as the primary source of your new friend is the water. That is where we derive our power from. The ability to harness the rest comes from that source." She pointed to the oak tree in the yard. "Why do you think I sent you those trees? Through them you are still part of us. We can use them for other things as well. This you have already seen."

"Alright, I guess I've seen all that," I agreed, looking over at the oak tree. "But where do I fit in with all this?"

"This will be difficult, my son." Her face became solemn and she grasped my hands again.

"As you know, Maria, your grandmother, loved you very much. It was her decision to place you under the spell that both protected you and hid your magical line. She did this willingly, although I can tell you now that it came at a great cost."

"I am not sure I understand," I said. "At what cost?"

Cacilia stood up, and turned away from me looking toward the oak tree. "Her immortality," was all she said.

"What!" I cried out. "What the...? Why would she do that?" I stood up and turned towards her. "That doesn't make any sense!"

It had been a crazy week but this was more than I could take. I still didn't understand half of what I'd stumbled into and all the explanations and magic stories in the universe didn't compare to the thought of losing my grandmother.

Charlie took that moment to go back into the house. He could tell I was upset and you know how dogs are. They think when you get angry that you're mad at them. I guess he calmed me down because his act of bowing down and slinking away made me stop and compose myself. It also made me realize that I had tears in my eyes.

Cacilia looked back at me. "Robert, I'm sorry. I know all of this is new to you, and in some ways, beyond comprehension. But be assured, what Maria did for you, she did willingly. Please sit," she said, gesturing back towards my chair.

"As I said before, we are daughters of the trees. Descended from the first nymphs to roam this world, we are of the world of the Fae. When I said immortality, I did not mean that we cannot die. Just that we seldom die naturally. We die in wars and from calamities. Some of us die if the tree that we are bound to dies, although sometimes we can live on if that happens. We can also be killed by another, which is why we are so careful. When Maria passed on to you that that was needed to shield you she passed on all her powers to close the circle. In doing so, she allowed herself to become mortal, doomed to die a natural death."

"But why would she have to do that? What could have made her do that, I mean I didn't even know about this until today. This doesn't make any sense at all."

"She had to do it, Robert, to protect you."

"But protect me from what?"

"Daughters of the trees, my dear Robert, daughters. Our power is passed from mother to daughter as was first decreed by Demeter herself. It was her will."

"So are you saying I should have been born a girl?" I was still confused. "I mean, don't the men in our family have any powers?"

"Not exactly, and yes, they have some. But the line that passes the purest blood must always be passed from firstborn to firstborn and that has always been female until you were born. It is not this way among all the clans, but it was in ours, until your mother changed all that."

"Okay, okay, so mom had a boy, I still don't know what the big deal is. What, am I tainted or something? How is that my fault? And what did she have to shield me from?"

"Tainted, an interesting word, but in truth, many did consider it an abomination. One that some argued could not be allowed to continue. So, simply put, it was felt by many that you should be put to death."

"Put to death! What the hell kind of people kill innocent children just for being born? Wait, forget I said that." I was learning fast that this world wasn't really much different than the one I was used to, so I told her so. "So in reality you, or I guess, we, are no different than anyone else, eh?"

"Again, yes and no," she replied. "You must understand that this was one of our highest laws. These laws have served us for thousands of years and in your case one that was broken by your mother, who did have a choice. When your mother decided to bear a male child she knew that she would have to break an oath that was given by the first born. She also knew that in doing so it would cost her all her powers in return. For only by sacrificing her powers to cause her child to be born a male was she able to do this. This she could only do if her love of your father was greater than her love for herself. It was only through the power your grandmother wielded that she was not put to death herself."

"This is friggin' nuts. What the hell kind of nightmare have I fallen into? Do I have to worry about being hunted by my family now that this has happened as well?"

"I do not believe so, your grandmother saw to that," she answered. "But I would still take care. I do not know what effect this incident has had. This was my fear when all this began. We did not know then, nor do we now, what will happen when a male is born pure blood of our kind. I believe Maria's spell, albeit damaged, will protect you from many of the effects, but it is still too early to judge," she said, sitting back down. "The magic of our kind comes from the earth itself and while many other lines have pure blood males, ours never has. But I will do all I can to help you."

"Okay, Cacilia," I said, looking over at her. "I need to exactly what we are...what I am." I was trying to get a grasp on all of this, which was not coming easy.

"We are of the Fae, born when the Earth was made. Our line comes from the Hamadryads and the Dryads. We are the spirit of the trees themselves, born of the oak. We are not the only clan; there are families that descended from other trees, the birch, the poplar, the ash, as well as others. Some were born of the water and others the land itself. All Fae are spirits of the Earth, sky or water. In mortal mythology we were apart from the Gods, but that is not true. Although we sprang from the line of Titans, Demeter became mother to us. She was Goddess of Fertility and keeper of the Law as well as one of the twelve Olympians."

"Alright, so are you saying we're Gods?"

"The Gods are a mortal concept. We are what we are. Mortals descended from apes, isn't that what they say? We descended from the earth. It is our abilities that set us apart from mortals, that which they call magic."

Well at least I was getting some answers; even if I wasn't sure how accurate they were. "Ok, next question then. Why would my mother do that? Break the rules and have a boy I mean, especially if she knew the cost?"

A smile lit her face. "She did it for love," she answered back. "Your father wanted a male heir and it was the greatest thing she could give him. So, her love for him created you. You see we do not need to mate to create a child as the seed is already within us. But a male can only come if joined with seed of another, like your father. Your mother, well, as I said, she was deeply in love with him. Although I will admit that the union was frowned upon. She kept it hidden for a time, but she had her mother's, your grandmother's, blessings, so we did not interfere. Besides, we just assumed that she would follow tradition.

"When you were born, there was much apprehension and discussion, but on your grandmother's council, we waited. Then, when you turned seven the signs appeared and we knew something had to be done. Of course, that's when Maria stepped in and offered the solution. She was the eldest of us and the most powerful, so no one doubted her. Her enchantment was woven and you remained mortal, or at least so we thought at the time. But, all were satisfied, balance had been returned and that brought harmony."

"Looks to me like something went wrong," I said, wondering about the world I had entered and the cost my family had paid to keep me from it.

"Perhaps, but now I wonder, maybe she knew. Either way we would not have doubted her." She stood up and looked down at me again. "Whatever has been done in the past is done. We must deal with the present, and the future."

"I need to know, were one of you responsible for my parent's deaths?" I wasn't sure if I really wanted to know the answer. They had died in a plane crash while on a weekend vacation trip. My father had been a pilot and it was not unusual for the two of them to fly somewhere in a small plane. They had even taken me along on several occasions when I was still a baby.

"It was not of our doing. There was nothing to indicate it was anything but an accident."

"Okay," I said, not quite believing her. "But where does this leave me, and what about the others? Seems to me that I might be right back where I started from."

"As I said, I do not believe so. Maria's pass to mortality has been made so the die has already been cast. I believe they will see this as I do. It is an unknown equation but the price has already been paid. I am more concerned with what will manifest itself now that the spell has been altered. I fear more the danger from others than that from within, especially after learning what has transpired."

Yeah, sure, why didn't I believe that? "What about my kids, are they going to start sensing something strange as well?"

"Jeremy and Nichole? But they are exceptionally bright already, are they not?" she said with a laugh. "I do not believe you have anything to fear. Although I am certain that they benefit from their heritage it would be unlikely that they would be affected by this. You would have known by now, I assure you."

I know every father says this, but it's true, my kids are bright. My son, Jeremy, he goes by Jay, is a Homeland Security agent in Los Angeles. He fast tracked to an anti-terrorism squad last year after a stint in the military. I already mentioned my daughter, Nikki. Both of them are well thought of at their respective agencies.

Well, at least something positive has already come from my so-called lineage. They both had successful careers ahead of them, and of course, I'm sure that their mother contributed as well. My ex, Lynn, was the CFO of a large technology firm in Los Angeles. She wasn't missing anything in the brains department either.

Before you ask, it was an amiable split. She accepted the offer in LA before I retired from the police department. We are actually still good friends and with one child in each of our respective cities we still see each other on a semi-regular basis.

"Robert, I must return. I know you have many questions and your powers are still uncertain. There is one who has offered to help. Bernd!"

"What's a Ber...," I started to ask, when suddenly something, or more accurately, someone, brushed my leg. I damn near hit my head on the patio ceiling coming out of the chair when the small, gnarled being appeared.

"Bernd is here," it...he said, turning to look up at me.

He was about two and half, maybe three feet tall. He was old, his skin was like aged leather but his blue eyes sparkled. He had a pointed white beard and he looked, well, he looked like a lawn gnome without the hat. Hell, he even wore blue pants.

"What the..." I gasped, looking down at the creature.

"I am sorry," Cacilia stated, "Perhaps I should have warned you."

She looked down at the creature. "Bernd, are you still willing to watch over him?"

"As I said Mistress, of course, of course, never fear. I will watch over the...," he stopped and looked back at me, "not so young master."

"Whoa, whoa." I said, looking at the two of them. Things were once again getting way too weird. "A Gnome? Who is this, what is he, and why do I need him?"

"Hrmph," was all the creature said, folding his hands across his chest and glaring at me.

"Robert, meet Bernd," she said. Then she turned to the creature. "Bernd, you remember Robert I believe."

The creature, Bernd, looked at me disapprovingly. "Aye, I remember when he was just a boy. Tall has he grown, but perhaps not wiser, eh?"

"We've met?" I asked as I eyed Bernd.

"Bernd served your grandmother," Cacilia answered. "He was there when she placed the enchantment on you. He has counseled members of our family since time forgotten. As for what he is, he is a Zwerg, a Dwarf. Gnome may also be an appropriate name, although they do not call themselves that. I believe Dwarf is the better name. He has agreed to stay here and watch over you. He can also teach you many things."

Bernd seemed to relax, but then shook his head. "Well, I can try and teach him. Stubborn he appears, but we will see, we will see." He walked over to me, his head just above my knees and looked straight up at me.

"Do not be concerned. Bernd will keep you safe, if he can." He turned around and started walking through the yard. "I must look over the grounds."

With that, he was gone. I walked over and looked around the pool area but I couldn't see where he went. "Are you sure about this?" I asked her as I turned and walked back to the chairs.

"Of course, I cannot stay, and Bernd has agreed to watch over you. I am concerned about what will occur now that the enchantment has been altered and you have been involved with these others. Beside, your grandmother was Bernd's favorite and he has not been the same since she passed. You will be good for him as well. I must go. Come, walk with me," she said, leading me back towards the oak.

Charlie had joined us as well.

"I will return if I can. Take care, and trust Bernd."

Then she stepped toward the tree and raised her hand. I saw her place her palm on the trunk of the tree. There was another flash of golden light and she disappeared.

Charlie barked a few times. He must have been startled by the flash. But his tail started wagging so I figured he must be okay or maybe he was just happy she was gone. I started to turn back to go to the house when Bernd took that moment to reappear.

"Friend," Charlie said, his tail now wagging like crazy. He ran over to Bernd and started licking him. I thought Bernd was going to get knocked over but he just rubbed the dog's head as Charlie sat down.

"It has been a long day, Robert, and the grounds are safe. You must get some rest. We will talk again soon," he said. He patted Charlie's head and, without a sound or any warning, disappeared.

Charlie stood up and circled around where Bernd had been. I thought he was going to search for him but instead he just walked into the house. Shaking my head I followed, heading straight to the bedroom.

I was tired and had too many questions. At least some of what I'd heard matched what Siegfried had told me. It's screwy when you don't know who you can trust. It was still early but maybe what I really needed was a good night's sleep.

Chapter 9

The morning started off quiet. I sipped my coffee out of a *Space 1999* cup and opened the paper. There was still no sign of the Dwarf, Bernd. Hell, maybe I dreamt my Aunt's visit.

Charlie was out in the yard. I'd only seen him for a minute when he decided I should get out of bed and feed him. With him around I don't know why I even bother to have an alarm clock. Then the phone rang.

"Robert, its Siegfried, have you seen today's paper?"

"I just brought it in, why, what's up?"

"I think you'll want to read the story on the front page of the local section. Read it and let me know when you're done."

I realized he was waiting for me to read it when the line didn't go dead. I opened the newspaper to the page and read the story:

Las Vegas – The badly burned body of a male was found earlier this week in Primm, Nevada, by a Las Vegas resident while motorcycling. Police stated that the unidentified male body was found in a ravine approximately two miles from the California border. Police believe the body had been in this location for at least a week. Detectives on the scene stated that they do not believe the man died at that location. A review of police radio logs indicated that electrocution was suspected.

The remains were removed to the Clark County Coroner's Office where an autopsy will be performed. Police declined to comment when asked if there was any connection to a similar electrocution incident outside of Baker last week.

In that case, police found the body of an unidentified male in a dry lake bed outside of Baker, California. A police spokesman stated that the body had been electrocuted, and placed in the desert by persons unknown. There is speculation that the man had been the victim of an unreported industrial accident and placed at the lake bed to avoid investigation by authorities.

"So I take it you think there is a connection with my incident at the hotel," I asked after reading the column.

"Yes, my sources in the California incident tell me that the coroner there described the body as if it had been hit by lightning numerous times. That's as close to the magic you witnessed as mortals would be able to describe." Siegfried hesitated for a moment.

"I believe it also means that they used magic to torture him. The report indicates it took several strikes before he died."

I wondered if this was the same call my daughter had been on. It had to be. How many electrocutions could there be that warranted a direct call to the head of Homicide. "What about the Primm victim, any word?" I asked, shifting into detective mode.

"Nothing definitive but our sources on the local PD indicated similar wounds. If it is the same dark Mages, you may have saved Mr. Milagre from a similar fate."

I considered his words. I also wondered who his sources at Metro were. If it was true, then the reason for the attack had to be more than just a kidnapping. I was going to have to do some digging as well. "Siegfried, have you heard any reports from anywhere else?"

"Not as of yet, but my people are looking."

"Ok, so my intervention could have stopped or at least slowed them down."

"It would appear so," he replied. "But again, we just don't have enough information yet. I have increased the guards on Mr. Milagre and the property as well but I am concerned you may also be a target now. In my experience, those who practice dark magic are vengeful and do not take interference well. I know their magic did not have the same effect on you but there are many ways to kill."

"So I've heard," I said, trying to sound confident. "Let me know what else you hear. I may have some people I can call on this one. Thanks for the heads up. I'll be careful."

"I will. One more thing, Mr. Milagre has someone who is in need of your services. Would you be willing to meet with him tonight? I was told to tell you it would be worth your while."

"Sure, where and when?"

"There is a local bar that is frequented by our kind, Danu's, I will text you with directions."

It just figures, Danu's...shit. What was I gonna say, sorry, I beat up some Werewolves there, can we go somewhere else? "I know where it is."

"Do you?" He seemed startled but not surprised.

That was disconcerting. I wondered if he'd heard about the fight.

"Good, we will see you there at 8:00 p.m.," he said as he disconnected.

So someone else had gotten zapped. Where was this going to lead? Well, at least on this case I had a place to start. I was just going through my contact list looking for O'Malley's number when the phone rang again.

"Hey Dad, what's up?" my son asked as I put the phone to my ear.

"Jay, just getting ready to go the office, how are you doing?"

"Fine, Dad. Hey, I got a case that needs some follow-up in Vegas. Just wanted to give you a heads up that I'd be in town and make sure I could stay at the house."

"Of course, and since when do you have to ask," I said, mentally preparing a shopping list. "When you going to be in town?"

"Probably sometime tomorrow but it'll be the early evening before I can meet up. I have some things scheduled in the early afternoon. I'm hoping to be there for two to three days. I thought if we get the time maybe we could get some fishing in."

"That'd be great, I should be clear, I'll let Nikki know you are coming."

"She already knows. I just got off the phone with her."

"Why didn't I know that? But I'll touch base with her anyway so we can coordinate a family dinner."

"Ok, but no meatloaf, I had that with Mom yesterday."

"Damn, you know that's my favorite," I joked, then added, "I guess you'll be stuck with my recipes then." Growing up, Lynn, my ex, had always fixed the family favorites and I'd done the barbecuing and experimenting. I'd actually worked my way through high school and my first two years of college as a cook before joining the force so I rather enjoyed it.

"I'm sure we'll be ok," he said with a laugh. "Gotta run then, I'll see you tomorrow, love you."

My kid's always told me they loved me when they hung up the phone. It was nice that some things hadn't changed. Since Jay was coming to town, I bumped my call to O'Malley down the list and dialed my daughter.

"Hey Nikki, I just talked to Jay. He's coming into town, you gonna be free to do dinner tomorrow night?"

"Absolutely," she answered. "We're actually working a case together so we'll be spending some time together. Is that cool or what?"

"Yes it is," I commented, "which one is that, if you can talk about it?"

"It's the electrocuted guy from Primm. The autopsy is scheduled for tomorrow and since I handled the crime scene I caught the case. It's a weird one, too."

"Oh really, I saw that one in the paper today and O'Malley mentioned that you'd called that one in. What's the deal on it anyway? It sounded like he got hit by lightning."

"I wish it were just lightning. He must have been hit at least seven times and there hasn't been a storm in a month, really weird," she answered. "I just found out that Jay has four others almost exactly like it."

"Four, damn, the paper just listed the one out of Baker. That is weird. What do you guys think? You got a lead on what's going on?" I wished I could tell her why I was really interested but I wasn't ready to have that conversation yet, if ever.

"Our guys are leaning on some kind of industrial incident cover-up but Jay doesn't think so. He hasn't said too much though, you know how he is. But Dad, why else would they send him? He works anti-terrorism and cases like that. I just hope it's not some kind of weird weapons thing, that's all we need."

"Well, with you two on it, I'm sure the case will be resolved in no time." I said, acting the proud father.

"Ha, ha, ha," she chuckled, "the Hoskins kids save the world!"

"Damn straight!"

"Well, I'll let you know if I hear anything else. I've still got some evidence to process from yesterday so I have to get going. I'll see you soon, love you, Dad."

"Love you too babe, talk to you soon."

O'Malley was next but his conversation was short. He had Hoskins' coming out of the woodwork with both my daughter and son involved so he wasn't chatty. That was alright. I figured I'd learn plenty when I saw the kids tomorrow.

Hell, I wasn't going into the office today anyway so I called Mal to see if he'd had any luck with the drives from my computer. I knew it was magic that fried them but it would be interesting what he dug up, if anything. As I figured, Mal hadn't learned a thing but he told me he wasn't giving up. I let him know I'd check in over the next few days to hear about his progress.

I spent the rest of the day with housekeeping duties and shopping. Pretty boring stuff, but hey, when you have a house, there's always little things that need attention. Like the lawn being mowed, the pool being cleaned and weeding the garden. It was a nice day so I didn't mind. That's one nice thing about working for yourself; you get to set your own hours. I was lucky, business had been good lately and I was caught up. I wish I could always say that.

I was just getting a drink in the kitchen when realized I still hadn't seen the Dwarf. I went out into the yard and figured I'd try to use some of my new found talents. Charlie was just coming around the corner of the house so I called out to him. "Charlie, where's the Dwarf, Bernd?"

He dropped the bone he was carrying and looked up at me. Then he turned his head sideways and I heard a mental shrug. He went over to the oak tree and sniffed for a minute all around it. He turned his head from side to side a few times sniffing the air. Then he looked back at me and said, "Bernd gone." Then he walked back over to where he'd dropped the bone, plopped down and began chewing it.

Well, that was informative. I just shook my head and went back into the house to clean up and then get some shopping done. What had I expected, the Dwarf's itinerary? I guess he'll show up sooner or later.

Chapter 10

I left the house around 7:30 p.m. and headed for downtown to see what Mr. Milagre had set up. I got off on the Boulevard and drove down to Oakey. When I got close, I drove around the neighborhood a bit to make sure there was no one from the other night waiting for me. Everything looked ok so I parked next to the tour bus lot and walked toward Danu's.

I opened the heavy outer wooden door and then paused after going through the inner doorway. I saw that Delia appeared to be working alone tonight. She looked up at me as I walked in but gave no hint of recognition. She had to remember me, but if so, she wasn't acting like it. I wondered if Siegfried had mentioned we were coming.

I took a seat at an empty table and watched her for a bit. Damn, she looked good. Was she really some kind of Vampire? She was wearing a red silk blouse with just the right amount of cleavage showing and creased black slacks that fit, well. Let's just say they fit perfectly. There was something else about her and it wasn't just her beauty, although her green eyes were definitely enchanting.

Just then Mr. Milagre came in through the doorway. As I stood to greet him I saw that he was accompanied by another, shorter man. This one looked to be in his 60s with a full head of gray hair and dressed casually in expensive clothes. He didn't seem the Vegas type, especially compared to Milagre who was impeccably dressed in a black tailored suit.

"Robert, I'm glad you could make it." He turned toward his companion.

"William, this is Robert Hoskins, I believe he can handle what you need."

"Excellent," the man said.

I knew Milagre was Fae, but William, although I could sense some magic about him, appeared to be mortal. I wondered how they were connected.

We sat down at a large table. At that moment, the door opened again, and looking over, I saw Siegfried and another man come in. I nodded as he walked by and took a stool at the bar. His partner moved closer to the door and sat down next to someone who had already been here when I arrived.

"I hope you don't mind?" Milagre said as he waved at the bartender to come to the table. "It seems that Siegfried likes to keep a closer eye on me these days. They won't disturb us."

"Probably a good idea," I answered. "I don't fancy a repeat of the last time just yet."

Milagre didn't comment so I glanced over at William but he was quiet as well. The bartender chose that moment to arrive at the table.

Milagre stood up and gave her a hug. "Delia, let me introduce you," he said, turning toward us. "William you already know, and this is Robert Hoskins, a friend of ours."

William waved and I stood up.

"Hello, a pleasure," I said as I extended my hand. Two could play at this game.

Delia took it and gave me a friendly shake. "A new friend, well then, Robert, Danu's and I welcome you." She was still acting like the other night had never happened. She turned back towards the table as I sat back down. "Now my friends, what can I get you?"

We ordered drinks and as she went back to the bar, I turned to William. "So, tell me what I can do for you," I asked.

"Straight to business, I like that," he said with a laugh, then turned to Milagre. "What have you told him?"

"Nothing yet," he replied. "I wanted to leave the specifics to you."

"Very well," he began, "here's the job. I need something delivered to a woman who ran the mitt camp, uh, the fortune telling booth. She was known as Pythia, the Oracle. She and I worked the carny circuit years back and all I know is that she's now supposed to live somewhere around here."

"Alright," I said, "but it would help if you could tell me her name."

William looked thoughtful for a moment, and then replied. "I knew her as Deborah but her real name was Diantha. She used to go by the last names of Medea and Kent but I can't swear that she still uses them."

He reached into his front pocket and pulled out a leather pouch. It looked old and well worn. He loosened the rawhide tie and looked around the room for a moment as if he wanted to make sure that no one was watching. He pulled out what appeared to be a green oval stone on a fine golden chain. It looked like jade but I couldn't be sure. As he lifted it out of the pouch by the chain I saw the stone had a design on one side, almost like an eye. "I need to return this to her and it needs to be handled delicately, and soon."

"Fine," I said, "you need me to find an old fortune teller named Deborah or Diantha and give her back her property. So what am I missing here?" Come on, there had to more to this story.

William was about to answer when Delia returned with our drinks. She served the two of them, and then placed a beer in a frozen mug in front of me.

"This is one of our specialty brews that we make here on the premises. It's a light lager but don't be fooled, the alcohol content is higher than most. I hope you like it," she said.

I took a sip and answered back. "This is good."

She looked pleased and gave me a wink. "Let me know if you want anything else."

First she ignores me and now she flirts with me, at this rate I was never going to figure this girl out.

"It was after the war, you see, the Great War mind you, W W One," he said, pronouncing it just like that, W W One." William continued as he put the pouch back in his pocket. "I was running this little carnival. Nothing elaborate, you understand, but we did ok. We even had a regular circuit in the New York area." He stopped to take another drink.

I was surprised to learn of his longevity. If what he was saying was true, and I had no reason to doubt it, he had to be over 100 years old.

"Anyway, as I was saying, I had this little carnival. So one day, outside of Cooperstown, I meet this gal, Deborah. God she was beautiful. She makes me a deal you see. I let her join the show and she grants me long life and prosperity. I gotta tell you, I thought she was some crazy gypsy at first even if she was pleasing to the eyes, if you get my drift." He seemed lost in his memories for a moment but then went on.

"Anyway, she showed me things that I hadn't even dreamed of and we did well together. Made a lotta scratch, hell, I was even happy for a time when we lived together. I never grew older, just like her. Everything was fine for a long time."

"So what happened?"

"It was like this. Debbie, I mean Deborah; well...she liked to wander a bit. Do you understand?" he asked, waiting for me to say something.

I assumed he meant she was unfaithful to him, so I said so.

"Exactly," he answered, "and it used to make me angry. Times were a lot different then. But what could I do? She had powerful magic and she could make people do things. But like I said, I wasn't happy about it. After a while we started to argue about it a lot but she wouldn't change."

"She used to tell this story about the jewel around her neck. Said she'd been given it by the Gods back in the old days. So, I figured that's where her powers came from. Well, one day, after one of her little...excursions...I took it from her while she was sleeping. Clean up and left her behind, I did. That was about, oh, 60 years ago, I guess."

"Didn't she look for you?"

"She might have, but without the necklace I don't think she was much more than mortal. No, I grabbed a train and headed out west. Changed my name and face and started working in the movie business. I never saw her again."

"So why now?" I asked.

"Well, this necklace doesn't work as well for me anymore. Aw hell, it doesn't work for me at all, you see. Truth is, I'm dying, but I need to set things straight before I go."

"Alright, why me?" I asked, knowing that Milagre, at least, had a reason for choosing me for this job.

"Well, after I got to California I got married, had me some kids as well. Now, Deborah, she has got to still be pretty upset. Once she gets this necklace back...well...there's no telling what she might do. She could be quite temperamental." He almost looked embarrassed.

"Look, I'm not afraid for me. I've had a good life, longer than it should have been. But she may want revenge and I don't want my family to suffer for my mistakes. They're as mortal as I was before I met her. Do you know where I'm coming from?"

"I think I do," I nodded. "But I have a few questions."

Milagre held up his hand. "Rob, before you go on, let me tell you why I recommended you. It's my belief that the spell you carry will offer some protection to you from anything this woman might do when the necklace is returned. I'm not saying it won't be dangerous but I believe you offer the best chance of success, for both of you."

"There's always risk," I said, "but it sounds as if you don't think she's lost all her abilities."

He shrugged. "I know William believes that because she never came after him but my people are not as sure of that as he is. I don't doubt that she lost a lot of power when it was taken from her. But I do believe she may have retained enough, at least as far as her ability to sway others, if nothing else."

I thought about that for a few seconds before answering. "Ok, so she may still be able to influence people. What else?"

"At the very least I find it hard to believe this is her only gift. William tells me she could foretell the future and had power over men. She may have received other gifts over the years as well."

"Well, if that's the case, why was William able to steal the necklace? Surely she would have foreseen that, or at least one would think so."

"Not necessarily," Milagre continued. "You may not be aware of this, but magic in mortals can be very specific and if the giver himself wanted to limit her abilities...no, I'm guessing she couldn't see her own future."

"I get it," I chimed. "Someone may not have wanted the student to become the master."

He chuckled at that. "A good way to put it. I also believe that even when she gets the necklace back she won't be able to determine how powerful or what, exactly, you are. That should give you the advantage."

"What do you base that on?" I asked, eyebrows raised.

He got a serious look on his face. "Because even now, as when I first met you, I cannot sense anything extraordinary about you. I have never encountered that before."

"Interesting, I take it that it's a good thing we're friends then," I said, not sure how to take the look on his face.

Milagre just smiled. "That is true, and I want you to know that if either of you were not trusted friends, I would never have brought him to you."

I turned back to William. "Okay, what exactly do you want me to do?"

"Just return it and get her oath that she will not harm or even contact my family, ever. You'll need her oath, nothing less will bind her." William reached back and pulled an envelope from his pocket. "Here's $5,000 to get you started. I'll pay you another 15K when you complete the task. That should cover any expenses and your time. Everything I know about her is in that envelope with the cash. What Eddy's people know about her is in there as well," he said, handing me the envelope.

I opened it and ignoring the cash, removed the papers William had mentioned. "Hmmm," I said as I glanced through them. "Ok, I'll need the jewel and a few more minutes of your time."

"Whatever you need," he replied, handing me the leather pouch.

"What name did you go by when you were with her?"

"I used to go by the name of Billy Kent."

Something didn't feel right about this deal and it wasn't just the obscene fee I was getting. It sounded like he'd done pretty well by her, too well. I hate to get moral but she deserved something for his theft. "How would you feel about sweetening the pot a bit?"

"What do you mean, isn't 20 large enough?" he asked, glancing at Milagre.

Milagre just shrugged his shoulders. "What do you have in mind, Robert?"

"Well, according to what I've read here, she's supposedly lost her youth and is now an old woman. Seems to me she might be owed something for, let's call it, William's use of her property. I'm also thinking an incentive wouldn't hurt to make her forget about him."

"It might not be a bad idea, Will," Milagre remarked, thoughtfully. "A token of good faith could go a long way and you can afford it."

"Are you working for me or her?" William asked indignantly, and then sighed at Milagre's impassive face. "Fine, lemme figure it out when we get back to the hotel."

"I'll discuss a fair amount and have it ready for you when you need it," Milagre said, grabbing William by the shoulder. "Now that business in concluded, let's get back to the hotel, we've taken up enough of Mr. Hoskins' time."

They stood up and Milagre gave Siegfried a small wave as the two of them started to walk to the door.

Siegfried looked over at the other two bodyguards who got up and exited in front of them.

I put the envelope and pouch in my pocket and then Milagre stopped and walked back to me.

"How much do you want him to ante up?"

"Whatever you think is fair," I answered. "I just want some leverage if she decides to balk at anything."

"No problem, besides, William really can afford it and it may go a long way if getting the necklace back restores her powers. She could come in useful. I would be very happy if she would ally herself with us. She would be an asset to my business."

"Good point; I'll see what I can do," I said, thinking I should have figured there'd be an angle.

He turned and left the bar so I retrieved my beer and walked to where Siegfried was sitting.

"So I take it you accepted the job," Siegfried asked as I sat down at the stool next to him.

"I did, but I'm not sure it made William very happy. I changed the terms a bit." I shook my head. "I suppose he'll get over it."

"I believe it's not the type of matter that just anyone will be successful at. Besides, you are taking all the risk, therefore, you set the terms," he said, draining his glass.

"So what's the deal with William, how do they know each other?" I asked, waving at Delia for another round.

"William Harrison, retired Hollywood financier and entrepreneur," he recited, rising and placing money on the bar top. "Delia, thank you, but none for me, I've got to get back to work." He turned his attention back to me. "Mr. Milagre has known him since the 50's. He used to run clients to Las Vegas from Hollywood when this was still a small town. They partnered up in the junket business, Mr. Milagre here in Vegas, starting a small casino, and Harrison in Hollywood, sending actors and other industry professionals here in a fleet of small planes. They did very well."

"I guess they did," I commented as Delia placed another beer on the bar.

She smiled and went back to the other side to clean some glasses.

"I've got to get back to the property," Siegfried continued. "I wanted you to know that everything my people could find out about the woman will be in the envelope Harrison gave you. We still have a few queries out but the rest is up to you. Please be careful. This is your first step into a world that as you have already learned can be very dangerous. Things are rarely what they appear. If you need anything, and I mean anything, please contact me. I will do what I can to assist you."

I peered into my mug and then looked back at him. "Thanks Siegfried, I appreciate it. I have a few tricks up my sleeve as well, I'll be careful."

"Ha! Excellent," he said, slapping my back, "Then I bid you farewell. Duty calls."

As Siegfried left, Delia came back over to my side of the bar. Putting away some glasses, she glanced over at me. "You want another one?"

"Sure, and thanks for not saying anything."

She poured a mug and slapped it down on the bar in front of me. "Hey, the less I know the better. I want no part of any dispute Milagre is involved in."

"Dispute, what dispute?" I had no idea what she was talking about.

"Fae," she uttered with an air of contempt. "You never change." She put her hands on her hips. "I don't know why Milagre has you screwing with the Weres and I don't want to know," she said, throwing down her towel and walking away.

"What the hell are you talking about? A minute ago you're being nice and now we're fighting. What is it with you?" I asked loudly.

She spun around and came back, leaning over the bar with her finger in my face. "I can't afford to have Milagre mad at us so I played nice, this time. I will only say this once. Never use me as an excuse again! At least it makes some sense now, why can't you just leave us alone?"

Well, shit. She thought I'd used her as part of a plan of Milagre's to screw with the Werewolves. No wonder she was pissed. How was I supposed to deal with that? Should I even bother? The real bitch was I was stuck between a rock and a hard place. I couldn't let her think Milagre was planning some coup against the Werewolves, God only knows what that could lead too. On the other hand, Vampire or not, I liked her and I didn't want her to think I used her either. I gulped down my beer, ale, whatever it was. Women...I must be nuts, damn green eyes!

"Delia, wait!" I said in my best commanding voice.

She didn't turn around but I'll be damned if she didn't stop. I stood up and walked so that I was across the bar from her.

"Just listen," I offered. "Things are not what they seem. I need you to believe that."

She swiveled her head and looked at me. "Why? I ask you again, what has changed?"

"I don't expect you to understand but you have to believe this. Milagre didn't send me after the Werewolves and he isn't my boss." I wondered if I should have said master, damn supernatural crap. "It's exactly what I said, there's no conspiracy." I paused a moment, trying to decide what to say next.

"Look, I know you won't believe me but I really don't understand all this Fae versus Lil stuff. But I will make you this promise; I'll do what I can to make things better. I just need some time."

What else could I say? She either believed me or she didn't. I doubted anything I did was going to make a difference tonight.

"We'll see each other again," I said as I walked out the doorway.

Chapter 11

I had just pulled into the driveway when Charlie came bounding up to greet me. That's the greatest thing about having a dog; they always act like they haven't seen you in a month, even when they can talk.

I went into the house and threw my keys on the counter and then headed into the office to put William's jewel and the cash into the safe. As I opened it, I noticed the scepter I had taken from the young Werewolf the night I had first met Delia. I had forgotten all about it. I was just reaching for it when I heard something.

"Bernd is here."

"Do you have to do that?" I asked, rubbing my head where I had hit it on the safe door when he startled me.

"You have been busy," he exclaimed, walking to the safe and picking up the scepter and bag. He held each up and examined them. "Tell me how you acquired these."

"Just like that, huh?" I replied as I stood up. "Who are you anyway? I mean, really, what are you? Did you really know my grandmother or are you just Cacilia's watchdog?"

He just stared at me with his hands out.

I walked up to him and took back the items, holding them where he could see them. "If you must know, this one I got as part of a job from another Fae," I said, holding up the pouch containing the jewel. Then I held up the scepter. "This one I took away from some punk ass kid that turned out to be a Werewolf. A week ago I'd only read about them in fairy tales, mind you, and now, well let's see...now I got Werewolves, Fae, Lil, and God only knows what else crawling up my ass. Oh yeah, I also got Dwarves."

I knew I was ranting, but sometimes when you get angry you just have to get it out. Once I stopped yelling I looked at him. He looked a tad irate, well shit, that couldn't be good.

He rose to attention, his body straight and tall, or as tall as his 3 foot or so would allow him. For a second it was almost humorous but then I got a good look at him. He didn't look like some lawn gnome you find in the back yard anymore. He looked tough, like some creature you read about in an epic adventure. There was a light in his eyes and his voice was proud and he spoke clearly.

"From the earth my people sprang and for ages we have watched over the lands and water. I am no mere Dwarf and I am not a spy. We were here before you came and we will be here after you are all long gone. We do not offer our guidance to just anyone. I am Bernd! I have counseled your family since the Dryad first walked this Earth and I counseled Maria, your grandmother, whom I called friend. It was her wish that I come to you when you needed me and I am here. Do you doubt me?" he asked, walking over and looking straight up at me.

I didn't know what to say.

Then his face grew less stern and his appearance changed back to what it had been before.

Charlie chose that moment to come into the room. He sat down next to Bernd and I heard him say "Bernd, friend."

How could I argue with that? Besides, I had to believe him. Dogs are great judges of character.

"I'm sorry. It's just been a tough week. Maybe you are what you say. But this is all new to me and I'm beginning to wonder who I should trust," I exclaimed. "Hell, I'm not even sure what I've become."

He gestured towards me. "It is not what you have become, it is what you have always been. It was just hidden from you. The world turns and we turn with it. I cannot change the past but know that we all have a destiny even when we do not realize it. Let me help you to where yours leads as Maria would have wanted me to."

Damn, now I had a destiny. What do I say to that? Especially after the week I just had? I put the two objects down and sat down on the ground, my back to the safe. "Alright Bernd, what do you want to know?"

He picked up the scepter. "Tell me again how you acquired this?" he asked, examining it with his gnarled hands.

I told him about the fights with the Werewolves, and about Delia.

"She is a Lilin and yet you came to her defense, interesting."

I stood up and walked over to my chair and I sat down. I watched as he picked up the jewel and walked over beside me, leaning on the leather couch.

"What's the deal with that anyway? What happened between the Fae and the Lil? Siegfried said there was a war but isn't it long over? Why does it look like everyone still hates them?" I asked.

"So many questions and we have just begun," he answered. "I will try and answer them all in time, but first, this scepter." He held it up and twisted it in his hands. "This is a staff of office. You say you took it from a boy?"

"Well, a young man I guess you'd call him. He was carrying it in his pocket. When he started to shift I stopped him. How did I do that?" Damn, not even a minute and I'd asked another question. I looked down at him and just shrugged my shoulders.

"Do not be so hasty, there is much to learn. Let us deal with this first," he lectured. "As I was saying, this is a symbol of power. I do not believe that the true owner would let it go so easily."

"What exactly is it?" Oh, damn, more questions.

"Werewolves are pack creatures and as such only one can lead. This is an ancient symbol of command. It symbolizes the bearer's rule without having to bare fang and claw over every disagreement. Interesting to find it here, it is one of the old ways. Much has changed since *The Fall*. He must come from an ancient pack. I doubt the true owner will be glad to see it missing." He looked thoughtful.

"Wait," I interjected, "when I was fighting at the bar, the father...I could sense his line. I remember it was something from France, old, I remember something like 300 B.C."

"You sensed his line, very good, Robert. That explains much about the scepter, and about you. It is indeed very old. Why the boy carried it, I cannot say, as only one who leads can wield it. Perhaps it was stolen. Whatever the reason, it could be a useful tool to exchange for the pack's allegiance, especially now that you have bested three of them."

"What do you mean it can only be used by one who leads? It worked for me."

He gave me a funny look, twisting his head. "Did it now? What did you see?"

"It was during the fight, right after I took it from the second kid, the one that was taunting Delia. It burned with blue fire."

"Indeed, well, that is interesting. Such things are possible after all. Now, about this stone," he continued, picking up the leather pouch.

Why did I get the feeling he wasn't telling me everything?

"This is a dragon's eye," he said, emptying the pouch into his hand and lifting up the stone and its golden chain.

"A dragon's eye? You don't mean a real dragon's eye do you? Like from a real dragon?"

"Where else would a dragon's eye come from? They are rare, very rare indeed. This one has been gifted at least once. Return it you must." Looking closely at the stone, he continued. "While a scepter may be passed in succession, this cannot. It truly can only be used by the one to whom it was gifted as it is the magic that binds it. Since it has already been bound to the one that it was given it will be safe to deal with."

"I kind of figured that since William didn't seem to have much luck with it"

"Yet another link to your line. It is said that Apollo slew the dragon at Delphi and gave the eye to the Oracle. In doing so he granted her the gift of youth and long life as well as other powers over men."

"You mean, the Apollo, the Greek God?"

"Yes, the twin brother of Artemis. But he was no God, although he was worshipped as one. A powerful Fae was he but this is a story for another time."

"What happened to him?"

Bernd sighed and then walked closer to me. "Faded during *The Fall*, as did the others when the magic dwindled and their followers deserted them. That is the fate of those who aspire too high and fail. Even the Gods are not immortal. A good lesson, is it not?"

"I guess so," I said, thinking I knew what faded meant. Cacilia's comments about the Fae had been similar. "I had planned on returning it. Any tips you care to share?"

"She will be cunning. If it is a bargain you must strike be cautious of her words. She must have been exceptionally gifted in her own right. Apollo would not grant such power to just any mortal. He must have thought greatly of her. If there is a ritual, you must follow it, but forget not her cunning. I must leave it to you, a fine test of your abilities, as well as your craft."

A ritual? That was helpful — not. My disappointment must have shown.

"If she is indeed the oracle she could be a valuable ally. But she will know the Fae. You must charm her as Apollo did," he said with the hint of a laugh. He handed me back the pouch and scepter. "You will know what to do when the time comes."

Charm her? What did that mean? "Whoa, whoa...Where are you going, I thought we were going to talk?" I yelled as he started to walk toward the doorway.

"Come, I have something you must see," was all he said.

I started to put the scepter and jewel back in the safe, but the Dwarf interrupted me. "…and bring the scepter."

I scrambled to follow him. We were in the backyard when he stopped and turned back towards me.

He raised his arms chest high, his palms pointing outward. "Within these walls and trees is your land. I have claimed it for you. Here is sanctuary as best as can be offered. Outside these walls there is danger. The Mages you killed will not easily be forgotten. Others may want vengeance, there you must be cautious, but this land I will make as safe as I am able. I have whispered to the earth. It and the trees will guard their gates from outsiders."

Charlie took that moment to appear, Bernd reached over and petted him. "Charlie, too will guard, as he always has, and there is another…one who sees the worlds that he cannot."

"Another?"

"Lucinda," Bernd called out.

I looked around not knowing what to expect. Suddenly a black cat jumped out of the oak on the other side of the pool. "A cat?" I asked, caught off guard.

"But of course," said Bernd. "Who better to guard you from evil?"

The cat ran over to him and rubbed up against his legs.

Bernd bent down and looked at it. "Lucinda, do you accept the charge?"

She walked around his leg, then sauntered over to me and sniffed. She began to twirl around me, rubbing her head against my leg, as cats do. "I do," I heard her say in the same loud type whisper as when I heard Charlie in my head.

What do you say to a cat? "Ok, Lucinda, thank you, I guess. I hope Charlie doesn't mind sharing."

I looked over at the dog and felt only a mental shrug. Not exactly an endorsement, but then again, he wasn't chasing her across the yard either. I took that as a good sign. Then Lucinda trotted off around the corner of the patio with Charlie following.

"The scepter, Robert," he said, motioning to me. "Try it now."

I held it out in front of me and concentrated but nothing happened. I tried it again a few times but it remained cold. So much for a repeat performance. "It was only when I felt the rage about me that it worked before," I commented.

Bernd just grunted. "Kneel," he commanded as he walked over to where I was standing.

I knelt down and bowed as he placed his hands on the sides of my head. I heard him muttering something but I couldn't make out the words. I felt pressure in my head, like I would have if I had a head cold. Suddenly, it became unbearable, but then he let go. "What was that about?" I asked as I shook my head, the pain and pressure subsiding.

"Maria's spell was like a dam, holding back the magic within you. The attack by the Mages has pierced a portion of Maria's spell; I have opened this gap a little wider. Magic is like water and begins as but a small trickle. Eventually it will flow faster until it becomes a mighty river. Do you understand?"

"But what about when I fought the Werewolves? That was no trickle."

Bernd took my hand and pulled me up. "Sit," he said as he gestured towards one of the pool chairs.

I walked over and sat down.

He took a stance that reminded me of a college professor lecturing his student. Ok, so he was short and dressed funny, but you get the idea.

"Even though you were not aware of it, the magic has always been part of you. Once hidden, it is now free and will respond when called upon. That is what occurred when the two began to shift into their other selves. The magic sensed the danger and answered your call."

"My call, what? But I couldn't control it, how did I call it?"

"Even untamed it is part of you. Time is needed for you to adjust to it and it to you. I have done what I can to aid that adjustment." He stood in front of me and gestured toward the scepter. "Let us see what you can do now. Do you remember what it felt like when you used it before?"

"Yeah, sort of," I said, looking down at the scepter. "It was like it became an extension of my hand."

"Good, good, then that is what you must make it become again. Try it now."

I held up the scepter and tried to will the jewel to light. Nothing happened. I tried to concentrate harder but still nothing happened. Finally, I willed myself to calm down and then just tried to feel the wood in my hand. Still nothing, wait...slowly I felt something happening. It wasn't the *red rage* feeling like I had had before. This time is was gradual. Then the awareness of everything around me began seeping in as well. I felt the scepter in my hand and it did become part of me.

I opened my eyes and saw the jewel glowing. Ok, so it wasn't as strong or as bright as it had been the time before but it was glowing with a steady flame. I looked over at Bernd. His arms were crossed and he was stroking his beard.

"Excellent. Well done, Robert," he murmured.

The flame went out and I lowered the scepter. Then I remembered something he said. "Wait a minute. I thought this would only work for the one who leads. Isn't that what you said? So how can I make it work?"

He looked thoughtful for a moment and then answered. "Many things can alter such a claim. But the simplest explanation is often the case. Do you recall where you believed the creature's line to be from?"

"Yeah, like I said before, somewhere in France, why?"

"The wood is oak as is your line. Those same forests were home to this Were's line," he answered, acting as if that would explain it.

"So, what does that mean to me?"

"Did you not listen to what Cacilia said? he asked, looking irritated. "Maria was eldest, leader of the Dryads. You are her line."

"I heard her say eldest but she never said that she was the leader. How does that help me, I'm male, remember. That seemed to be the big deal breaker to Cacilia."

"Pfaa!" he groaned, looking flustered. "I had hoped to teach you slowly, when you were more prepared." He walked directly in front of me and pointed his finger at my face. "Hear this, Robert. You are descended from the first born. Male or female, it matters not. You are the rightful heir. The magic knows this even if the others do not wish to acknowledge it! The Dryad are Fae and the forest is their domain. The creatures within owe them their allegiance. That scepter was given to them by your line. You are Fae, do you understand now?"

Wonderful, I'd had a nice, fairly normal life, good job, money in the bank, and then, *wham*, everything changes. Oh sure, it sounds great, but I'm getting too old to watch my back for every Tom, Dick, or Fae upstart that wants to take me out. Oh yeah, I need that like a hole in the head. "Yeah, I get it. I'm some bastard king of the Faeries." Now I was gonna have to watch my back for real. I stood up and began pacing around him.

"The timing sucks Bernd. Why did this have to happen now? I'm pushing 50 and my knees are shot. I sometimes need glasses to read and I sure as hell can't kick butt and take names like I could 20 years ago."

"Stop thinking like a mortal," he said as he struck me lightly on the leg.

I felt an electric jolt pass through me. I started to say something but then noticed my hands. They were changing color and the skin had become tighter. I grabbed my face and it didn't feel right. Even my hair was longer. No, not longer, but there was more of it. The rest of me felt different, too. Stronger, wait a minute...not just stronger, younger! What the hell! I jumped up and ran back to the house and into the bathroom.

Looking at me from the mirror was a younger version of myself. *I looked 25 years old,* young and virile with a full head of black hair.

Ok, ok, it's not that I was bald or anything, but I had definitely receded a bit and had a lot of gray showing. I stretched my arms and legs and felt the difference the years had made.

Bernd walked up behind me, he didn't look angry anymore. "Yes, this is your true self, when seen as a Fae."

"Holy shit," was all I could say. "What am I going to tell my kids?"

"You need tell them nothing," he answered. "Do you remember what you looked like before?"

"Of course I do," I said, feeling my face and still in shock.

"Then remember," he said, taking my hand and pointing the other toward the mirror.

I stood there and thought about it. As I watched, my old face started to appear. Slowly, like I was watching a movie. In a moment I looked as I did before. But there was a difference, I still felt like I was in my twenties.

"While you remain in the mortal world it would be best if you appear as you do now," he said, letting go of my hand. "I hope it is enough that you now know your true self as a Fae."

I rubbed my now receding hair line and laughed. "I think I like the other me better."

But I was used to the old me and so was everyone else. Changing back and forth could be confusing. Bernd was right, better to look like this for now. Could Fae like Milagre and Meredith do this? It made me wonder what they would look like.

Bernd chuckled as well. "Perhaps, but it would give you away to more than just other Fae and that we must not let happen just yet. Danger still haunts you and there is still much you need learn."

Great, more danger, I thought to myself.

"Bernd, why do I still feel younger?"

"Your grandmother's spell made you appear to age normally. While you may not live forever, it would take much more than a mere 50 years for a Fae to begin showing the signs of aging that a mortal would have at this time. Your strength has returned as well. It was the spell that made you feel mortal."

"Is there more?" I asked, waiting for another ball to drop.

"More," he answered, "there is always more."

I followed him into the kitchen and we sat down at the table.

"I was not trying to deceive you, Robert, but I hoped that I could teach you properly. So much in such a short time must appear as quite a burden and there is much I do not yet know. The Mages attack on you and the fights with the Werewolves has made that burden even more difficult. Your powers are just making themselves known. It will take time to learn."

"It's certainly been a whirlwind," I commented. "So what now, what's my next move?"

"That, my young Fae, is up to you. I have opened the gap and you have taken the first step. But only you can decide your future. Fate has offered you a new beginning. But there is danger. You must be cautious. Reveal not your true self unless absolutely necessary. It will take time for the magic to develop to its true potential.

"No, Bernd. I mean what now? Do I have to do anything about this heir thing? I'm not sure of Cacilia and what if I don't want to be the leader of the Dryads? Do I have to watch my back every second? I had more questions, but that would do for a start.

"What do you want to do?" he asked as he stood there watching me.

"I have no clue," I admitted. "Just a week or so I thought life was pretty good. Now, sure it sounds great, but I don't know anything about magic and I never asked for any of this. What do the rest of my, family, I guess we should call them, think? Are they going to be happy about this?"

"I will handle the others, for now," he answered. "There will be a reckoning but it need not be today. As to the magic, it is part of you. The magic will follow its true path and that path is through you. Do not fear. I will guide you. As to the rest, there is time to decide. There is still much I must learn before I can counsel you."

"What do you have to learn?" I asked, incredulously.

"It is too soon to know what you have become. But we will see how you progress. I can say no more."

This was too much to think about in one sitting. I wasn't really happy about the "for now" or "I can say no more" part either. But what could I do?

"Fine, we'll figure it out."

A smile appeared on his face. "Indeed! Now, it is late, you should rest." He stood up and headed towards the patio door.

I had a million questions, but there were a few things I still wasn't clear on and now was as good a time as any. "Wait, can you answer something else for me?" I asked before he could leave.

"Yes?"

"What's the deal with the Lil? I know what Siegfried told me, but you never answered my earlier question. Is there something significant there?"

"Ah, the Lilin, or the Lil, as they are often called. Tell me, why does this one interest you?" he asked as he walked back to the table.

Well," I stuttered, "I don't know." Ok, that wasn't very truthful. "Look, there was just something about her. To be honest, I'd like to get to know her better but she seems to think I'm trying to set her up or something."

"Another long story," he said as he hopped up on the stool next to me, his legs dangling over the seat. He made a motion with his hand and a pipe appeared.

I watched as he put it in his mouth and puffs of smoke began to drift lazily up around his head.

"Curious, actually it is. Out of all the people you should come to the aid of, that this one was a Lilin."

"Why is that?"

"Ancient enemies are the Lilin and the Fae. For centuries they battled one another. Near the end the Fae triumphed. There were but few Lilin that remained at the end of the last battle. Those few remaining sued for peace with the Fae. They would have been destroyed but the Elves intervened. Elves have always worshipped life, you see. Even so, many argued against it. One Fae lord held back, herself swayed by the Elves, and agreed to accept their surrender under terms. As she was one of the most powerful, and therefore influential, the others followed her decree.

"In exchange for their surrender, and their oath, the Lilin were bound by her words. They were allowed to live but little else. They were banished from the lands of the Fae and forbidden regular contact. Many fled to foreign lands. Many others became a servant class. Their ability to convert others was limited.

"After *The Fall* the Lilin scattered and even today are still shunned by many of the Fae, although it is said that the Elves still watch over them. That is why she fears you. The pact that was made still binds them. She fears that you wish to trap her and by doing so rekindle the last war."

"Ok, but what does that have to do with me personally?"

"It was Demeter that decreed their fate. She was the Fae Lord who accepted surrender. Therefore, my young Robert, you are the only one that can change that fate as you are her royal heir," he answered with a grin.

"You're shitting me? Oh, she's gonna love me now," I groaned.

I thought about that for a second. If I held the key to their future, I could change the rules. But what about the original reasons behind the war? Would I be reopening the floodgates if I did that? I just didn't have enough information to know what to do. When it rains it pours. "Bernd, isn't this a bit too much of a coincidence? Everything I do keeps being linked back to the old Gods."

"As I said, the world turns. Never let it be said that Fate is not endowed with a sense of humor. And do not forget the scepter. You must decide if the true owner is worthy to have it returned."

Oh great, my first duty of office.

"I must go, we will talk more." He paused for a moment near the doorway. "Do you have a sword?"

"What...a sword, no, I don't have a sword," I answered, sputtering. "Who keeps a sword these days?"

"Hmm, can you wield one?"

"Yeah, I guess so, why?"

"You are Fae; magic is not your only weapon. Even you are not invincible, a good blade stops both fang and claw. Perhaps I can find one for you." Then he went through the doorway and was gone.

Just great, I thought to myself as I locked the back door. I should have known there had to be a reason my grandmother had made me take fencing lessons all those years ago. I grabbed the scepter and put it into my briefcase. Shit, now I had to find a way to deal with the Werewolves without getting killed.

It was getting late, but wouldn't you know it there was still one thing I had to do. I grabbed my keys and drove to the Wal-Mart for cat food and a litter box.

Chapter 12

I thought about staying in bed all day after my conversation with Bernd but I knew that that wouldn't accomplish anything. Besides, I actually had something to look forward to with both the kids coming over for dinner. So I headed down the stairs to start the coffee and then jumped in the shower and got dressed.

Filling a black *Battlestar Galactica, the original series,* cup, I grabbed the paper and went out back to enjoy the morning sun. Charlie was lazing on the lawn but there was no sign of Lucinda. If I remembered correctly, cats slept a lot during the day. I was sure she'd pop up when I least expected it since she had come from Bernd.

I had a million things going through my mind so it was hard to concentrate on the paper. I was getting something new thrown at me almost every day. I was hoping to keep my kids away from it but this murder and Milagre's attack would probably make that impossible. Even if I hoped that wasn't the case, I knew it was going to come up sooner or later but I just wasn't ready to give the King of the Faeries announcement just yet. The last thing I needed right now was too much time to think. So I went back into the house, cleaned up my mess, and then headed down to the office to find something to do for the next few hours.

I wasn't at the office long before O'Malley called me back. He said he had an hour or so to kill before the autopsy (yep, that's what he said, pun intended) so he was calling in my offer of a cup of coffee. He asked me to meet him at a popular cop breakfast spot called Mary's Diner on Decatur. I hopped in my car and jumped on the freeway. He was already there when I arrived.

Mary's is an old restaurant that's been around since the 60s. The décor probably hasn't changed much since then, either. The walls are filled with knick knacks and old photos of Vegas in its heyday. Advertisements of popular shows adorn the walls. Sure, they're a tad yellowed, but the place is always clean and the food's good. The coffee isn't bad either. I came in through the back door and met Ray already in a booth with a steaming cup in front of him.

"Hey partner," he called out, shaking his head from side to side as I sat down. "I've got Hoskins' coming outta my ass this week with that boy of yours coming in today. The kids tell you what was going on?"

"Nikki mentioned the electrocution when I called her, but that was it. All I know is what you told me and what was in the paper" I replied as the waitress came over. Technically that was true. I didn't have any proof that Milagre's incident was connected.

She poured me some coffee as Ray looked deep in thought.

"I guess they got a string of these working in the Southwest," he said. "Of course, I hadn't heard about them until just now and that doesn't make me very happy." He drained his cup and motioned to the waitress for another. "Listen, the autopsy's in an hour. I want you to tell your boy that I'm gonna be pissed if they try and cut me out of this. This asshole's mine and I'm not gonna stand for any Fed jurisdiction crap."

Ah, so that's why he really wanted to meet. Like I said, he doesn't like others getting in the way of his investigations. Fortunately, I knew how to handle that one. Now he was gonna owe me a favor and with the sudden complications in my life that was probably a good thing. I pulled out my cell phone and dialed Jay's number.

"What's up Dad? I just pulled into the courthouse," he exclaimed as he answered.

"I'm sitting here having a cup with Ray, he says he's gonna see you at the autopsy."

"Yeah, we're supposed to meet in an hour."

"He wants to know if you are gonna pull any jurisdictional crap." I glanced over at Ray as I said it. He just gave me a dirty look.

"Let me speak to him."

I handed Ray my cellphone.

They talked for a minute or two before he handed it back to me.

"Still there?" I asked as I put the phone to my ear.

"Yeah," he chortled. "You'd think he knew me better than that."

"Well, sometimes it just makes you feel better to hear it."

"I guess. Hey, I gotta get inside. See you tonight, all right."

"Sure," I answered as he disconnected.

"You happy?" I asked as I put my phone away.

"You know how the Feds are. At least I can talk to Jay," he answered.

"So what's the deal here anyway?" I asked, hoping he would share a bit of information.

He looked around the restaurant, acting as if he may not want others to hear. Fortunately, the place was pretty empty with the breakfast rush over. At first he said nothing. Then, as if deciding it was safe, he answered.

"Rob, you know me. I've been a cop for over 30 years but I've never seen anything like this. Shootings, stabbings, hell, I've seen people killed with almost any weapon or household item you can imagine, but this one is different. Someone's got something new, and it ain't pretty. I want this bastard, Rob."

"I thought it was supposed to be lightning or maybe an electrical accident," I commented, remembering what Nikki had told me.

"Yeah, well, those wounds were too precise to be anything but deliberate. I'm telling you, someone's developed something new." He leaned closer to me over the table. "Rob, I shit you not, this guy looked like someone shot him with a friggin ray gun right out of *Star Wars*."

He straightened back up and picked up his cup. "Of course, nobody wants to say that, so it's an industrial accident or lightning...My ass. I just hope the autopsy gives us something. They're supposed to have copies from the other ones as well."

"That is weird, Ray. Come on man, there's got to be a logical explanation." I guess I could have asked if he'd checked to see if any dark Wizards could be behind it but I just didn't see where that would help.

Then he said something that surprised me.

"Well, I guess my grandmother could have been right and Dullahan do walk the Earth and shoot fire from their necks," he said, falling quiet for a long moment as if gauging my reaction.

When I didn't say anything, he continued.

"Hell, that's as good an explanation as any I've got. Anyway, I've got to be going," he said as he drained his cup, winking. "I have a few stops to make on my way. Oh, and thanks for calling Jay, I owe you one. Let me know if you hear anything," he added as he stood up.

"You got it, Ray. Be careful, okay?" I added.

He just nodded as he walked toward the doorway.

Hell, what was that about? He was closer than he thought, not that some Irish demon was stalking Fae, but it was as good an answer as any. Who were these guys? What had Milagre said? Something about trying very hard to make sure the two worlds didn't meet. It didn't appear that everyone followed that rule. I pondered that for a moment wondering if O'Malley's comments meant more than they seemed.

I didn't like this. First, I didn't have enough information about the other victims or even the Mages for that matter. Of course, at this point I doubted anybody else did, either. Second, the victims had to be Fae, or something like it, and now that I was part of that world that was something I needed to learn more about. Not that it helped that I'd already gotten myself in the mix by defending Milagre and taking out two of the bad guys. And third, both my kids and even Ray were more involved than I liked, way too involved. How do I protect them? Could I even protect them? I didn't have a clue. Well, never let it be said I ran from a fight. I'd just have to play the hand I was dealt. I'd think of something. I finished my cup and left the restaurant.

I decided I'd stop by Mal's on the way back to my office.

He was puttering behind a computer when I walked in the back door of his place. He looked up when I walked in, and then he frowned.

"Where in the hell did you get this shit?" he asked as he stood up.

"Like I said, a client," I answered, knowing that wasn't what he wanted to hear. "Did you find something?"

"Did I find something?" Mal answered, walking to another computer. "It's what I didn't find. Nothing you gave me makes any sense. The CD is written to but blank; the memory stick is burned out in a way that makes absolutely no sense; and the drive, well, the drive is fried in ways that I would have told you were impossible if I hadn't seen it myself." He turned the monitor so that I could see the screen.

On it was an image of a disc platter - a part of a disassembled hard drive where information was stored, I could see what appeared like damage on its surface. "That's unusual," I said, pointing to the platter's picture.

"Unusual? That's not unusual, it's, it's, hell, I don't know what it is," he answered, looking frustrated.

"What is it exactly that you found?"

"OK, look here," he pointed to the damaged section of the drive as he clicked a few keys and magnified the image. "These areas are totally obliterated. I found these blank sections all over the drive. There's no magnetic material on them. No magnetic properties left to the surface, well, at least as far as I can tell. Whatever was written on them is gone and it can't be recovered. They're not just wiped, Rob, something systematically erased those areas but left other parts intact." He stood up and picked up a piece of the hard drive case that I had given him. "It's like something went over every bit of this drive and removed stuff, at the bit level. The microscopic level, Rob, and there's roughly 100 gigabits per square inch here. I don't know anything that can do that."

"Do you have any theories?"

"Yeah, nanobots, if they existed," he answered, shaking his head. "No, I don't have any clue, but whatever did it, I want one! Can you tell me where you got this from yet?"

"Not yet, can you hold out for a few more days?" I asked, waiting to see if he was going to punch me. I could see it was driving him crazy that he couldn't figure it out, but he probably would slug me if I told him the truth.

"You're gonna be the death of me, you know that?" he said, pulling out a chair and straddling it. "Rob, this isn't just a new program, damn it! This is way beyond anything I've seen before. Where the hell did you get this? Can't you tell me anything?"

"I got the stick from a client but he isn't the computer type," I answered, knowing I had to tell him something. "I've gotta meet him again so let me see what I can dig up. But we have to keep this quiet, ok?"

"Quiet, yeah, no problem, I don't want men in black suits kicking my door down at 3:00 a.m.," he answered as he stood up. "Damn, Rob, this is hot stuff." Then he twirled and looked at me, a nervous expression on his face. "Rob, I need to know...do I have to worry about men in black suits? Not that I care mind you but it pays to be prepared just in case they might be coming."

"Relax, Mal. No one knows I brought it to you. Hell, no one even knows I have it except one person and he's my client. He's not gonna say anything as long as it doesn't get out."

Ok, so it was only partially the truth, but I had to have Mal keep a lid on it and I certainly couldn't tell him everything. Although if bad shit kept happening, I was gonna need friends like him on my side. Still, he didn't look satisfied. I thought he was going to lecture me some more but then he picked up the hard drive parts and walked over to where I knew he kept his safe.

"I'm putting this shit into the safe and wiping my drives for now. But I still want some answers."

"Alright, I gotta get to the office myself." I walked towards the doorway. "I'll find out for you what I can." I had no idea yet what I was going to tell him down the road. "Oh yeah, I almost forgot, how's the database coming?"

Mal had been slowly buying up public data from various governmental agencies as part of a plan to sell information online. Tax data, revenue sources, all public data that could be sold to real estate agents, mailing companies, salesman and the like who needed that sort of data as part of their business operations.

"Why, you making a mailing list?" he asked, sarcastically, as he closed the safe door. He was upset with me but what could I do

"Nah, just trying to find someone," I replied. "I'm hoping they made some tax payments or maybe got a license or permit."

He pulled a card out of the pocket of his shirt and wrote something down. Here," he responded, handing me the card. "It's not public yet but that'll get you in. It's still slow until I index it all but you can enter your queries and it'll email you when it's done."

"Thanks."

****

My office was quiet when I got there. Hailey was on the phone so I grabbed a cup of coffee and just nodded a hello. I went through my inbox as the desktop booted up and then checked my email.

Once that was done I accessed Mal's database web page and entered in queries for a Deborah Medea. Just to play it safe I added the Diantha and Kent names. It was a longshot but it was worth a try. The database contained records from several Nevada counties, including Clark and Washoe and their surrounding areas. That would perform a search anywhere within a hundred miles or so of Las Vegas and Reno. After that I closed my computer down and left the office.

Chapter 13

I got home and did a little last minute cleaning and then kicked back to wait for the kids to arrive. It felt weird, but I also had a chat with Charlie and Lucinda to try and act like regular dogs and cats. Then I told the cat I was calling her Lucy. I'm not sure she liked that.

Nikki made it to the house first with Jay following about a half hour later. We spent the best part of the next several hours rehashing old times, enjoying dinner (steak and shrimp on the barbecue) and just catching up. Jay played ball with Charlie and Nikki fell in love with Lucy. It was such a nice time; I almost forgot what my life had turned into...almost. After the dishes were all put away I fired up the outdoor fireplace and we sat down, cocktails in hand.

"So Jay, tell me about your new case. I hear it's the same as Nikki's body in the desert."

"Actually, I'm glad you brought it up, Dad," he said, shuffling in his chair. "It's a bizarre one although you know we aren't really having this conversation." He always said that when we talked about work.

"Bizarre?" I asked. "What's so strange about it?"

"It's the autopsy results," Nikki chimed in. "They don't make any sense."

"In what way?"

"Well, there's no argument that the guy was electrocuted. There's clear evidence of that," she answered. "But the wound pattern and tissue damage are not consistent with normal electrocution injuries."

"What do you mean?"

Jay sat forward and answered. "Ok, Dad, it means it's really friggin weird." Then he stood up and moved in front of us. "You see, electrocution injuries follow similar patterns."

"Yeah, they're supposed to follow established scientific rules," Nikki added.

"Hey, are you telling this or am I?"

"Sorry little brother, I just wanted to make sure Dad understood."

I took a drink and said, "Whoa, guys, slow down. Jay, please go on."

"Alright, Dad," Jay continued, "it's like this. If you get electrocuted there are certain things that usually happen. Body parts are supposed to react in certain ways. There can be exit and entry wounds, such as burns at the point of contact. High water content parts, like nerves and blood vessels, are good conductors of energy so they offer low resistance and move current. Bones aren't so they usually heat up...Now, if it's a lightning strike, you can have..."

"I think I'm getting lost here," I said, getting up to refill my glass.

Jay just grinned. "Sorry, next time I'll leave the science discussion for Nikki. Anyway, the point is that there are certain anomalies in the examinations that aren't consistent with established rules of science and that's got people worried."

"Ok, what are the anomalies?" I asked, sitting back down.

"Nik, you want to explain?" he queried, plopping back down in his chair.

She took a drink and then put the glass down. "Well, without getting all scientific, it boils down to this," she answered. "The tissue and other body damage are inconsistent with known electrical injuries. That means we are dealing with an unknown source and type of energy, something new. No one seems to be able to identify what it is but we know it's different."

"Wow, seems like you two have got your work cut out then," I answered, trying to decide how I should continue. "So, Jay, what do you think it means?" I asked, remembering what Ray had said. "Has someone developed a real working ray gun, like in *Star Wars*?"

"Honestly Dad, I'm not sure. I have to continue on the premise that it's some new form of energy, but whether it's purely a weapon or someone's just using it as one, I just don't know."

"Well, with several people dead, it seems like more than a weapon than just a source of energy," I pointed out, shaking my head.

"You would think so," he answered. "But if someone had developed a new energy source there'd be a ton of money in it. I know they assigned me due to the terrorist angle, but think about it. If you were going to develop a terrorist weapon, why would you use it on rich people individually and then try to hide it? I mean that's not the actions of a terrorist. You'd want to strike fear in large groups of people. These are individual deaths and they've been too quiet, something just doesn't add up."

"Tell him about the spooks," Nikki interrupted.

"Spooks?" I repeated. "What, is the CIA involved, too?"

"Who knows who they work for?" Jay retorted. "But get this, I get a call from DC this morning that these two suits wanted to observe the autopsy. I sent a car to pick them up from the airbase and take them at the coroner's office."

Nikki gestured wildly. "Dad, these guys were absolutely spooky! Real *Men in Black* types, like the kind you hear about investigating stuff from Area 51!"

"She's not kidding," Jay continued. "They stayed for the autopsy and then we had to take them back to the base. They never said more than a few words the entire time, just stood there watching and taking notes."

"They were beyond weird, Dad, I mean they looked like a couple of ghouls," Nikki added.

"So you don't know what agency they were with?" I asked, wondering what their significance was. Could there be a government agency that dealt with non-mortals? That was a scary thought.

"Hell no, DC didn't tell me and I didn't ask," he answered. "Really friggin weird. Whoever they are, they had full military access and clearances I didn't even know existed and I was told to give them whatever they wanted."

"I thought this was like the fifth body," I noted. "Were they at the other autopsies?"

"No, not that I know of. But they didn't call my team in until they found the third body so my reports wouldn't have hit DC till last week."

"Hmm, beats me," I said.

Nikki leaned forward. "Dad, I know you still have a lot of contacts, see if you can find out who they were?" she whispered as if someone else may be listening.

That was my girl. She still believed that I could find out anything. Of course, in this case, she might be right. "Well, that sounds like it's more up Jay's alley," I said, chuckling.

"Not me," he replied. "I've learned not to ask too many questions when it comes to anything out of Washington. Those DC guys would classify the morning paper as secret, you know what I mean?"

We all laughed. Jay wasn't saying anything I hadn't said in the past when it came to dealing with Feds, even if he was one himself.

I turned back to him. "So, tell me about the victims. You mentioned that they were wealthy. I mean, if you can't talk about them, I understand."

"Oh crap, Dad, I've already said enough to get me suspended," he said as he laughed. "Anyway, I still don't have all the info yet, but it's not just the money. It's that they dealt in a lot of cash. Two of them were in the entertainment business, movies and video distribution, I think. One guy was connected to the adult entertainment industry; him we have a file on. The fourth was a rancher/farmer." He turned to Nikki. "I haven't seen the final on today's guy, did you hear anything else after I left?"

"Other than he was a regular Vegas player? No, your guys were with our detectives, but that's the last I heard," she shrugged.

"Ok," Jay said. "Metro identified him as a high roller. I'll find out what else they have in the morning. But the point is they all seem to have had access to large amounts of hard cash."

I didn't think of a rancher or farmer as having access to large amounts of cash, so I asked him about it.

"Yeah, multi property payroll services, believe it or not. Migrant workers, farm hands, all paid in cash. That one caught me off guard as well."

I had enough to think about so I let the conversation drift off to other things. Nikki, who had to go to work early, soon left. Jay went to get ready for bed and I cleaned up the mess. I had just closed the dishwasher door when Jay came back down. He had his cell phone in his hand and was taking it down from his ear.

"Sorry, Dad, that was the office. It looks like I have to head back earlier than I had hoped. We'll have to postpone fishing," he said, putting his cell phone in his pocket. "I'm really sorry."

"I know how it goes, maybe next time."

"Well, as soon as we get this one wrapped up they'll owe me some vacation time." He reached in the cabinet for a glass.

"There's cold bottled water in the fridge," I said, assuming that's what he wanted.

"Great," he replied, pulling his hand away. "Hey Dad, you know the suits we were talking about?"

"The not-CIA spooks?" I asked.

"Yeah," he continued, "remember when you did that work on quirky religions and black magic stuff?"

"Sure, what about it?" I wondered what brought that up.

"Well, I just got off the phone with Darrell; he was the agent that played driver for them."

"Ok."

"He just told me that when he was getting ready to drive them back to the base he overheard them talking about some kind of black magic mumbo jumbo."

"Black magic?" Now I was getting interested. "What did they say?"

"Well, he said one guy made some kind of comment about Necromancers and blood wands but he stopped as soon as he caught Darrell listening. What do you think that was about?"

"Maybe they were just bs'ing." My guts clenched.

"I don't know, these guys didn't seem the chatty type and Darrell said they gave him the creeps." He walked over to the fridge and grabbed a bottled water and then turned back to me. "Ok, humor me for a second. Let's say the government has a special section, like the old project Blue Book. Only this time, it's not about aliens, but voodoo and sorcery stuff. Is that too crazy?"

"It sounds a little farfetched to me but who knows where the government is concerned. I can tell you that there are a lotta folk out there who believe in that stuff." Shit, he'd probably hit it right on the nose. I wondered if they knew about me.

"Yeah," he replied, "but governments do weird stuff all the time, believe me, I know. Even the Germans did that in WW II, looking for old relics that were supposed to be magical."

"Look, Jay, is there something you know that you aren't, or can't, tell me?" I asked, trying to get to the heart of the matter.

"That I know, not really," he said. "I didn't want to mention it in front of Nikki but there are rumors about other teams getting observed by these kinds of guys on weird cases. So I was just wondering if you ever got that when you were working that stuff."

I took a moment before answering. It had been 20 or so years since I'd worked black magic and witchcraft cases. I'd even written a paper on the subject for the Department way back when. I tried to decide what information I could give him that would help. I mean, how do you tell your son that you just found out that you're a magical being yourself?

"Well, I do still have a few contacts in the Wicca and witchcraft world and they do believe in magic. I guess my only advice to you is to never discount anything. I mean, even if you don't believe, their beliefs are real to them. Besides, it's like I always said about Christmas."

Jay started to laugh. "Yeah, yeah, I remember...even if your friends don't believe in Santa Claus you have to give him the benefit of the doubt because there are always a few presents under the tree that you have no idea where they came from. Thanks Dad, and good night. I'll see you in the morning." He turned and started to go upstairs.

"Listen, Jay, I know you can't ask too many questions," I said.

He paused at the foot of the stairs.

"But like I said, I still know a few people. I'll keep my ears open and see what I can find out. Just let me know if you run into them again or if anything really weird happens, ok?"

"I will, Dad, I know it sounds a little crazy, but thanks."

I walked up the few steps and gave him a hug. "Nothing in this business would surprise me, you know that. I'll let you know what I can find out. But you stay safe, there are a lot of crazies out there and you're in the thick of them."

"I will, Dad, and good night," he headed up the stairs.

Later, as I lay in bed, I promised myself that I would do whatever I could to protect them from the world I had been thrown into. Although I admitted to myself that sooner or later I was going to have to find some way to tell them. I just hoped it would be later rather than sooner. Although their safety was my prime concern, I had enough going on at the moment to be worrying about what their reaction to my new found situation would be.

Chapter 14

The next morning, Jay came into the kitchen just as I was pouring a cup of coffee.

"I'm gonna head over to where our latest victim was last known to be staying at here in town and drop a subpoena, then I'm heading back to L.A. I'll try to come up next month unless business brings me here sooner." He paused as I handed him a cup, raising an eyebrow. The mug featured Fox Mulder from the *X-Files*. "Are you trying to tell me something?" he asked with an inquisitive look.

"No," I said, chuckling, "just thought you'd get a kick out of it."

We sat down at the kitchen table.

"So, where was he staying?"

"Comped suite at the Neptune's Landing. Apparently he was a whale from Japan. You know much about the place?" A whale was a heavy gambler. It was a term known to every casino employee, as well as most Vegas folks.

I almost spilled my coffee; it would have to be the Neptune. "As a matter of fact, the head of the place is a client of mine and his corporate security guy is an acquaintance. I can introduce you. It might make things work smoother."

"That'd be great, Dad. Can you arrange it? It'll take me an hour or so to get the paperwork from the U.S. Attorney. How do you want to play it?" he asked with a smile on his face.

I knew it would give him the opportunity to make a new connection in town as well as make things move faster.

"Do you trust them?"

"I have no reason not to at the moment, but it's your case. I can call him now and set something up, or if you'd prefer, we can drop in on them cold." I left that decision to him. I didn't want him to think I was stepping on his investigation.

"Yeah, go ahead and call, I don't want to be too difficult. See if we can meet him around 9:30, if that's ok," he replied.

"Let's find out." I picked up my cell phone and dialed Siegfried's number.

"Do you want me to tell him anything?"

"I'd rather wait," he said, shaking his head.

Having been in his shoes and knowing that I couldn't tell him anything different, I nodded. Siegfried answered almost immediately. I put the call on the speaker. "Robert, you're up early, what can I do for you?"

"Hey, Siegfried, I was wondering if you time to meet up this morning, say around 9:30 or so? My son is in town and had a few questions about something he is working on."

"Ah, yes, the agent," he said. "Can you tell me what this is about?"

"Well, I'm really not in a position to comment. It's his case so I'd rather have him discuss it with you, if you don't mind."

Siegfried didn't hesitate before answering. "Of course, I understand your position. Do you want to meet here?"

I looked over at Jay and he nodded his head. "That would be best. Where do you want us to meet you? We'll be traveling in two cars."

There was a short pause. "Why don't you ask for me at the security podium by the cage? I'll come down when the first one of you arrives."

"That'll work," I answered. "See you then."

"Thanks, Dad," he said as he got up from the table. He drained his cup and placed it in the sink. "Well, I'm gonna head to the Vegas office then. So I'll see you there at 9:30?"

"I'll be there," I said as I followed him to the front door.

****

I arrived at the Neptune's Landing around 9:15, parked in the main lot and went inside. I headed to the cage area where the security podium was located and gave the guard my name and waited. Moments later, Siegfried came out of a side door.

"Robert, how are you?" he asked, shaking my hand.

"Good, Siegfried, Jay should be here any minute."

We made small talk until Jay showed up. After introductions, we went into the back toward Siegfried's office. His office was large and well-furnished, indicating his position in the hierarchy of the business. There were some interesting artifacts as well, all relating to his Viking ancestry, Viking art on the walls and examples of weaponry behind glass cases.

He sat down behind his desk as we sat in the plush chairs in front.

"Well then, Agent Hoskins, how can we assist you?" Siegfried asked, clasping his hands.

"I have a subpoena for some records for you. Your company is not the subject of my investigation. Rather, it's for records about an individual by the name of Chitose Shoda. He was known to have stayed here recently." He handed the subpoena to Siegfried.

Siegfried looked over the paperwork, appearing stunned for a moment, then recovered quickly. "Mr. Shoda is well known to us. As you have a subpoena, we will, of course, provide you with whatever you need. But, please, can you tell me what this about?"

Jay looked over at me before answering. "Mr. Shoda's body was found a week or so ago, we believe he was murdered."

Siegfried picked up the phone and dialed a number. "Please tell Mr. Milagre that I have Mr. Hoskins and his son, Agent Hoskins with Homeland Security here in my office. We need to speak with him immediately." There was a short pause. "Thank you, we'll be there in a moment." He looked back over at us. "This is very disturbing news. Chi was a good client, as well as a regular guest. He and Mr. Milagre have been acquaintances for years. I think he will be better able to answer any questions you may have."

Siegfried stood up and we followed him out the doorway. He stopped at his secretary's desk and handed her the subpoena. He gave her some instructions and then asked us to follow him to Milagre's office which was around the corner from his. Once there, he asked us to give him a moment and we waited in the outer office as he went in to see Milagre.

"So what do you think, Dad?" Jay asked as Siegfried closed the door behind him.

"I think you caught him off guard. He looked quite concerned."

Jay started to say something but Siegfried came back out and waved for us to go in.

"Tell you what," I said as I turned to Jay. "This is your gig, son. I'm gonna wait out here while you do your thing."

"Ok, thanks Dad," Jay answered, smiling.

I could tell he knew I was recognizing that this was his case and I'd done my bit with the introductions. Hey, you gotta let them grow up sometimes. I sat down in one of the plush chairs and watched him walk into Milagre's office. I grabbed a magazine and sat back to wait.

Siegfried came out a few minutes later. "They will be a while. Would you care to wait in my office?"

"Sure," I said as I stood up.

When we got to his office he went straight to his secretary's desk. "How soon will those records be ready?" he asked her.

"Michael is handling it," she replied. "Everything the subpoena requires is computerized. I told him to rush it. We should have the file in the next 15 to twenty minutes or so."

"Very good, him in when he arrives."

I followed him into his office and he closed the door behind me. I took a chair as he sat down at his desk. "I'm sorry I couldn't tell you more before we got here," I said.

Siegfried leaned back and ran his fingers through his thick, blonde hair. "I understand. It's just a shock. Shoda was well respected and he was a powerful Fae. That would have been Mr. Milagre's fate had you not intervened."

"I figured he was one of us. What was he?"

"The Japanese are very different from us, Robert. Here, although well hidden, the Fae have integrated into modern society. But there the worlds remain apart." Siegfried said, rubbing his temples. "Shoda was an exception, he was a go between. He moved freely between both worlds. I understand his services were much sought after. His passing will leave a considerable void. It concerns me a great deal."

"His death?" I asked.

"More so the reasons behind it. Unfortunately, I do not know a great deal about his activities. What I do know is that Shoda was our only contact with the Eastern world. His passing closes many doors. I do not know when they will be open to us again."

"Well, it gets worse," I said. "There are at least 4 others that I know of. I am guessing they're Fae as well. From what little I've learned each was wealthy, so probably powerful as well. I don't have their names. But the question is, who's taking out the Fae, and why?"

"If we assume Mr. Milagre's was the last, then your dispatching of the attackers seems to have curtailed their activities, at least for now," he replied.

"So it seems, but for how long?"

I could see that Siegfried was thinking about that as well. He started to say something but was interrupted by the phone. Picking it up, I heard him tell them to send him in.

"Here are the reports you requested," said a young man in an Armani suit as he walked into the room. He handed a folder to Siegfried.

"Michael, this is Robert Hoskins," Siegfried said, introducing me. "Michael is my assistant chief."

"A pleasure to meet you, sir," he answered.

"You as well," I replied.

"Michael, anything out of the ordinary on this trip?" Siegfried asked as he shuffled through the papers he had been given.

"No, sir, as usual, he didn't book in advance and we did not receive an itinerary. He dined on property and we have no record of any visitors or out of the ordinary activity."

"Thank you," Siegfried said. "Check with other staff. If any other information becomes available, notify me immediately."

"Yes, sir," he replied and then turned and walked out of the office.

Siegfried picked up the phone. "I have those records, sir," he said. "Unfortunately, there is very little here. Yes, sir, I'll take care of it."

As he hung up the phone he turned towards me. "Your son will be on his way back here in a minute. Hopefully, Mr. Milagre was able to provide some useful information."

"Well, I am sure he'll appreciate anything you can do for him."

"Have you told him about the incident with Mr. Milagre?" Siegfried asked shrewdly.

It was my turn to run my hands down the back of my head and neck. "Hell, Siegfried, I don't know if I should tell him anything, but he's my kid, you know. He's also running this investigation. He has no idea that I took out two of his suspects and I don't know how to tell him without revealing the rest. I gotta be honest here, Siegfried, I don't like lying to my kids, but what can I do? I'm certainly not prepared to tell either of them the truth about all this just yet. Hell, I doubt they'd even believe me."

"A difficult position to be in," Siegfried agreed.

"He's got enough on his plate as it is and I'm knee deep in this mess and it's getting complicated." I stood up. "I'll have to play it by ear. If these killings place him or my daughter in any more danger than they are already in I'll have to try and find a way to tell them. But for now, I'm hoping we've slowed them down a bit."

"One thing at a time then. I hope you know that I will help you in any way I can." The phone rang and he answered it. "Very good, send him in."

After Jay came in, Siegfried gave him the information he had requested. We chatted for a while and then the three of us left the office and walked back to the casino to head our separate ways.

"OK then, Dad, I'll call you soon," Jay said as he prepared to leave.

"Alright, let me know what you can and I'll follow up on what we discussed," I replied as I hugged him. As he walked away I turned to Siegfried. "Have you got a few minutes?"

"Of course, would you like some coffee? We have an excellent coffee house on property."

"Lead the way," I answered.

The Neptune had several European style coffee stands throughout the property. Each one was themed after a different region. We walked through the casino and wound up at a little shop with a Mediterranean theme.

"How are you coming along with Williams' case? Any luck on locating the woman yet?" Siegfried asked after we'd ordered and taken a seat at a table in the back.

"Slow going right now," I confessed as I sipped my Latte. "I've got searches running and some other inquiries out. If they don't pan out I'll start hitting the streets."

I looked over at him and made a decision. Siegfried had been straight with me so far, and to be honest, I was gonna need a friend like him.

"My sources say that the jewel is a dragon's eye and that it was indeed gifted to an oracle from ancient Greece."

That got his attention.

"A dragon's eye, then she is indeed from Delphi. Hah! Who would have thought she was the one true Pythia." He took a deep drink. "She would be a valuable ally indeed. I hope you can locate her."

"I'll find her. Whether or not she'll cooperate, we'll just have to wait and see."

"I did not know that you had other Fae sources," he said, looking at me intently.

"Yeah, well, things have moved kind of fast lately. But first, there's more going on here than we know about, Siegfried, and that bothers me. We need to find out why these Mages are going after Fae? I know I took out two of them but I have to believe they'll try again."

"I agree," he nodded. "As you know, I have increased security at the property as well as on Mr. Milagre. But without further information about our adversaries there is only so much I can do. I have inquiries out to all my sources. Do you have any thoughts?"

"No, I wish I did, for now that's all I think you can do. I'm going to be doing some more digging as well." I sat back and took another drink and then turned back to Siegfried. "I'd like to discuss a few other matters as well. Jay mentioned something that I want to learn more about. Have you ever heard of any government agency that investigates nonhuman activity?"

Siegfried gave me one of those raised eyebrow looks as sipped from his cup. "Yes, I know of them. They have contacted Mr. Milagre on several occasions. It is said that many government s employ such agents to protect themselves. Why, has your son been approached by them?" He put down his cup.

"They were at Shoda's autopsy and Jay was wondering about them. My daughter met them as well. She described them as spooks, as in evil spirits, not agents."

"There are those in the government that know the Fae exist. These beings monitor magic for them, or at least magic that would threaten the government. It is rumored that many are half-breeds, humans, but with Demon blood. Historically, they were persecuted by the mortals of Earth in the old times, who thought them evil and unclean.

"Legend has it that some made pacts with the sovereigns of the realms they resided in, protection of the king's title and lands against attacks by magic in exchange for a safe haven. They seek out those who would harm their masters and report their findings. Governments today are no different than they were then. Does it not make sense that they would employ them to protect their interests from others?"

"I thought all Demons were evil, and when you say half breeds, do you mean a physical half breed, such as with a Demon and other as a parent?" I hadn't considered such beings would exist or that the government knew about the Fae but it did make sense.

"Exactly, a union between a Demon and a mortal would produce such a being. The universe is supposed to be in balance, if the Fae can visit and live here then it makes sense that Demons can as well. But they come from the Underworld. A very different place than the world we know. But in many ways they are similar to the Fae, so it does not seem unusual that they would breed with mortals just as the Fae have. But as to them being evil, I am not sure that is the right word," Siegfried answered.

"I'm not sure I understand. If not evil, then what are they...and similar to the Fae?"

"If the Fae could war against each other over petty trifles then how can all Fae be good?" Siegfried pointed out, leaning over towards me. "Demons are said to be no different. There are many types of Demons and some are indeed evil, but I am certain that there are Demons who want only to be left alone and live in peace. I do not know all their history but it is said that when the Gods first took up arms to battle one another they discovered the secret to summoning the higher Demons as warriors, opening a long-closed portal to their lands. While many came because they were bound and returned to their homes when the spell binding them was broken, others came willingly, seeking new lands to conquer."

Siegfried paused a moment, then sat back in his chair, looking at me intently. "As for them being like the Fae, they are creatures of magic with similar lines and powers. I have been told that the higher Demons are great warriors and are considered formidable opponents."

"Great, this just gets better all the time," I said, leaning back. I placed my cup down and leaned towards him. "Now, I have another problem I need to discuss with you."

"Another problem? You have had a busy week."

He had no idea.

"What can you tell me about Werewolves?"

"Werewolves?"

He started to say something about shape shifters but I interrupted him.

"Sorry, I don't mean Werewolves in general. I meant the ones that are local. Are there many and what are they like?

"I know a few," he answered with a look of concern. "Can you tell me what this is about?"

I told him about the incidents with Delia, both in the street and at Danu's. I didn't get too specific about my power or lack of control of it but I could tell he got the general idea. When I told him about beating the Werewolves and taking the scepter his eyes widened.

"You took that from one of the boys? But how..." he asked, shaking his head. "Wait; first tell me, what did the older man look like? Are you sure he was his father?"

"Light skinned, about 6', 2" and well-built but with dark hair and a beard...and the kid called him Dad," I answered.

"...and the Corvette was red. It must have been Ben Turner. He's been a thorn in the side of Martin for years. He has a boy about the right age as well, also named Benjamin. But stealing the scepter? That is a bold move."

"Ok, who are they?"

"Sorry, Robert, Martin Chibeaux is the pack leader of the local Weres. Ben Turner is also a member of the pack. Their families have been at odds for generations. He's been testing Martin for years now. He wants control but doesn't have the strength, or the following, to challenge Martin. But to steal the scepter, that is bold...and foolish as well." He shook his head. "Turner's line is old, but not as old as Martin's. Nor is he strong enough to lead. He is a fool." Siegfried slapped his hand on the table. "What do you plan on doing with the scepter?"

"Find a way to return it most likely. But what about this Martin, what will losing the scepter do for his position? I understand it is supposed to be a symbol of leadership."

Siegfried looked thoughtful for a moment, and then answered. "Well, that it is. But if it was common knowledge that it was missing I should have heard of it before now. I doubt Turner has said anything, especially since it is no longer in his son's possession, and Martin would be searching for it on his own. He'd never announce it publicly unless he had no choice. It may just be a symbol these days but it is a potent one. While the loss would not end his rule, it would be a sign of weakness that Turner could exploit."

"Well, Turner's an ass. So do you know this Martin guy well? Is he a good leader?" I asked, since I didn't know anything about him or local Werewolf politics for that matter.

"Martin has a good reputation among the Fae," Siegfried commented. "I've dealt with him on a few occasions and he takes care of his people."

"Ok, I'd like to meet him if that's possible? I have enough on my plate without me getting into a war with some Werewolves because I have his scepter. But let's keep that info under the table for a while. No sense making myself a bigger target."

"Perhaps I can make a discrete inquiry." He leaned back in his chair and gave me a serious look. "Let me give the matter some thought. Now, are you ready to tell me how you fought three Weres and defeated them?"

I paused before answering and then I decided that if I was going to include him in the bad things going on, I owed him the good things as well. "Honestly, Siegfried, I'm still not sure. When they shifted it was like something switched on inside of me. I've tried to repeat it, but so far except for a small test, it's only worked when I've been attacked."

"Well, I cannot say what the spell has hidden from you, but consider this, first you defeat two of the three mages that attacked Mr. Milagre and then Meredith did not sense you when we met for lunch. Later you saw the Faerie and then defeated three Weres. That is not the work of a simple Fae, not even a Fae warrior. I do not know what you truly are but it seems that you are more than just a Dryad."

He shook his head, laughed and stood up. "You have certainly made my life interesting. I will keep this conversation between us for now. Mr. Milagre will want to meet after what he has just learned from your son. I will let you know if I discover anything else, take care until we meet again." He grasped my hand to shake it.

"Of course," I replied, "and you do the same."

"I will be in touch when I have learned something," he added, dropping a bill on the table for a tip. Then he walked out of the restaurant.

I finished my cup as I thought about what he said. What had I become? Without an easy answer I wandered out of the coffee shop towards the casino. As I walked through it I watched people as they played their games of chance. I could feel the magic in the air swirling about.

Formed by the wishes and prayers of the people and pulled out by the talismans and spells situated around the casino. A few of them had talismans of some sort or another as well. A rabbit's foot in the hand of one young man, an old coin in another, a lucky necklace being worn by an old woman, things like that.

People seemed happy, but I guess that's how Milagre uses his magic and makes a profit at the same time. It was strange; I'd been thrown into this world of homicidal Mages, Faeries and battles with Werewolves and all I could think about at the moment was that there had to be a better way to use the magic.

I guess I was being altruistic. What Milagre was doing was no different than anything else the Fae had done in the past, or humans for that matter. It saddened me a bit as I was again reminded that this world and my old one were not so different.

Chapter 15

Like I said, new found Fae or not, sometimes my job is just boring. I spent the next couple of days just catching up on mundane work. I hadn't heard back from Siegfried but since I still had casework coming in from regular clients I stayed busy. The rest of the time I did what normal people do; went shopping, got gas and did the yard work. Even Charlie and Lucy were quiet. To be honest, it made me kind of nervous. I couldn't shake the feeling that it was just the lull before the storm. Even Bernd hadn't come around. Well, at least no one had tried to kill me in a few days. That was a good thing, right?

I had just finished mowing the lawn when my phone went off. It was an email from Mal's database. It had found something. I accessed the site from the computer in my home office. Reviewing the information I learned that someone by the name of Deborah Kent had paid a license fee to work in a brothel in late 99.

What? I had guessed that she'd be a little old for that. As I read the rest of the file I realized that it was for some type of contract employee, not a working girl.

The brothel I knew. It was named the Venus and it had closed down about 10 years ago. It had been a popular place in the 60s and 70s and had been located outside of Pahrump. Now closed, it hadn't been able to compete with the more modern places that cropped up south of town. Big money had been invested in those houses and places like the Venus had slowly faded away.

Thank God I worked with Hailey; her rolodex just might offer a name. I dialed her at the office. "Hail, it's Rob, didn't you used to know a few of the working girls in Pahrump?"

"Sure, I still have a few contacts. Why, what you got, or are you just lonely?"

"You wound me," I said as I laughed. "I had a call to return some property to a girl, that's all. Apparently she used to do some work for the Venus. I was hoping you might know where to start looking for her."

"Well, she'd have a license if she worked there."

"Maybe, but this one was apparently not a hooker."

"Well, let me check my files." There was a pause and I could hear her rummaging around on her desk. "She could have been anything. Let me see...ah, perfect! Mattie Truesdell. Mattie was a manager there before they closed down."

She gave me Mattie's number. "Once again, you owe me."

"As usual," I jested as Hailey laughed.

"You bet your ass, and one day I'm gonna collect!"

"If this helps me find her, I will, of course, give up some of my commission. Is that acceptable?"

"It's a deal!" she said as she hung up the phone. Her rolodex had come through again.

I called Ms. Truesdell next. At first she was hesitant about speaking with me. However, once I told her I worked with Hailey she agreed to meet with me. She gave me her address in Pahrump and we made an appointment for the next day. I hadn't told her too much on the phone, just that I was trying to return some property to the family of a client.

I spent some time doing computer searches of properties in Nye County with owners by the name of Kent. Finding three, I printed them out, figuring I would take them with me in case one of them was hers. Then I called Siegfried to let him know I would be on Deborah's trail tomorrow. After some discussion, he agreed to contact me in the morning to make arrangements for William's additional peace offering.

With things looking up I went back outside and played ball with Charlie. Lucy decided to join us as well, although she just sat and preened herself. After a while I went inside to clean up. I was just getting ready to hit the shower when the phone rang. It was Siegfried.

"Siegfried, what's up?" I asked as I answered.

"I have that package from Mr. Harrison for you. Will you be available in the morning? I can run it by your house if that's convenient. I have some early runs in the northwest side of town."

"That'd be great, know where I live?" I asked, already sure what the answer would be.

"Of course. How does around 8:00 a.m. sound? I should be finished with my other business by then."

"That's fine, just buzz me at the gate when you arrive and I'll let you in."

"Excellent, I'll see you then."

I looked down at Lucy and Charlie and said, "Ok, you two, my friend Siegfried is coming by at 8:00 in the morning. He's like the Fae but I'm not sure if he can talk to you like I can, so act accordingly." I almost felt silly lecturing the animals but I hoped they'd understand.

Lucy sat back, licked her paws and gave me a look like she had already figured that out. Charlie, on the other hand twisted his head and asked, "Friend?"

"Yes, Charlie, he's a new friend, but I'm not sure he'll have time to play ball," I laughed. "I guess it's ok if he thinks you're smart, though."

He started wagging his tail. "Friend is good," was all he said. He trotted off to patrol the yard. I had a feeling Bernd's order to guard the place was something he took seriously.

I spent the rest of the evening just thinking. Considering my life the past couple of weeks, I needed to try and process what was happening. Unfortunately, I didn't find any answers. My last thought before falling asleep was wondering where the Dwarf was when I needed him.

The next morning I decided to wear a suit in case I needed to make an impression. I was just putting my tie on when I heard the phone ring the gate alarm. Picking it up, I answered and buzzed Siegfried in.

Both Charlie and Lucy were waiting at the front door as I went down to the front room. I opened the front door and saw Siegfried getting out of a black Cadillac Escalade. He was carrying a large satchel. Lucy stayed inside but Charlie immediately burst through the door to check him out. I didn't hear a word from either pet so I figured my comments to them last night must have worked. It was still strange when they obeyed like that.

Charlie ran up to Siegfried and stopped a few feet away. Siegfried paused a moment and then knelt down and started talking to him. Charlie stole a quick glance at me and I gave an imperceptible nod. He went over and allowed the big man to pet him.

"What a handsome dog," Siegfried said, standing back up and walking towards me.

Charlie followed, wagging his tail.

"Yeah, he is," I agreed and shook his hand.

"I'm surprised he didn't bark at me when I pulled in."

"Well, he knows if I let you in you must be ok." I motioned for him to come into the house.

"So he's well trained?"

"You'd be surprised at what he can do," I said as I laughed.

Charlie started to come into the house but I stopped him. "Charlie, check the yard." I hoped he wouldn't make me look bad but he immediately halted and ran to the gate, then took off around the perimeter.

Siegfried stopped and took a long look back at the hitching post. "This is interesting; do you get many that arrive on horseback?" he asked with a raised eyebrow.

"I like to be prepared," I answered with a grin.

As we walked in, Siegfried commented on the wooden floors and ceiling beams. I gave him the short version of the ownership history of my house.

"I tried to keep as much of the original as I could. I know the distressed look is in fashion but I can honestly say these floors came by it naturally."

"Well, you did an excellent job restoring the place. It's a nice change; there is so little history in this city."

"Yeah, we do tend to implode everything," I quipped, meaning the tendency of most old hotels to be imploded to make way for the new ones."

We sat down at the kitchen table. Lucy followed, appearing to keep an eye on the satchel. As we sat Siegfried opened it and removed a package. Lucy jumped up and placed her paws on the opening, trying to peer inside.

"Lucy, relax," I said, as I reached around and pushed her aside.

"...and a black cat, you do have interesting friends," Siegfried said, placing the package on the table. "This is from William, $50,000.00 in $100 dollar bills, Mr. Milagre hopes that will be sufficient to make her happy."

"I think it'll work," I said as I moved the bundle to my side of the table. "Does he need a receipt?"

"I don't believe that will be necessary." Siegfried said with a smile. He started to reach toward the satchel again but Lucy moved to intercept his hand. "Have no fear, little one, this is a gift for your master."

I was surprised when Lucy backed away but I also noticed she wouldn't take her eyes off Siegfried's hands. Well, so much for her being low key. It was also obvious to me that Siegfried had some understanding of my companion's abilities.

Siegfried removed a larger package and placed it on the table as well. Removing the leather wrapping he took out what appeared to be another seax. This one was a little different than the one he had shown me the other night but every bit as detailed.

"It's incredible," I commented as he removed it from the scabbard and held it up for me. It was a beautiful weapon, single edged with oak leaves and runes inscribed on the blade. The hilt appeared to be made of a dark hard wood wrapped in leather. The pommel was silver, shaped like a ball, with a raised oak leaf on the top. The quality of the workmanship was amazing.

"This one was also crafted by my family, as is the one I carry. This is a magical weapon designed for fighting evil. It is my gift to you." Siegfried handed it to me, hilt first. "The blade and pommel are made of a variety of metals that are deadly to the Fae as well as others," he said.

"I'm honored, but why?" I inquired as I accepted the blade from him.

"First, you saved my employer and in doing so prevented dishonor to me. As I have said before, you have placed yourself in danger. You have also become my friend. This blade may protect you when others cannot. Although in the old times they were worn in the front, at the belt, this one can be worn under the shoulder, concealed." Siegfried unbuttoned the top of his shirt and pulled it aside to show the one he carried.

"I don't know what to say."

I slid the blade back in the scabbard. While it hadn't been very long since my situation had been revealed, Siegfried had become the closest thing to an ally and friend I had, outside of Bernd in the Fae world. But this was unexpected. I almost felt guilty that I had not trusted him sooner.

"Say that you will wear it," he said simply.

"It will be an honor to wear such a blade," I replied and removed my jacket and unbuttoned my shirt as Siegfried helped me put it on in the same way he carried his. The holster was designed to be easily pushed forward and the blade removed. The fit was perfect. I could hardly tell it was there.

Charlie took that moment to come into the house and drop a ball at Siegfried's feet.

"Charlie, not now," I said. "Sorry about that, he loves to play."

Siegfried picked up the ball and tossed it down the hallway. "It's fine. Well, would that I could stay but I have other duties," he said, standing up as Charlie ran back with the ball. He turned to Lucy and petting her said, "Keep watch over your master, little one."

I'll be damned if she didn't purr!

Then turning back to Charlie he added, "you as well," as he tossed the ball again. "Well, I must go."

I got up to walk him out.

"Be safe, and carry the seax. We can discuss things further after your trip."

"Good idea, and thank you again," I said as we walked outside to his car.

Once he had left I went back into the house, grabbed my coat and gun, as well as the package Siegfried had dropped off, and then headed out to my car for my trip to Pahrump.

Chapter 16

The drive to Pahrump is about an hour or two from Las Vegas. The difference depends on which side of the Valley you're coming from. For me, it's about an hour and a half, if traffic cooperates. Although there are a few things to look at, most of the trip is just desert. At least it gave me an hour to reflect on the past week.

Last month I'd been just a normal guy, taking care of my business, my house, and talking to my kids now and then. Now, things were different. I mean, hey, think of the simple pleasure of playing ball with your dog. You throw it, he runs, catches it and brings it back. You do it again and again. It's fun to do. At least it was fun for me and Charlie.

Now, I'm not saying it isn't fun anymore but the dynamic has changed. Especially when I throw the ball, miss the grass, and it ends up in the rocks. Now he gives me a dirty look and I wince when he tells me that it was a rotten throw. As if I didn't already know that!

On the other hand, I have to admit it's kind of cool finding out I can do magic even if I haven't mastered it yet. It puts a whole new perspective on all the fantasy tales I read as a child. All of a sudden I'm living them. The downside, of course, is that there's folks out there that want to kill me. Not to mention having to kill them, dark Wizards or not.

Alright, I'll admit it, it's still pretty cool. I mean, come on, how often do you get to carry a Viking dagger? I know I used to be a cop and all that. Being a cop or PI may sound glamorous but it's nothing compared to this. Of course there were a few things that still bothered me. The least of which was that I didn't seem to be able to summon up the magic at will and when it did kick in it was almost uncontrollable. Bernd had said it would take time but I still had the feeling he wasn't telling me everything. Then there was the bastard king thing. Damn, if I was some Faerie king, shouldn't I feel different? Where was this all leading? What was I missing I asked myself for what must be the hundredth time?

I arrived in Pahrump a little after 10: and wound my way around town till I arrived at Ms. Truesdell's address. It was an older house, well-kept, with a chain link fenced front yard. The one thing that makes Pahrump different from Vegas, other than being a small town, is that it's still a rural community. There were goats grazing in the front yard and chickens as well. You don't see that in Vegas too often, at least not the goats.

I parked and went through the gate towards the screened door, dodging goats as I made it up the short stairway. The door opened before I could knock.

Standing there was an attractive blonde woman in her 60s. She was dressed in Wrangler jeans and western shirt and wore reddish leather cowboy boots. Her hair was pushed up, like they used to wear, and her sparkling eyes were brown with a hint of hazel. "You must be Mr. Hoskins," she stated with a smile.

"I am, and you would be Ms. Truesdell?"

"Yep, but call me Mattie," she said with an almost southern accent and held open the screen door. "Any friend of Hailey is welcome here. She said you were a good fellah."

"You talked to her?" I asked, entering the house. The room was decorated in what can only be described as American cowboy. Gnarled wood chairs and leather furniture that offered a Texas-style flair, there was even a pair of antlers used as a hat rack.

"Yep, a few minutes after you called. A girl can't be too careful these days. I hope you don't mind," she remarked as she gestured for me to sit on the couch.

"No, not at all, better safe than sorry."

"Well, she didn't tell me you were such a nice dresser. I don't get many handsome men in suits here these days, unless of course they're trying to sell me something," she laughed. "Can I get you something to drink? I just made some fresh coffee. I have sweet tea as well."

"Coffee would be nice. Cream and sweetener if you have it, it's ok if you don't." I looked around the room as she went into the kitchen. The cowhide rug, twisted wood chairs and other western memorabilia reminded me of an old movie set.

"Here you go," she said, putting a mug of coffee down in front of me minute or so later.

I took a sip as I admired the logo on the cup. The mug was from the old brothel. The logo had the name Venus and a caricature of the statue of the Venus di Milo, only a bit more animated, if you get my meaning.

"That's an original," she said. "I saved a bunch of them when we closed."

"I collect old cups myself although I don't have any like this," I admitted, admiring the artwork. Then I got down to business.

"I don't want to take up too much of your time so I'll get down to why I am here. I'm looking for a woman named Deborah Kent. At least, that's the name I think she went under. I understand she may have had some dealings with the Venus before it closed."

"Before we get to that," she said with in a serious tone. "I'll need to know why you want to find her. I'm not in the habit of talking about folks needlessly, friend of Hailey or not. I know what you said on the phone but I'd like to hear it in person. If she's in any trouble, well, I'll need to know that, too, you understand."

I took a sip of the coffee, it was quite good. "No, she's not in any trouble and it's not confidential. I've simply been asked to return some property to her. It's an item of jewelery if you must know. The person who possessed this item wants to do the right thing and has agreed that I will not provide him with her location, assuming I do find her. You have my word on that. I hope that explains it enough."

"I can live with that I suppose," she said, looking a bit relieved. "To be honest, she was a nice lady, even if she is a bit different. I'd like to do something that will help her out." She seemed to make a decision. "Ok, I'll show you where you can find her."

She got up and went into a desk next to the front door and grabbed a pen and paper. She sat down and wrote down the directions to where she said Deborah was last staying. She came over with the paper, and then hesitated, the note still clutched in her hand. "Be careful when you see her. Like I said she's different."

"Different, what does that mean?" I asked, looking up at her.

"Well, it's just that Deborah is very nervous around strangers. I know that you're doing something good for her, but still, you need to be careful around her."

I watched her closely. She looked almost scared as she handed me the note. "Mattie," I said as she sat back down, "can you be a little more specific? I'm not here to harm her, only to give her what is hers."

She sat down on the couch besides me. "I know that. I guess you could call her eccentric. She never liked strangers, especially men, and I got the feeling...well I got the feeling that she was running from something."

"Any idea what she might be running from?" I wondered if it could have something to do with the necklace.

"No, and I never asked. But she'd get queer if anyone asked any questions about her past." She looked over at me with a thoughtful but serious expression. "A lot of folks in that business are running from something, even if it's just themselves. You learn not to ask. Just be careful." Then she gave me a smile. "It's a good thing you're doing for her. You just may need to convince her of that before she'll talk to you."

I looked down at the hand drawn map. It showed an old trailer near another closed brothel I knew a little of called the Ash Meadows Sky Motel. It was next to an old airport runway northwest of town. She said it was about a 30 minute drive.

"Ok, Mattie, thank you," I said as I patted her hand in a reassuring way. Then I started to get up.

"Wait just a minute."

She got up and took my now empty coffee cup and went into the kitchen. She returned a moment later and handed me the cup. "Take this with you," she said, "for your collection."

"Wow, that's very nice," I replied, admiring it as she handed it to me.

She shrugged deprecatingly. "Well, it was a good house and maybe you'll remember us when you drink from it."

We walked to the doorway and she opened the screen door and held it for me.

"I surely will," I added and thanked her again as I walked out to my car.

Afraid of strangers, I thought to myself, how do you get by in a brothel if you're afraid of strangers?

Chapter 17

I headed out of town and then up Bell Vista Road. This eventually turned into Ash Meadows. Turning off the main road I headed up a dirt road and drove around some type of strip mine that blocked the view of the old airstrip that had served the brothel in the 60s.

Coming up parallel to what looked like a small hotel, I spied the abandoned brothel. Its chain linked yard and empty pool was now filled with leaves and other trash. I drove a little further past where the road curved and parked the car near a stand of cottonwood trees where the crude map said she was supposed to live. Not expecting to need it, I left my gun under the seat and put my briefcase with the cash in the trunk. Then I removed the necklace and started towards where the map said the trailer was.

Pausing beneath the trees I looked around and finally saw the roof of a trailer to my right. It was barely visible behind some large brush. The place was concealed by the vegetation but it fit the description Mattie had given me. I walked across the deserted lot and then around the large bushes until I could see the old trailer. It wasn't much to look at but it was situated in a nice spot. As I skirted the property I saw there was a natural spring just off the side of the trailer. A well-tended garden was not far from the door.

There was something else, too. Not necessarily dangerous, but concerning. That was the problem with my magical abilities. I hadn't learned them from childhood or in a school. They just kind of showed up, or trickled out, as Bernd had believed they would. The magic must have been in the on position because I sensed a warning feeling. I knelt down and looked around before continuing.

The trailer sat on a parcel of-semi cleared desert. It looked as if someone with a grader had just swept a path so the trailer would be level. That's when I noticed the perimeter. It was a lighter color than the regular desert sand. I reached down and scooped a bit up into my hand. The outer line was some kind of salt, courser than table salt, maybe a sea salt variety. The inner line appeared to be crushed eggshells and maybe some type of pepper and herbs. Something else was there as well. Crushed bones, maybe?

It looked like some kind of spell had been cast to protect the occupant from evil spirits. It must not have been too powerful of a spell because I figured a threat would kick-start the magic like it had in the past and this one didn't seem to be having any real effect on me. Maybe it was a good thing I had no evil intentions. I saw a few other potential magic-related items as I walked towards the door. Mint grew in the garden and not all the desert sage had been cleared from the yard. There was also a crude Gorgon's head carved into a piece of wood hung above the door. I think I liked that the best.

As I approached the stoop a gray cat bounded up the steps and stopped on the porch before the stairs. It turned to watch me.

I knelt down and heard a meow.

"What are you?" I felt her say. Hmm, so I guess it's not just my animals that I can talk to.

"A friend," I answered. "Or at least, I hope to become one. Where is your mistress?"

"She is not my mistress," she purred. "You are not like the others, but she will still not see you."

"Well, I have come a long way to see her and see her I must," I said, getting up and walking up the stairs. I will never understand cats, I thought to myself as she bounded away. I raised my hand to knock on the trailer door, wondering who the others that visited might have been.

"Hello, Ms. Kent," I called, knocking louder. The door finally opened a bit and I could see a woman's face.

She looked very old, with wrinkled skin and long gray hair. Her eyes, however, were blue, and I could still see the youth in them. She was dressed simply in a rumpled and faded blue dress that hung loosely and she was barefoot. "I don't want any, go away!" she barked, closing the door on me.

"I just need a moment of your time Ms. Kent, or should I call you Diantha," I responded, blocking her from fully closing the door. "I think you'll want to know what I have to say."

"How do you know that name?" she asked, holding the door open a crack.

"I was told to find you, by an old friend."

"I have no friends," she replied, and started to close the door again.

Now I don't normally take the forceful approach when approaching a witness or a target, but hell, I knew what she was, or at least what she'd been. I doubted I would be facing a lawsuit here. "I really need to speak with you, Mrs. Kent." I pushed the door open a bit.

She backed away and then lunged forward towards me. I spun to the side and reaching out, grabbed her wrist. With my other hand I removed the dagger she had held in it. I'd like to say my magic protected me, but to be honest, it was probably just the years of police training. Looking at it, I realized it was very old and appeared to be made of silver.

"Why are you here?" she asked as I let go of her wrist and followed her into the trailer's small living area.

"As I said, I've come at the request of an old friend." I held up the dagger. "Not exactly a pleasant way to greet someone," I said, slipping it into my belt.

"You forced your way in. Why shouldn't I protect myself?"

She had me there.

"What do you want then? I am just an old woman, leave me be," she exclaimed as she sat down at a small table. She rested her head in her hands, looking all the part of a frail, dejected old woman.

"A moment of your time is all I ask. I am looking for a Diantha, who used to work in a carnival under the name of Pythia. Is that you?" I asked, standing across from her.

"Why do you want to know?"

I looked around the place. It was small and sparsely furnished. Nothing more than an old loveseat, the table she sat at, and in the corner, a three-legged stool. That room led to a small kitchen on one side and what appeared to be a bedroom on the other.

The stool interested me. It was about four feet high and looked as if it was made from bronze. There was also a shallow dish of the same metal on the stand next to it. Everything was old but the stool still looked beautiful. According to legend, the real Oracle at Delphi sat on just such a stool when she had her visions. "An interesting piece," I said as I walked over and began tracing the serpent design on the seat with my fingers. "It looks very old."

"It's just an old stool," she said as she stood up and walked towards me. Moving between me and the stool she placed her hand on the seat and then turned towards me, her attitude changing. "Why are you here?"

"I told you. I'm looking for a woman named Diantha Medea or Kent that used to work in a carnival with William Harrison."

"Do not speak his name," she proclaimed. "Leave now if he sent you!"

Wow, I could feel the strength in her words, but I knew I had who I had come for. Now I also understood why Milagre had warned me about the power of her voice. Despite her appearance of old age, influence oozed off of her as she spoke. I could almost see it, like wisps of smoke flowing outward from her.

She turned away from me for a moment and I thought she was going for another weapon but she turned back and pointed to the door. "I command you to leave!" She must have expected her words to have some effect on me and I saw that she was startled when I didn't move.

I almost laughed, thinking mind tricks don't work on me...but I thought better of it. Besides, I didn't know if she'd even seen *The Phantom Menace*. I looked her over for a moment. "I think not," I said instead.

"You are of the Fae," she noted, appearing startled and with just a hint of fear creeping into her voice and expression.

"Look, let's just start over. I'm Robert Hoskins and I have something that belongs to you." I pulled the pouch out of my pocket and opened it, removing the necklace. I held it up to show her. "Look familiar?"

She walked towards me slowly, as if in a trance. "The eye, has Apollo forgiven me then?" She took the necklace and fell to her knees in front of me. There were tears in her eyes.

I have to admit that caught me off guard. I knelt down next to her, watching as she held the necklace in her hands and cried. Apollo, where the hell had she been all this time? "Apollo is gone. He will not return to this world," I answered.

"Gone," she gasped, "but he was High Fae, one of the Gods! I knew that they fled this world but surely they will return."

"I'm sorry, but he's not coming back."

High Fae, what the hell was a High Fae? If I really was a bastard king and the heir of Demeter, being male, would I fit the bill? I needed to find out more, but without revealing too much, or my lack of knowledge.

"Then I am lost, for only he would return it to me. Wait," she asked, looking hopeful. "What of Artemis, or Hephaestus, or even Poseidon? Surely one of them must return."

"They too are gone. Gods or not, they destroyed themselves."

"Destroyed themselves? Then the Eye is lost to me," she muttered. "What is left? Only one of the most high could have saved me."

"Perhaps there is still something I can do."

She stood up, her tears of grief replaced by anger and frustration. Fool, it is worthless now," she said as she held up the necklace. "This is a dragon's eye, once lost, it is but a curse. Only by gift can it be returned if it is to be of any worth, and even then, only if gifted by one the Gods. Look at me! At least five thousand years of life was granted, true. But by losing the Eye my youth and beauty have fled. How do you not know this?" she screamed, pulling at her hair. "Lost, I am lost!" She threw the necklace on the floor and walked back over to the stool.

Five thousand years, damn! Well, at least she was back to her mean spirited self. I picked the necklace up as I stood. Change of plan—if I really was what Bernd said I needed to find out what that was. Nothing like living the fantasy, not to mention that I knew that while she may have lost her youth she was still much more than just an old lady. Besides, Werewolves were after me and I wasn't satisfied that my parents death had been an accident. And lest I forget, someone out there was killing powerful Fae. The world was turning fast for me and it wouldn't hurt to have another ally at this point.

"Ok, so you want to keep feeling sorry for yourself or do you want to get out of this dump?" I asked, trying a different approach.

She was leaning over the stool, her head resting on the raised seat. "There was a time when I would have had your eyes and tongue pulled from your head for such a remark, whatever you may be," she proclaimed. She swept her hands down the front of her body. "Don't you see? I am trapped in this decrepit form because of the actions of a human I favored. A foolish mistake that I must pay for till the end of time. What then, is left?" Her tears had stopped and her sorrow had been replaced with anger. Still, that beat an old lady sobbing.

"Well, anything's gotta be better than hiding out here," I said as I plopped down on the loveseat and gestured with my arms around the room. "You may not look young, but you still have power in your voice...and they do say that 70 is the new 50 these days, or at least so I've heard."

She didn't catch the humor.

"Come with me. If nothing else, you'll be more comfortable." I didn't tell her that I'd try to figure out how to make the necklace work, besides; I might not be able to.

"Whom do you serve and how did you come upon the Eye? Tell me this before I give my answer," she asked, standing upright and staring at me, defiant once again.

I sensed a hint of change in her voice. This wasn't the poor old pissed off grandma bit, this was something more. "I'll tell you what; I have some time, I'll answer yours if you answer mine." Oh great, now I'm speaking in rhyme.

"Agreed," she answered, perking up at the comment.

Well, that was quick! "As to who I serve, I serve no one in the way that I think you mean. As to the necklace, there I do serve a purpose. A friend asked me to find you and return it. I got it from the man that took it from you, I already told..."

"Do not speak his name," she yelled, cutting me off. "May he be cursed and suffer Hades' punishment for all eternity. She walked over to me, her hands on her hips. "Why do you mock me?"

"Mock you?" I asked as I stood up. "How have I mocked you?"

She pointed her finger at me. "Do you truly expect me to believe that you were not sent by my enemies? You know the Eye is now lost to me. Who sent you to torment me?"

I reached out and gently removed her hand from in front of my face. "I promise you, Diantha. What I have said is true. The one that took the necklace regrets his actions and wants only peace before he dies. He is an old man now. No one has sent me to torment you. The old Gods are gone, good or bad it's a different world now. Surely you know this to be true."

She pulled her hand away and looked down. "Regrets, he knows nothing of regrets, may he burn forever. But the Gods, augh...I feared it was true. I prayed that it was not, but it has been so long. What a fool I have been."

"So what happened?" I wasn't sure if she was going to answer.

"Very well. I was deceived...he did not understand what I was, nor did he understand the power and curse of the Eye. I did love him, as best I was able, but it wasn't enough. He betrayed me," she said after a moment, and then she turned and walked back to the table, sitting down. "Now I am only what you see, an old woman."

I walked over and sat down across from her.

"I have not heard from Apollo in over two thousand years. But still, I did not think him truly dead, only in hiding. I thought that he would be angry when he returned and saw that I had lost the Eye, so I hid." She hesitated, and then continued. "The Gods, do you know what happened to them?"

"I was told they fought amongst themselves and then faded from this world as they battled one another and their followers turned from them. Why it happened I don't know. I can tell you that the rest of the Fae still exist, as do other creatures." I leaned back in my chair. "You called them High Fae, what did you mean?"

She gave me a look of disbelief. "You do not know the story of the High Fae? What are you?"

Damn I hate that question. I thought that if she was a danger to me I'd feel it, so I was ready to give up a little to learn more. It's such a bitch when you don't know who you can trust.

"There's no easy answer to that question," I said. "Look, I'll keep it simple. My parents died when I was young. I know little of my heritage other than that my mother was of the Dryad. I've never heard of the High Fae, though, what are they?"

"It is said that Gaea chose among the children of her children a handful of Fae to be above the others. These were the High Fae who became the Gods. They could be terrible to behold. I myself saw Apollo slay the dragon when I was but three and twenty years. From its blood he granted me long life and later gave me the Eye which restored youth and beauty," she explained.

"Why did he give it to you? Was he in love with you?"

"Ha, in lust perhaps, but love, never," she answered. "Gods they may have been, but capable of love? I do not think so. But he did care for me. When things went bad he ordered me to flee the temple. But true love, no, he desired my gifts, as well as to bed me." She must not have liked the look I gave her.

"Pah...," she said, throwing her arms up. "You see me now only as an old crone, but then, oh if you could have seen me then. Before the Eye was lost to me men groveled at my feet just to be near me, they threw themselves off of cliffs if I spurned them..."

"Ok, I get the picture," I interrupted, "and the rest of your gifts?"

"They are still with me. The Eye may have strengthened them but do not think I am powerless," she replied defensively.

"I did not mean to offend you," I responded quickly, then changed the subject. "Look, here's the deal. With a few conditions I can take you to a place with much better accommodations and make sure you are paid well for your services. Interested?"

"Perhaps, name the terms."

"The one that took the Eye from you is dying. Swear to do no harm to his family and let him die a natural death. For this I will see that you are paid handsomely for your troubles. I may also have a job offer for you."

She balled her fists and shook them at me in anger. "Whoreson, you would take away the one thing that I have yearned for, retribution for his betrayal!"

Whoreson? I didn't remember ever hearing that term before.

"Vengeance belongs to the Gods," I countered, since I thought she would understand that. "Besides, he's already dying, what more do you want?"

"I would see his head on a pike at my door. You ask much of me." She was silent again before continuing. "What else do you offer?"

"You will be paid $50,000 cash for your troubles.

"Have you heard of the Neptune's Landing in Las Vegas?"

"I know of it," she answered.

"Eddie Milagre runs the place. He is a Fae of water, a Nereid, I believe. He could use someone like you, as could I. I will see that you are paid handsomely and treated well for the use of your powers."

"Gaea curse you should you deceive me, Fae, but I have no choice." She stood up and pointed her hand at me. "I may have lost my youth and beauty but there is still life and power in me. I would be foolish to waste any more of it here. I will agree to your terms in principle. Do as you have promised and I swear not to harm he who betrayed me or his family. But know this, my oath is to you and no other. You must see that the agreement is fulfilled."

"Agreed," I replied. I got up and reached out and took her hand to shake it, she just snorted.

"I will need the stool and a few other things." She looked around the small room for a moment before continuing. "Let me change clothes and then you can get me out of this 'dump' as you called it."

She was awful cheery for someone that I thought would be angry over the deal. I wondered what I'd missed.

When she came back out of the small bedroom she was a different woman. Her hair was combed and she had changed into a white blouse and jeans. She was even wearing sandals. She had a small bag and after taking one more look around the trailer she asked me to bring the stool and then headed directly for the front doorway.

I put down the stool and opened the door for her. I had barely followed her out and was just going back to retrieve the stool when the attack came—this time I had no warning.

Chapter 18

Someone grabbed her right in front of me and then I was thrown against the door, my stomach and chest burning. It was only a second later that I threw the Werewolf that had attacked me across the trailer's small front porch. I barely had time to register the bloody gashes as I looked down at myself before the second beast attacked. I reached for my gun and then remembered I had left it in the car. Not one of my better decisions. Luckily my magic decided to kick in at the same moment and I saw red. Better late than never I thought to myself.

Before I even realized it I was up and catching the Were as he leapt towards me. At the same time I found myself grabbing the dagger I had taken from Diantha and plunging it into the beast's chest. Blood spurted as he yelped and went limp. I pulled out the dagger as I tossed him aside, his blood coating my arms. Once his blood hit me I knew it was one of the Weres from my first encounter.

I went over to the first attacker who by now was unsteadily trying to rise. I picked him up by the neck and slammed him into what was left of the railing and then threw him over the raised deck. He yelped as he hit the rocky desert floor. I knew he was badly injured and watched as he shifted back into human form. I should have known. It was Mr. Beat It. He didn't look like he was going to be getting up for a while so I turned to check on Diantha.

The beast holding Diantha was like none I'd seen before. He reminded me of a creature out of a bad horror movie. Even so, thanks to the magic, I knew what he was, or more accurately, what he wasn't. He wasn't what I would call a Werewolf; instead he was like some half-breed mutant that hadn't grown correctly in the womb. He stood upright on two legs like a man. He was a half human; half wolf-type creature that looked like someone had mixed up the pieces during assembly. Securing the dagger, I pulled the seax Siegfried had given me from its holster at my shoulder. It felt comfortable and was a more versatile weapon.

He held Diantha with one claw-like hand by the throat. She couldn't talk, hell, I doubted if she could even breathe. It pushed her neck to the side and I could see the drool dripping from his fangs onto her. He just stared at me and growled, appearing ready to bite. Beneath the stench I could smell his scent, similar to Mr. Beat It's line, yet not quite. I could also smell his anger; there was no fear. I didn't know anything about Were culture but I was surprised that this beast had been allowed to live. He reeked of corruption.

Before I could move the creature thrust forward and bit down on her neck. Blood gushed from the wound as he raised his head and roared. I had tried to get to her in time but I was too late. Lunging forward I grabbed his head by the mottled fur and hacked through his neck with the seax, wrenching it from his body. The blade glowed as blood continued to pump and his headless form fell over.

I bent down and cradled her blood-soaked body, not even registering what else the beast's blood could tell me. Taking her hand I looked at the gaping wound and torn flesh sure that nothing, not even magic, could save her.

In that instant the red faded and the rage left me. I felt drained, yet still I held onto her, lifeless in my arms. I started to lay her down when I felt her body twitch. Shocked, I watched as the wound began to gurgle and slowly close, healing right in front of me. Her eyes opened and she gasped, coughing and screaming in agony.

"By the Gods," she finally cried out, "I have not felt such pain in many a lifetime." Then she started laughing hysterically and I watched, dumbfounded, as she pushed away from me and stood up, her white blouse covered in gore.

"My Fae Lord, you are as good at deception as Loki ever was." She continued laughing as she stomped her feet and held up her blood soaked arms. She rubbed her face and neck with them.

I guess she really was immortal after all. She was also as mad as a hatter. "I thought you were dead," was all I could say.

"My time is not yet up my glorious Fae. Besides, it would take much more than these mangy beasts to kill me." She kicked at the headless form as she spoke and then knelt down in front of me. "But why the charade my noble Fae? Am I not worthy? Surely you can forgive me the loss of the Eye and return it to me. I will serve you as I served Apollo. Remember, it was he that abandoned me, not I that abandoned him. Please, allow me to serve you."

Well, shit, what the hell was this about? "Why are you kneeling? Stand up," I said as I lifted her back to her feet, not really processing the words she had spoken.

I looked around at the mess. The two Weres had reverted to their human form. The *whatever* it was still looked the same. I walked over to Mr. Beat It and rolled him over. He was still breathing but out cold. I had probably given him a concussion. The other one was dead; it was his partner from our previous encounter.

How could I have not known they were here? Why hadn't the magic kicked in sooner? Shit, I didn't have any answers and I needed a clean-up crew. What the hell else could happen? Oh yeah, Diantha. I turned to look at her. An old crone drenched in blood. I had a vivid image of a scene from *Army of Darkness;* thank God I wasn't looking for an old book.

"Please my Lord, I beg of you, complete the ritual and I will serve only you," she cried.

"What are you talking about?" I asked as I tried to decide what my next move should be.

"There is no need to hide it from me. Gift me the necklace and I will serve you as I did Apollo."

Did that mean what I think it did? "What exactly do you think you saw?" I asked, trying to retain some semblance of control.

She came over and knelt before me once again. There was a momentary pause as she eyed me. "Ah, a test then," she cackled, and continued. "Very well, I saw you, one of the High Fae, strike down his enemies. I saw your wounds heal and felt the wrath of a God as you struck down your opponents. I have spent more time with Gods than most mortals and Gaea herself granted me the sight. I felt you wield the same power as Apollo once did. There can be no mistake."

Could it really be true? I placed my hands on my chest and stomach; the wounds were still there but they had stopped bleeding and there was no pain. From bastard King to High Fae, whatever that was. What the hell was next? "Tell me of the ritual should I decide to return the necklace to you?" I asked as I holstered the seax and pulled the chain with its oval stone from my pocket. Then I yanked her back up to her feet, hell, isn't that why I came here?

"Surely you...of course, the test continues. Blood has been spilt, it remains only to gift me the Eye in water that flows forth from the Earth and take me as yours and the spell will be complete."

Take me as yours? "You're kidding right?"

She didn't say anything for a moment and then looked down at her gnarled bloody hands. "Ahh, you jest. Come, come, there is a pool just around the corner."

Before I could protest she grabbed my hand and led me around the trailer. There was a small pool that must have been fed by the underground hot springs that this area had once been famous for. She pulled me towards her into the water, now turning red as the spilled blood mixed with it.

"The necklace, place it around my neck," she said as she bent down to submerge herself in the warm water.

Staring at the old woman before me I tried to decide what to do. I wasn't averse to giving her the necklace, hey, maybe it'd even work. But what if it didn't? Between that and the battle I'd just been through I had too much going on in my mind to think clearly.

Oh, what the hell. I started to place the necklace around her neck and then stopped, something was happening. The magic began to kick in again and the stone, the Eye, was glowing. I reached into my pockets and beltline and threw the dagger along with my cell phone and wallet onto the desert sand a few feet from the water. The seax I left holstered.

"...and your oath?" I said, the necklace frozen just inches from her head, the stone glowing brighter.

"I will serve you as I served Apollo," she answered.

I placed the necklace around her head and watched as it dropped to her neckline. "Holy shit," was all I could mutter as the transformation began.

Green tendrils of magic flowed from the stone into her. Then, it was as if time started turning backwards. It was incredible to watch. Her hair lost its gray and turned jet black and became curly. Her wrinkled skin became taut, the age spots fading and her skin changing to a healthy color. She rolled around, ripping off her torn blouse. I watched her breasts and stomach becoming firm. Seconds later, the transformation was done. She was now a young woman in her mid-twenties and I'll be damned if she wasn't as beautiful as she claimed to have been.

"Complete the ritual," she begged as she unbuttoned her jeans and pulled them off.

I watched as the tendrils of magic reached out to me from the stone on her breast, I hesitated.

"You must complete the ritual for the spell to work, I must be bound to you," she cried as she reached for me.

She wasn't kidding. As the first tendril of smoky magic touched me I felt it speak to me and there was recognition. Then there was knowledge. There was much more to being Fae then I could have imagined, and it wasn't all nice. Blood, sex, power...they were all there. But so was the beauty of the forest and all living things. It seemed like I was taking it all in for an eternity but it was actually only a few seconds. I could now understand why Diantha needed me.

She had been granted some type of foresight, born with it by chance or granted it by Gaea I really couldn't tell. Apollo had somehow given her long life, but it was the stone that was the eye of the dragon that would give her the youth and beauty she craved for and make her extended life bearable. But she could only have that back at the behest of one of the Gods, or at least these days, someone like me.

The stone had opened something inside me and it was waiting for me to decide. I looked down at the now beautiful woman. "So be it," I answered, and removed the rest of my clothes.

The human side of me winced briefly at the carnage that was still nearby, but the Fae side of me reveled in it. The magic surrounded us as I entered her. I had thought for a moment that this might be a purely physical act, performed only to bond the magic for its purpose, but I was wrong. If anything Diantha was more sensual and aggressive than I could have imagined. We finished with her on top, holding me tightly as we climaxed together.

When she stopped shaking she leaned over and kissed me, there were tears in her eyes. "You will not regret this, my noble Fae," she whispered.

Then the magic dwindled and my head cleared. I didn't know what to say.

She rolled off of me, laughing again, and then walked back into the deeper water, rinsing herself off. By now the pool was clear.

I watched as she poured water over herself. It was hard to believe that just a little while ago she'd looked so old. Damn, that was a visual I didn't need at the moment. But she was beautiful now, and deadly as well. I would have to be careful with her.

"Do you like what you see?" she asked with a mischievous grin on her face.

Oh yeah, she was dangerous. I stood up and then rinsed off as well. "I'm not complaining," I jested. "But now we've got some work to do."

I strode over to where I'd thrown my cellphone, picked it up and dialed the only number I could think of.

"Siegfried," the voice answered.

Without too much detail, I told Siegfried where I was and explained about the two dead Weres. I walked around the trailer to check on Mr. Beat It; he was still out cold. I told Siegfried about him as well.

"Are you secure for now?"

"I think so," I answered. "We're far enough away from anywhere to have any witnesses."

There was a short pause and I heard him talking in the background. "Do you have the scepter with you?" he asked when he was finished.

"Yeah it's in the car, why?"

"I can have a team out there in an hour or so; I should be there soon afterwards. I will explain it then, perhaps we can kill two birds with one stone."

"See you then," I said as I disconnected, wondering what he had in mind.

I went to my car and popped the trunk. I grabbed a bottle of antiseptic but the gashes were closed. They were still red but already healing. I shook my head at the sight. My suit was wet and torn so I grabbed some jeans, a t-shirt and tennis shoes from my emergency bag and threw them on. Then I grabbed some cuffs and hooked up Mr. Beat It. He was still out but why take chances. I went into the passenger compartment and grabbed my gun from under the seat. I did a quick inventory, seax...dagger...gun...Ok, now I was actually prepared.

"What are you doing?" a still naked Diantha asked as she walked up behind me.

"I've got to sort this out." I looked over at her. "Do you have any clothes?"

"Of course, but why worry about them?" she asked, meaning the bodies on the ground. She bent down and looked at Mr. Beat it. "This one still lives; shall I kill him for you?"

"No, I may need him. I have some people coming to help clean up this mess."

"Clean up? You are a God. You can do what you will," She remarked, as if it was just that easy.

I could tell we were gonna have to talk. I turned around and gently grabbed her by the shoulders. "Diantha, be that as it may, this is not the age of Gods. Remember what happened to the last bunch? We're gonna have to do things a bit differently these days. Now, I need you to find some clothes and then I'm going to do as I promised."

She looked at me quizzically.

Then I spent some time explaining again what had happened to the old Gods and the situation today as I saw it.

"I still don't understand," she responded, looking around at the carnage. "What is different? You are a God; you have the right to slay those who oppose you."

I could see that this was going to be difficult. It was like she had already forgotten the time she had spent in hiding or that this was the modern world. "Perhaps that's true. But as I explained, I'm not ready to reveal myself to the world just yet. You are one of the few that know my secret. I'm going to have to ask you to bear with me for a while. Can you do that?"

She was silent for a moment and then I saw the light bulb go off in her head. "As you wish, what would you have me do?"

I could tell she liked the idea of being a confidante but I couldn't help but wonder what else she was thinking. I hoped she would keep to her oath, at least for the most part.

"First, I need you to get some clothes on. Then we need to talk."

She nodded and headed back to the trailer.

While she was gone I moved my car closer to the trailer and then dragged Mr. Beat It to a better position (at least for me). He was still out cold. I went through his pockets and found a set of keys. So he had to have a car somewhere nearby. I concentrated on the concept of his car and an image appeared in my mind. It was parked on the other side of the old brothel. Damn, that was amazing; maybe my magic was finally starting to work on demand!

Then I caught myself. Here I was trying to tie up loose ends and clean up a crime scene. Did I mention I killed two people, again? Of course they did attack me first, and they weren't exactly people, but still. Sometimes you have to wonder if the fantasies of becoming something else are really worth it.

I didn't have long to ponder that question as Diantha chose that moment to come out of the trailer. She was wearing another old pair of jeans and a Venus T-shirt. I have to say it; this time she looked a damn site better. It would still be a little while before Siegfried could arrive, time to get back to reality.

"So how's it feel being back?" I asked as I leaned back against my car with Mr. Beat It on the ground beside me. "You have any idea what you want to do?"

She stopped a few feet in front of me. "I told you I would serve you as I did Apollo. I will hold to my oath."

Damn, maybe she did really mean it. If so, this was definitely a different person than the one that I met earlier tonight. "Ok, about that, I made you an offer tonight, are you still interested?"

She looked at me questioningly. "But that was before you gifted me the necklace."

"Look, let me put it this way," I said as I stepped closer to her. "I meant what I said earlier. This is a different world than the old one. Your oath is appreciated, but I'm not like that, I don't need you to serve me as you did Apollo. What I need is someone I can trust. I'd rather earn your loyalty than demand it, if you can understand that. Don't get me wrong, I'll hold you to your oath when necessary, but..."

She crossed her arms and interrupted me, again. "You are the strangest God I have ever met. You can do anything you want yet you wish to negotiate." She shook her head as if I was crazy.

Hell, maybe I was. "Think of it this way, a kiss is much sweeter when freely given, wouldn't you agree?"

A smile crossed her lips. "I believe I do," she said as she put her arms around my neck and kissed me. "What next then, my Lord?"

"First, you can stop calling me that. Just call me Robert. Next, can you keep an eye on this idiot while I go check out his car? We have some guests coming in a few and I want to see what's in it. We're going to turn all this over to them. Oh, and I may need your assistance when they get here, you up to it if I need you?"

I thought I might know what Siegfried had in mind with the kill two birds with one stone remark. But even so, it never hurt to have two in your hands.

"My powers have not been lost, if that's what you mean. I will do whatever you need," she said. She looked again at the unconscious Mr. Beat It and then gave him a swift kick. "Are you sure I can't kill this filthy beast for you?" She gave me a pleading look.

"I'd rather you didn't."

We talked a bit more and when we finished I walked down the dirt road about half a mile until I got to the old building. The car turned out to be a van parked on the far side that was not visible from the trailer or the dirt road that led to it.

I tossed the van and found the both kid's wallets and keys under the seat. The back was rigged with some type of animal cage. It was clean but still smelled of corruption. It made sense as the beast hadn't seemed to be something easily controlled. I went through the rest of the van with a fine tooth comb but there was nothing else of interest there. After going through the wallets I sat down for a bit, trying to decide where to go from here.

Close to an hour later I slammed the van door and started walking back to the trailer. I turned when I heard cars. There were two SUVs coming down the road towards me. I stopped as the first one pulled up next to me. The passenger rolled down his window. It was Michael from Siegfried's office; he had turned in his Armani suit for black fatigues.

Chapter 19

"I heard you could use some assistance," he said with a smile as I waved the dust from my face.

"That was fast," I remarked.

"Where do you need us?"

"Just around the corner there's a trailer. You'll see my Lexus," I replied as I pointed the way. "There's one still breathing by my car and two down in the yard. There's a girl, too, she's with me."

"Siegfried is about 10 minutes behind us," he added as he rolled the window up and the SUV's pulled ahead.

By the time I got back to my car Michael's people were already bagging and tagging the two stiffs. Diantha was nowhere to be found and Mr. Beat It was in the backseat of one of the SUV's. One of Michael's people appeared to be giving him medical aid. Damn, who'd of thought it? There really was a clean-up team for these kinds of things.

Michael himself was stooped over the area where the beast had fallen. He stood up and walked over to me. "The lady asked me to tell you she was going to wait in the trailer. You're full of surprises, Mr. Hoskins," he said.

"As are you, Michael, and call me Robert. I appreciate the help."

We shook hands and Michael turned and looked around the trailer, surveying the scene. I hadn't noticed it the first time I had met him. But this time I could sense something magical in him. He was a lot like Siegfried but the scent wasn't as powerful. Maybe they were related in some way? My magic was acting more consistent but I still didn't feel the intense information gathering ability that I had when I was in battle mode.

"No problem. Siegfried told me to handle whatever you need."

"I apologize for asking, but I'm curious, do these kinds of things come up often around here?" I asked with a smile, hoping I wasn't being too inquisitive.

"You know how it is," Michael replied as he shrugged his shoulders. "There's not that many of us so it's not too bad most of the time. The hardest thing is keeping the mortals out of it. But hey, it is what it is." He eyed me curiously. "What's your beef with the Weres, if you don't mind me asking?"

It was my turn to shrug my shoulders. "I've run into these two before. I guess they didn't like the reception I gave them the last time. They must have brought along the beast thinking he would give them an edge. Oh, and I found a makeshift cage in the van they were driving."

We both watched as two of his people lined the body bags behind the second SUV.

"That's going to have a few people asking questions," he commented.

At that moment Siegfried pulled up in his black Escalade.

"Back to work, Siegfried's going to want to see that thing," he said as he began to walk to the black SUV.

I watched as Siegfried got out of the Escalade and talked to Michael. There was one more thing—there was a Were in the car with him. This magic thing had its benefits. It had to be Martin Chibeaux. I couldn't see him but I could sense him. I trusted Siegfried so I wasn't worried. Besides, that explained why he wanted to know if I had the scepter. If anything, the day was just getting more interesting by the minute.

Siegfried leaned in the car to say something to him as he opened the door and stepped out of the passenger side. Chibeaux was a big man with dark brown hair with a smattering of gray above the ear and on his goatee. He looked my way briefly then walked with Siegfried to the body bags.

I popped the trunk of my car and found a long sleeve shirt in my kit and put it on. Then I removed the scepter from my briefcase and dropped the leather bag the necklace had been stored in over the jeweled tip. I slid it into my back pocket and covered it with my shirt. It stuck out quite a way but I hoped the shirt would hide it. I had an idea in mind but I figured it was better hidden, for now. Grabbing the wallets and keys, I closed the trunk and made my way over to them.

Siegfried saw me coming and said something to Chibeaux who nodded and walked over to where Mr. Beat It was being attended to. Siegfried came my way and met me halfway.

"Thanks," I said as I shook his hand.

"You haven't seen the bill yet," he said with a laugh. "But seriously, this problem aside, how did it go with the necklace and the female?"

I was startled a moment. Siegfried was more concerned about the necklace than he was the dead Werewolves. How often <u>did</u> this kind of thing occur? But then again, it did make sense. Siegfried was a warrior and was probably used to things like this happening and Diantha was potentially quite a prize as well.

"She's willing to come with us for now. We need to get her a place at the Neptune for starters and she's probably gonna need some help with paperwork and other things to bring her up to date."

"That can be arranged. So you've convinced her to work with us?"

"Let's just say I've made quite an impression on her," I answered. I thought about what else to tell him. "She considers the deal we made personal. I hope Mr. Milagre won't have a problem with that," I finally added

"He trusts you, as do I. As long as you aren't thinking of going into competition with him in the casino business I doubt there will be an issue."

"We should be good then," I said, gesturing toward the SUV. "What about Chibeaux, how's he taken me killing some of his pack members?"

Siegfried turned to look at him, not commenting that I apparently already knew who he was. "He didn't say much until he learned of the creature and confirmed that Turner's son was involved. Apparently he was unaware of its existence. That is not a good thing for a pack master, especially with the other problems within their group"

I shook my head. "I wouldn't think so".

"I did not tell him what you have. He is nervous. He knows Turner's people are moving against him and does not know where you fit in. He has asked for my assistance should they try to do anything outside of pack law. He is well thought of by the Milagre's and has assisted me in the past. For those reasons I had to agree. Do you plan on returning the scepter to him? The Fae community is still small and the attacks still worry me. It would not hurt for you to become allies. Whether a foolish move or instigated by Turner himself these events will turn some of the Weres against you."

"Good point," I said as I clasped his shoulders. I felt a smile coming on; that idea was looking better and better. "Let's go cement that alliance."

I started walking toward the pack master, not sure if I should feel good or bad for what I was going to do. Siegfried didn't know yet what I was becoming but he was about to find out. I just hoped Diantha was everything she was cracked up to be.

"It would be best..." Siegfried started to say as we walked towards the SUV.

"I have an idea," I interrupted. "Introduce me, and follow my lead."

I watched as Siegfried raised his eyebrows. "As you wish," he replied.

Chibeaux stepped away from the SUV as we walked up. Siegfried stepped between us and introduced me. I didn't know diddly about Werewolf culture but I was guessing that I had to get some formalities out of the way if I didn't want another enemy. But still, I took a less than subtle approach.

"Mr. Chibeaux," I began, "Siegfried has informed me that this attack was not sanctioned. Considering that fact I hope that this meeting can alleviate both our concerns."

Both Siegfried and the pack master seemed surprised at my opening. I thought I glimpsed a hint of anger flash in Chibeaux's expression as I spoke. I didn't need magic to sense that.

"I also wish to apologize to you," I continued. "I had a prior run in with these individuals and I am sure that had I come to you sooner this altercation may have been avoided."

My apology seemed to soften his mood. "Their actions were unacceptable. It is forbidden to attack the Fae without provocation or sanction. Can you tell me what happened?"

"Of course," I answered, and then gave him an overview of our encounters starting with the incident when I first met Delia. I purposely left a few items out.

"All this over a Lil?" he asked, incredulously. "I can understand Turner's anger at the bar, but this? And they brought a beast as well. What else is going on here?"

"That I can't answer." Well, at least not yet. "I didn't find anything of value in their van, either." I handed him the wallets and keys. "These were all that were inside, it's pretty clean, but there was a large cage in the back. I assume it was for the creature."

As he took the items, I asked him about the Turner kid.

"He's unconscious but alive," he told me, looking concerned. "Things are moving faster than I anticipated."

He turned to Siegfried. "Even with his son involved, Turner will try to use this to his advantage. This may be pack business but politics is politics, especially when outsiders are involved. I may still need your people if he tries to make a move outside the law. I'm going to have a difficult time without the..." He stopped suddenly and looked at me. I could have sworn he was sniffing.

"No normal Fae could do what you did to these Weres." He pointed to the body bags. "Beasts like that are killed at birth because they are almost always uncontrollable if allowed to live. You are more than you appear."

That was an understatement.

"Siegfried has told me that you are Fae and tells me also that I can trust you."

"I'd like to think so."

"Things were much simpler in the old days," he remarked. "There aren't a lot of us in the Valley, let alone the new world. There was a time when pack business was kept private, now it's impossible. There are too few Fae here for us to remain apart. I didn't know any of the Dryad were here but my line has a long history with your clan. Maybe you can be of assistance as well."

Finally, he'd given me the opening I needed.

At that moment Michael returned and whispered something to Siegfried, who nodded. Then he turned to Chibeaux.

"We're ready to remove the bodies. I assume you want them kept for a tribunal. Turner will be taken to one of the healers. Do you have anyone to guard him or should I take care of it?" Michael asked Chibeaux as two of his men moved the body bags to the other SUV.

"Yes to the bodies. As for young Turner, can you handle it until I send someone over? And I want this kept quiet until I make the proper arrangements."

Michael glanced over at Siegfried. I saw him give an almost imperceptible nod. "I'll see to it personally," he said as he waved to the driver of the SUV. Then he said goodbye and got into the one that Turner was in.

We stood silently as they drove off.

I turned to Siegfried. "Where will they be taken?"

"There are agreements among the clans for this type of situation," Siegfried replied.

"Good," I said and then turned back to Chibeaux. "I understand you have a problem. What can I do to help?"

Chibeaux hesitated for just a moment. "Something has been stolen from me," he began. "It's just a symbol used in ceremonies, but an important one. I thought Turner had taken it but now I'm not so sure."

"Can you tell me what you lost?" I asked as I glanced at Siegfried. I almost felt guilty...almost. I was going to return it to him, after all.

He didn't say anything but I could tell he was curious as to what I was playing at.

Chibeaux looked around, but there was no one else to hear us. "It's a scepter, given to my line ages ago and passed from father to son. For that reason alone I want it back. Turner has always coveted it." He held his hands apart about eighteen inches. "It is about a foot and a half long, made of oak with a sky blue jewel." Then he gave me a quizzical look. "It's interesting that the Dryad should show up now. Historically, the scepter symbolized my line's alliance with the Dryads of our original home."

I was afraid for a moment that he suspected me.

"But maybe it's just fate. Will you help me?" he asked.

I couldn't help it; I started to chuckle, then caught myself. "I have heard that fate has a sense of humor. But seriously, I believe I have a way to answer some of your questions. Come with me."

I turned and led them towards Diantha's trailer. It was time to forge an alliance as well as make a statement. Bernd had said to use the magic sparingly but I was hoping that a little extra now and then was ok.

I led them up the stairs to Diantha's trailer. I knocked, and then entered. She had replaced the stool to its original location and was standing by it when I came into the room. She didn't say anything but just watched as I stood at the doorway and motioned for Siegfried and Chibeaux to come in. Even in her jeans and t-shirt there was something special about her, and it wasn't just her looks.

"Diantha, this is Siegfried and Martin." I paused a moment as they nodded. "Gentlemen, this is Diantha, a priestess of the old ways. I believe she can be of assistance."

She walked forward and greeted them. "Ahh...a warrior and a wolf," she remarked and then she turned towards me. "How may I serve you, my Lord?"

I watched Martin as she stepped forward. He may have been skeptical of the old ways remark but she definitely had his attention. Of course, being gorgeous never hurt either. "Martin has lost something. I was hoping you could help him."

"As you command," she answered.

I gave her a cautionary look but she just rolled her eyes. Reaching to the wooden stand next to the stool she picked up a metal dish and handed it to Siegfried. "I will need you to fill this with spring water. You will find a pool outside behind the trailer."

He took the dish and went outside, then she turned to Martin. "I have bathed in the spring water and can do as commanded. Are you willing to hear my words?"

"Sure, I'll hear what you have to say," he said, doubt obvious in his voice.

Looking around I almost couldn't blame him. I mean here we were in a dismal trailer outside of Pahrump with a guy he's never met before. That guy just killed two of his Weres and now a hottie wearing old jeans and a brothel t-shirt says she's going to tell his future. Not exactly a recipe for a spiritual reading. I almost started to laugh but it was Diantha's turn to give me a dirty look as she walked to the kitchen and returned with a glass jar containing some type of leaves.

At about the same time Siegfried returned with the dish.

"Place it here," she said, motioning a spot on the small stand.

As Siegfried put it down she reached into the jar and removed a handful of leaves. "These are from the laurel tree," she explained as she crushed them and scattered them over the water in the dish. Then she walked over to a shelf and lit some incense in a small burner. In seconds the pungent odor began to fill the room. "Step forward and I will begin," she said as she sat down on the stool."

Martin glanced back at both of us before moving a few a steps in front of her. He still looked unconvinced.

Diantha closed her eyes and just swayed back and forth for a while, chanting something too quiet to hear. Then I saw her reach over and pick up the dish. She looked down into it.

"I will require an offering."

No one moved.

It was probably cheating but I removed the dagger I had taken from her earlier and stepped forward. The blade was still stained with the dead Were's blood.

"A blood offering?" she remarked, looking at me curiously.

"I must know if he is worthy."

Martin started to say something but was stopped by Diantha. "Remain silent," she commanded. Then she looked back into the dish. Slowly, a fog began to form, its source the dish in her hands.

I watched as she breathed in the smoky fumes.

It wasn't fog, or smoke, it was tendrils of magic. I wondered if Siegfried saw it as I did. She chanted for a few more minutes just staring into the water, the magic flowing first into her then toward Martin and back again. Suddenly she looked up at me, her face one of revelation. It lasted for only a second before she returned her gaze to him. I wondered what she had seen. She stepped off the stool and walked towards him, her eyes glowing.

"Few could sail the desert sands in such perilous times and find their way as you have. It has not gone unnoticed. Fear not your enemies. You need but pray to the Gods of your forefathers and they will gift you that which you seek," she proclaimed with outstretched arms. "Blessed by the Gods shall your reign be." Seconds later she collapsed and fell to the floor, writhing.

Martin didn't move but Siegfried was at her side before I was. Lifting her gently, she stilled, and he laid her on the couch. I walked over to her and felt her head. It was hot but she was already coming to. I ran to the kitchen to get her some water. By the time I returned she was sitting up.

"You could have warned me," she whispered as she took the cool cup and lifted it to her lips.

I didn't reply.

"What the hell does that mean?" Martin asked.

I stood up and faced him. "It means that this belongs to you," I said as I pulled the scepter out of my back pocket. The leather bag fell from the top as I pulled it out and then I felt the magic kick in.

Martin stood before me, almost in awe as I held it out and the blue jewel lit up. "How... " he started to say. He never finished, his eyes glued to the ever brightening jewel.

Once again the magic altered my perceptions. Information was flowing into me and I was struggling to process it all. I could see his strength and character. He was a proud man who did what he thought best for his kind, too few in numbers for his liking, and he worried about their future. I felt the betrayal of Turner as well. History aside; it was like a knife in his guts.

For a moment I felt like a voyeur. It made me feel almost guilty. I'd never asked for this God stuff and I wondered once again what I had gotten into. I didn't have time to continue with that thought. As with the eye that I had placed around Diantha's neck I felt something from this scepter. It wasn't as strong as before but I felt its wish to be returned to Martin. I also knew that he had not known of its true potential or power. The jewel showed me the wolf behind the man and I knew what to do. I placed it into his hands and he held it up in front of him.

As he took it the jewel brightened and then flashed at him.

"This belongs to you, creature of the forest," I said, remembering what Bernd had told me. "I offer the same as was offered your forefathers. This scepter of power proclaims your right to share our lands and borders and strengthens your magic. Friend I name you, and ally."

The jewel flashed brightly as I spoke, then dimmed.

He seemed mesmerized as he held it, but I saw him nod ascent. I stepped back and I felt the magic within me recede. Finally he lowered his hands. "What the hell are you?" he asked, moving his eyes from it to me.

I really hate that question.

"I would like to know as well," I heard Siegfried whisper as he came up behind me.

Martin was still staring at me. "...and how did you get the scepter?"

"Only a God could do such a thing," Diantha proclaimed as she got up from the couch.

Oh, great, I thought to myself, and she had phrased it without calling me a God directly. Never let it be said she wasn't crafty.

"First, as to the scepter, I took it from the Weres I fought when we first met. Since it was my ancestors that gave it to yours, I couldn't return it to you without being sure you deserved it."

"Is that supposed to make me feel better?" he asked, his face an expression of annoyance.

I felt the magic calling and I raised my hand; the staff began to glow again. "Answer that yourself. You now wield the power."

Martin held the scepter up. The annoyance turned to surprise and then to understanding. "I'm sorry, I never knew," he muttered. "All this time I thought it was just a symbol. I never believed the stories." Then he looked at me hard, the scepter still glowing. "You are a God!" he said as he started to kneel.

Shit, not again, I thought to myself. "Martin, please, just stand up, what did I say. You're a friend and an ally, nothing less."

"But...," he started to say as I pulled him to his feet, hoping this was not going to become a regular ritual.

"No buts. Listen, all of you." I turned to make sure all three of them were listening. I pointed at each of them as I spoke. "Diantha, I have your oath, but the rest is still true. Siegfried, you are my friend and kin, nothing less. Martin, I merely return to you that which was already yours. Besides, with what the scepter can do for you, you'll get an idea what I feel like these days."

I glanced at Siegfried. "Have you told him of the attacks?"

"Yes," Siegfried answered. "He has promised to lend trackers if we need them."

"Good. Diantha, I'll explain when we head to Vegas. But you two already know, someone's out there killing Fae and we have enough on our plates without complicating our lives with talk of Gods. Besides," I added, "I've got enough enemies. I don't need any more by throwing a wrench in the local hierarchy."

They didn't look convinced. Martin appeared weary but he nodded in the affirmative and Siegfried slapped me on the shoulder. I guess that was enough for now.

I left Martin in the trailer to rest for a few. Diantha was watching over him. He might have been a Werewolf but the scepter was a different type of magic. I guessed that between what the magic could take out of you the first time and finding out that the scepter was more than just an heirloom, it took some getting used to. Hell, I could sympathize. Outside I stopped at the base of the stairs.

"An interesting performance," Siegfried said, walking up and standing next to me. "I wonder what you have become."

"That makes two of us."

"Diantha seems to think you are a God. Are you?"

I stepped back and sat down on the stairs. Siegfried moved to sit next to me. "Damn, Siegfried, things have moved so fast I don't really know what I am anymore." I told him what Bernd had said about my lineage and that Diantha had called me both God and High Fae. Then I joked and called myself a bastard king. I don't think he found that funny.

"What do you plan to do?" he asked, watching me intently.

"I never asked for any this and I meant what I said. I don't want to be king of anything. The last thing I need is folks like Milagre and the others thinking I'm going to try and take over. We have enough problems without me threatening the status quo."

"What you want and what will be may be out of your control," he stated. "As I have said, the Fae are ruled by strength, strength in magic. And you, my friend, appear to have that in abundance. You will have to tread lightly; I cannot guess how the others will react to this knowledge."

"What about you Siegfried?" He startled me when he laughed.

"I will not betray my duties to Mr. Milagre but I do not abandon my kin. I, too, am your friend and ally. That has not changed." He slapped my leg as he stood up. "I believe it will be interesting to see where all this leads. Besides, as you have said, we have an enemy that must be stopped. We will need more of your magic if what he has done in the past is any indication."

"Well that's a fact," I replied as I followed him back into the trailer.

Once inside we grabbed Diantha's things and carried them out to the vehicles. Martin was going back with Siegfried and I would take Diantha. We agreed to meet at the Neptune.

"What about the trailer?" I asked Siegfried as we stood in the dirt road.

He grinned as he took something out of the back of the SUV and carried it inside. "I believe there is a problem with its propane system," he said as he came out a minute or so later. "We should go, it is better that we are well away before anything else that can attract the human's attention occurs."

That apparently handled, I got into my car. Siegfried followed me to Pahrump and then we took the highway back to Vegas. I knew things were about to get more interesting. Too many folks had seen the aftermath of what had happened. I was sure I was safe from regular people but the Fae were too close a community to keep many secrets from. I'd just have to see how this hand played out.

Chapter 20

The ride back to town with Diantha was anything but boring. She was a little irritated about the scepter. Apparently between its magic and the blood from the dagger she'd gotten quite a jolt. She figured it was another test. I didn't have the heart, or the inclination, to correct her.

I also got quite a history lesson from her. Well, her history at least. You'd think someone like her would have lived the high life, but to hear her tell it, it wasn't that great, at least not for the last 15 centuries or so. Even with the conflict between the Fae she'd done ok. But when they had started to disappear, things had gotten a bit dicey. Just because you can't die and you heal fast doesn't mean you can't feel pain. All this took a moment to sink in; it's easy to forget that she's over 2500 years old.

Then there was the Church. Things were difficult enough for a woman in those times, let alone a prior Oracle. She hadn't expounded but just reading between the lines it wasn't a pretty picture. She eventually came to the new world, America. There had been few Fae here so she didn't have that to worry about, but times had still been hard. Still, she'd survived. You could go a long way when you were young and beautiful in those days, and being intelligent and devious didn't hurt either. Well, as long as no one else knows, anyway. Those were her words, not mine. But there was always a downside. Laws didn't protect women much in those days and there had been some rough patches. She didn't seem to have any regrets, though, except maybe about losing the necklace. That part still nagged her.

Although I felt like she'd keep to her oath I wouldn't put it past her to try and find a loophole. You didn't need to be a lawyer to see that she'd probably already been thinking about it. Oh well, one more thing to keep an eye out for. I'll just add it to the ever-growing list.

When we arrived at the Neptune I followed Siegfried into the VIP parking lot (I didn't have to use my borrowed card and code this time). We pulled into adjacent spots and Martin got out of the SUV and walked over to me as Diantha as I exited the car.

"Thank you. Siegfried told me how to get in touch with you. I guess I owe you for the scepter. I already told him I'd keep this quiet. I think I understand our relationship. I won't forget."

"Listen, you don't owe me anything. Although handling Turner would be a favor I'd appreciate. I don't really want to be watching my back all the time."

"Trust me; he's on the top of my list. I look forward to working with you in the future." He took off towards the other side of the lot after waving goodbye to Diantha.

"That's it?" she asked as she walked around the car towards me. "You could have had anything you wanted from him."

I shook my head. "What did I say? It's a different world, remember? Besides," I added to placate her, "he won't forget me. And the scepter's magic is tied to me either way."

She started to say something but Siegfried came over to us before she could reply. "I have someone making arrangements for Diantha and they will have a suite prepared. Mr. Milagre is off property but Meredith would like to meet with you both."

Things were moving fast now but I had to go with the flow. "Sounds good," I replied. "Diantha, a suite work for you? Oh, I almost forgot," I said as I walked back to the rear of my car. I popped the trunk and got out the package containing the money I had for her. Walking back I handed it to her.

"Fifty thousand, as we agreed."

She opened the envelope and fanned the cash with her fingers without removing it.

"Don't you want to count it?" I asked.

"I trust you, my Lord," she answered with a giggle, stuffing the envelope in her pocket.

"Hey, what'd I say about that? Call me Robert."

"The old Gods were so much easier to understand," she declared, winking at Siegfried and linking her arm in mine.

He chuckled at her remark. Then we followed him to his office where the young woman I had seen the night of the incident with the Mages was already waiting.

"Diantha, this is Laera, she will see to your needs."

"Miss Diantha, would you come with me to my office for a moment, I have a few things to discuss with you. It shouldn't take more than 5 or 10 minutes,'" Laera said as she held out her hand for Diantha to follow.

Diantha gave me a quick glance and then accompanied Laera out of the room.

"She's going to discuss the accommodations and get a few housekeeping items in order. I think we should go over a few things while we wait for them to return," Siegfried said as he sat down at his desk.

I knew what was coming so I plopped down in one of the chairs.

"Meredith knows some of what occurred as I needed her approval due to the circumstances of your call. She should be here when Diantha returns. I'd appreciate knowing how much you plan on telling her."

He looked concerned but all I could think about was that line from the *Lord of the Rings* about meddling in the affairs of wizards. But what do you do if you find out you are one? Siegfried was one person I wouldn't cause grief, or at least any more than I already had.

"I'm gonna tell her the truth, Siegfried, what else can I do?" Well, at least a version of it.

He looked relieved.

"What can you tell me of the political situation? I mean the Fae political situation, what am I up against?"

"As I have said, in our world strength in magic is power. The Milagre's are the most influential Fae in the state. I believe you have met Mr. Cornwall. His is an ancient line but he sees his role as an advisor. Do not misunderstand, he wields considerable influence but he prefers to stay in the background."

Yep, that's a lawyer for you, I thought to myself. I asked a few follow up questions and then he continued.

"Martin has some power and he will earn more now that you have returned the scepter and he knows its potential. As to the rest, there are a few other clans in the area that wield some influence..."

We were interrupted by a knock on the door. Before Siegfried could say anything else it opened and Meredith came into the room. Diantha was behind and she came back into the room with Laera following her.

"Laera, refreshments for our guests," Meredith said, motioning to her. "Bring coffee and soft drinks and some assorted pastries."

"Would anyone prefer something stronger?" she asked, looking over at Diantha.

"Red wine, a nice vintage," Diantha said.

"Of course," Meredith replied and turned back to Laera. "My private reserve for our latest guest as well."

The girl nodded and left the room.

"So, this is the famous oracle, a pleasure."

"Mine as well," Diantha replied.

"I will have Michael working on some papers for you. Do you wish to remain as Deborah Kent?"

Wow, talk about a Faerie underground.

"List her as my mother; I would like to go back to using Diantha again."

Meredith sat down on the couch next to the desk. "Excellent, I am sure that can be arranged."

"Will I be staying here long?" Diantha asked.

"That will be up to you," Meredith answered. "Assuming you wish to remain in our employ we can find a suitable off-site residence for you. It will take a week or so to finalize your identity, after Edward approves, of course. I hope that will be satisfactory."

"My agreement is with my G—," she started to announce, giving me an 'oops' look that I just knew was staged. But hey, it might work to my advantage so I didn't say anything this time. "Excuse me, with Robert, if he is satisfied, so am I."

"I see," Meredith said, now turning to me. "Will that be satisfactory then?"

"Of course it is. Although her agreement is with me, she has agreed to use her abilities as part of her employment with you. I didn't set the terms but I'm sure you can come up with something that will be agreeable to both parties." Damn, now I was starting to sound like a lawyer.

"Fine, Edward can discuss the terms when he returns. Consider yourself a guest until we can negotiate a proper agreement," she said, turning back to Diantha.

Diantha didn't answer, but she looked pleased.

"Now then Robert, I would like to discuss a few things in private."

Siegfried stood up and motioned to Diantha. "Please use my office. Diantha and I can wait outside for Laera to return."

"That will not be necessary, Siegfried. I believe it would be better if Robert and I talked in my office." She looked back over at me. "Will you join me?"

"Sure," I answered as I stood up. "Siegfried, Diantha, I'd like to talk to you before I leave."

"We will be here," Siegfried replied.

I nodded and followed Meredith out. Passing Laera in the hallway Meredith told her to leave the food and drinks with Siegfried; she also mentioned that she and I were not to be disturbed. I followed her into her office which was next to Mr. Milagre's.

"Please sit," she said as she closed the door.

As I sat down she walked to a cabinet behind her desk and removed what looked like a large scallop shell. She placed it on the coffee table in front of the leather couch I had sat down on. Returning to the cabinet she removed an urn shaped pitcher and placed it on the table as well. With that done she sat down beside me. "It appears that I misjudged you, for that I must apologize."

"Misjudged me? What do you mean?"

She folded her hands in her lap. "I did not recognize you for what it seems you truly are. Your grandmother must have been very powerful to have wrought such a spell." She reached over and picked up the pitcher, pouring water from it into the scallop shaped bowl. "Still, I must be sure." She turned to me. "This is water from my home. Will you join me?" she asked as she reached out for my hand.

I took it and she moved it over the bowl. Smiling, she dipped our hands into it—and then we disappeared.

I had never felt the magic kick in as fast as it did. There was just a flash and I was no longer in her office. My senses were in overdrive as I took in what could only be described as a sea shore. Whoa, I wasn't in Kansas anymore. Hell, I wasn't even me anymore I realized as I looked down at my hands and felt my face and long hair. I was standing in the water facing a sandy beach in front of a grassy area. Behind me was the sea, the waves lapping at my ankles. There was something else, too, I was nude.

Well, shit! It was a good thing I was in my Fae persona, I thought to myself. I mean, at least I looked good naked.

It took only a moment to realize that with the change in my appearance also came the magic. This was definitely not the human world. I could feel the magic all around me and I knew that this was all Fae. I could hear and sense animals and birds all around me. It was incredible; they were so much more alive than I had ever felt creatures to be before.

I took stock of my surroundings, beach, lapping waves, animals and birds, some small trees and grasslands; it looked like somewhere out of a travel brochure. I was in cove, to my left was a rocky outcrop that reached into the sea and to my right was more beaches that ended in some kind of forest.

Was this the Fae world? Well, if Cacilia and Bernd could travel using oak trees then I guess Meredith using water shouldn't be a surprise. I looked around; I didn't see anyone or even sense anyone for that matter. Where the hell was she?

There was a gurgling sound and I turned around to see someone coming out of the water. Why, I wondered, did so many Fae look like elves out of stories? This one looked to be in her mid-30s and she was beautiful. She had long black hair and deep blue eyes with a hint of green with pointed elfin ears. It didn't hurt that she was nude, either. She had a strong, taut body and firm medium sized breasts. I would have done a double take had I seen her walking down any street. Then I did do a double take, it was Meredith. First Diantha and now Meredith, this Fae switcheroo thing was going to be hard to get used to.

"Are you just going to stare or will you hand me my clothes?" she asked with a smile.

I looked over where she was pointing and saw a sea green wisp of gossamer fabric on the beach next to her. I picked it up and handed it to her.

"Welcome to the Nereid realm," she said as she slipped on what I now saw was a tunic. She stared at me for a moment as if she was sizing me up, maybe she was. Then she sat down in the sand, gesturing for me to do the same. "You have never been in the Fae lands have you?"

"No, first time," I said with a nervous laugh. "Uh," I stammered, "would you have another one of those robes handy?"

She stifled a grin. With a wave of her hand the surf came up and deposited another tunic on the sand before my feet. I slipped it on, it wasn't much but at least I felt covered. She turned and gestured towards the grasslands. "I was there, you know. At the end, when the High Fae fought amongst themselves."

"I had no idea..."

"How could you? It was so long ago. Oh, I was young then, much younger than even you. I watched my mother die defending her Lord from Loki's armies. It happened right there," she said, pointing to a spot not far from the beach. "Not much later Neptune himself was gone and we were left to fend for ourselves."

"I'm sorry." I replied.

"Don't be, I don't blame you and that isn't why I brought you here. But I am Lady of our clan and that is why your coming concerns me. Not for me but for my people. It has taken us a long time to recover from those dark days and I would not wish for them to return. So I must ask you, why are you here and what do you want?"

I wondered how to answer that as we sat back down. "You know as much as I do." Ok, not entirely true, but a guy's got to have his secrets. "Besides, you invited me and you were there. Hell, I didn't believe a word you said until Charlie started talking to me."

She interrupted me. "Charlie, who's Charlie?"

"Charlie's my dog," I said, laughing. "Anyway, I thought you guys were all nuts. Then shit started happening and the next thing I know I'm fighting friggin Werewolves over someone called a Lil and well, here we are."

"Wait, a fight over a Lil? Do you mean that bargirl at Danu's?"

"Yeah, but that was just the precursor. I wound up with Martin Chibeaux's scepter and he wanted it back. Siegfried knew Martin so I took his side and that's about it where that's concerned." I lay back on the warm sand. "As to the rest of this High Fae stuff, well, you know most of it." I rolled to my side and propped my head up.

"Meredith, I can see the mistakes that were made in the past. Now, I don't know what really happened to the old bunch. But the way I see it, I have no reason to want to go down that path. Hell, we have enough of that kind of power play in the human world. So all I can tell you is that I don't know exactly why I'm here, but believe me, I have no desire to cause you or your people harm."

She sat there for a moment with her arms hugging her knees, just staring at the water. Then she lay back and turned to face me. "Had I not been there I would not have believed it," she said firmly. "But you are not Loki and we have never quarreled with the Dryad so I have no true reason to doubt you. Besides," she sighed, "you are High Fae. How do I quarrel with a God?"

"Enough with the God stuff. Can we just agree that I am no threat to you?" I asked, my turn to sigh.

She reached over and traced her finger along my cheek. I thought for a moment that she was going to kiss me but she pulled away. "Would that it were that simple."

That made me sit up, I had thought for a moment that things were going pretty well.

"You still do not understand, do you?"

"Understand what?"

"Oh, Robert, you really have no idea the world you have stepped into, do you? You are as a child...Please, I do not mean to sound condescending, but it is true. It has taken us two thousands of your human years to drag ourselves back from the abyss the High Fae left for us after *The Fall*. Did you think we would welcome their return with open arms?" she asked.

"Hey, I never asked for any of this. How many times do I have to say this? I am not them."

She leaned closer to me. "Tell me then—what of Cacilia? Have you even spoken to her recently?"

"What does she have to do with this?" I asked, wondering how she knew Cacilia.

"She is eldest, is that not how the Dryad rule? She will want to know what you have become and she will be waiting."

See what I said about fairy tales? What else was I going to have to deal with?

"Waiting? Waiting for what?"

"Let me show you something," she said as she stood up. Grabbing my hand she pulled me up and I followed her to the water. "Here, do as I do." She knelt down and placed her hand into the water.

I knelt beside her and did the same. At that moment I became one with the sea. The first sensation was my closeness to Meredith; it was if we had suddenly been connected. Then there were the others, I could tell there were thousands of them. It wasn't like I could read their thoughts; it was more like feeling a myriad of emotions, everything from contentment to fear. Fear of what, I wondered?

Then I felt something else, panic...no, concern, and then I felt someone, no...many someones coming our way. The feeling of concern became overwhelming and then I could feel the power in me want to take over. I pulled my hand out of the water. I looked back out over the sea and they began coming up to the surface, at least 20 of them. I'll be damned, they were Mermaids. Well, Mermen actually, and they didn't look happy.

I felt the power in me surge again and I fought to contain it. Had they actually been a threat, I probably wouldn't have been able to, but I could now feel they meant me no harm, at least not yet. They were waiting for Meredith. I turned to her.

She appeared wary but could see that I wasn't responding threateningly to their presence. She stood and raised a hand.

The feeling of concern diminished and I relaxed.

Although she hadn't said a word they retreated from the surface, all except one. He didn't approach, but stayed close, watching. I knew she had told them I was here and I also knew they had been ready to do battle, but only at her command.

"Testing me?" I asked, looking over at her. I could tell she knew I wasn't happy.

"My apologies, but I had to be sure."

"Sure of what? Did you think I was going to attack you, or maybe them?"

"No, not really, but I have not ruled for so long by being careless." She sat back down on the sand so I joined her. "Actually, I wanted to see for myself if you were truly what I believed you to be. Now I am satisfied."

"Really, what convinced you?"

"I felt your presence through the water. That is something I cannot do in the mortal world. Still, I could not quite localize it. You are not bound by the oak, as your people are. I have known the power of the Gods and I felt that same power within you...and that, my Fae Lord, is what Cacilia is waiting for as well. Confirmation."

I pondered that for a moment or two. I mean I hadn't seen Cacilia since that first visit. "Confirmation...and what do you think she'll do when she gets it?" I asked after a moment. "What would you do?"

"I cannot say how she will react. As for me, I would do as we are doing right now and try to gauge your intentions. She may decide to challenge you. Powerful you may be, but you are not invincible. She will know that as well. So, I ask you again, what do you want?"

I wish I knew the answer to that question. I'd already decided I needed friends so that was as good a place to start as any. I wasn't planning on starting a war with my own people and I also had to worry about the things the kids were involved in, so, it was time to get serious.

"Alright Meredith, here's something I do want. I am sure you've heard of the attacks on the Fae."

She nodded in agreement.

"I want your help in locating who's behind it."

"I would have done that anyway, but what do you have in mind?"

"Give me Siegfried for starters and I may want his help after I talk to Cacilia as well."

That seemed to surprise her.

"I'm not asking for him all the time, just that you make him available. As for the rest, I want access to some of your resources in the human world and no interference if I do have a problem with Cacilia. I also need your help in dealing with other Fae. As you've already stated, I know little of what I've become and I could use your guidance in that area."

Ok, that was asking a lot but it didn't seem unreasonable, besides she gained a God as an ally as well. Vain as it may sound, I figured that would appeal to her. "In return, you'll have full access to Diantha, except when I need her, of course. What else do you want?"

"I will not participate in a war with your Aunt. That path leads to a return of the old days."

"I'm not asking you to participate in a war. I just want him there to watch my back in case it comes to that. I need you to believe me. Whatever I may be I am not the same as the High Fae of the past. I don't want followers or slaves. I want only to be your ally, as well as your friend."

She sat quietly for a minute before responding. "Perhaps you are not as naïve as I first thought. I will agree to this alliance provided you acknowledge that being an ally does not mean we will acquiesce to just any demand, High Fae or not."

"I never thought that it did."

"Excellent, then it is settled. Business is concluded." She waved her hand at the last Merman (Merman, is that even a word), he dipped back into the sea and disappeared.

The water surged and again a wave glided up the beach towards us. When it receded there was a wine bottle and two wine glasses. I could only laugh at the thought of such efficient Nereid room service.

She poured some liquid from the bottle and handed a glass to me. She raised hers to mine and then took a drink. I raised mine as well and sipped. I wasn't an expert, but it was without a doubt the finest wine I had ever tasted.

"So what's next?" I asked as I set the glass down on the sand.

"We must bind our agreement in one of the ways Fae always have. Of course, we could just say a pledge, but I think this will be more interesting," she responded with the hint of a smile.

That said she pulled off her robe and pushed me back on the sand, kissing me. Before I knew it my robe was on the sand as well. I briefly wondered how I was going to feel when I dealt with her in her human persona. A few seconds later, I didn't seem to care.

****

The trip back was as fast as before but this time something was different. I hadn't come back, unscathed, as it were. This time I felt the magic still within me and there was something else. Almost like I was still connected; a wisp of me must still remain in the Fae world. I was also back in my clothes.

"Robert, is everything alright?" I heard Meredith ask as I shook my head to clear it.

Gone was the dark haired Fae I'd been with just moments ago. She'd been replaced with the silver haired woman I'd first met in what seemed so long ago.

"Do you ever get used to it?"

"Used to what?"

"The different people thing...young, old, all in a snap, I don't know, makes me feel, schizophrenic I guess."

Her eyes sparkled as she laughed and with a flash she shifted into her younger self. "You mean like this? Please, this world isn't ready for us again, you should know that. Come, you should get back to the others."

I stood up and walked toward the doorway where she was standing. Without a word she switched back to the human Meredith and we stepped out into the hallway. This was going to take some getting used to.

"Why then? I mean why hang out here in the human world? Your land, uh, I mean seas, seemed pretty nice," I asked as we walked down the hall.

"Ahh, but this is where the action is, as the humans are so fond of saying," she quipped.

What did that mean?

"One other thing, time works differently here. You'll find we haven't been gone nearly as long as you think."

Just as she said that I felt someone and turned to see Laera returning with a cart and some trays. We followed Laera to Siegfried's office and Meredith motioned her to go in.

"I will not be joining you but I do look forward to further discussions," she said with a wink.

"As do I," I whispered as she turned to leave.

"Oh, one more thing," she said, putting her finger to her lips. "There is still much about our kind you do not know. It may be best, how would you say, to keep a low profile until the time is right to announce yourself to the local Fae."

"Yeah, well, I don't seem to be having too much luck at that lately, but I'll keep it in mind," I answered.

Chapter 21

"I hope all went well," Siegfried commented as I walked into the room.

"I think so; it appears that at the very least we have agreed to an alliance."

Siegfried gave me one of those *Star Trek* Spock eyebrow raises then quickly composed himself. I almost blushed thinking he must know how some Fae sealed agreements.

"Thank you, Laera, just leave the cart," Siegfried said as Laera poured Diantha a glass of wine and then placed some trays on the desk.

She nodded and left the room, closing the door behind her.

"What did you want to discuss?" Siegfried asked as he grabbed some food from one of the trays.

I grabbed a sandwich and a bottle of water and sat down on the couch next to Diantha. All I really wanted to do was go home and top off a bottle of tequila. Hey, it'd been that kind of day. But I needed to set a few things in motion before I could return to my not so normal anymore life.

I explained my deal with Meredith for some of Siegfried's time and a few other things I needed, including a discussion about what I could tell Mal. I had the feeling I was gonna want him involved in whatever I was going to be dealing with. Other than that it was pretty simple:

I needed Siegfried to make sure Diantha got settled and then give me a few days to figure out my next step and get my mortal life in order. I still wasn't sure where all this was going to lead. Business concluded, and with a kiss from Diantha; I headed back to my car for the drive home.

****

I slept the sleep of the dead. Well, it would have been the sleep of the dead had it lasted a tad longer than only 4 hours. But at least I slept undisturbed. Needless to say I was tired and a little cranky this morning.

I poured fresh coffee into my newly washed Venus brothel cup and sat down at the kitchen table. Slowly inhaling what was in my opinion the mortal realms closest equivalent to nectar of the Gods, I savored my first sip. Then reality set in. Bastard King of the Faeries, now what the hell am I supposed to do? Oh, hell with it, it is what it is. I was gonna have to deal with it no matter what.

A couple other things were bothering me. Where was Bernd? I figured he'd pop up when something new happened. Yesterday had certainly been something new, that's for sure.

"Charlie!" I yelled, standing up to look around for him. Hearing the doggie door I turned to see him coming into the house, his tail wagging away. "Charlie," I asked, have you seen Bernd?"

"No Bernd," he said, and then turned around and went back out to the yard.

I was gonna have to work on his conversation skills. I was about to look for Lucy when I felt something familiar. Looking down, she stopped rubbing against my leg and sat down, just staring at me.

"Have you seen Bernd?" I asked, suddenly feeling like I was in a scene from Doctor Doolittle

She just sat there for a second. "He will come when he is needed," she said and then she, too, headed for the doggie door and into the backyard.

I take it that means I'm on my own. Fine, I thought to myself as I grabbed my cup for a refill. I was just getting the pot ready for next time when my cell phone rang, I looked at the number. "Siegfried, what's up," I said as I answered.

"I know you said you needed a few days, but I thought you'd want to know that your final payment for returning the necklace is ready for you."

"Great," I replied, thinking a few extra bucks in the bank never hurt. "Does that mean Mr. Milagre is back?"

"No, he called me this morning. At his direction it will be at the cage for you to pick up," he answered. "He also said he is most anxious to speak with you when he returns."

"I'd like to speak to him as well. I'll pick it up on my way into work. Thanks."

"You're welcome, oh yes, Diantha is settled in and further arrangements, as discussed, are in progress."

"Sounds good, give me a day or two to complete what I need to do and we can go over the details."

"As you wish," he replied and then disconnected.

I finished getting the pot ready and cleaning up then grabbed my keys and headed for the Neptune to pick up my check.

As promised, there was an envelope waiting for me at the cage. But it wasn't a check, it was cash. God, I love casinos. And it saved me a trip to the bank. Money in my pocket I headed to the office to arrange a week or two off to get this Fae thing under control.

Hailey was sitting behind her desk as I walked into the office. She looked up and smiled.

"The prodigal son returns," she said. "I hear you talked to Mattie, how did it go?"

"It went ok," I answered, if only to hear her ask for more details.

"Ok, what does that mean? Did you find the woman, or not?" She stood up and went to refill her coffee cup, muttering something about me being ungrateful.

"As a matter of fact, I did. Oh, I almost forgot," I said, reaching into my pocket and removing her portion of the money I had split up while still in the car. "If I remember correctly, I promised you a finder's fee, didn't I?"

"Hmm, I do seem to remember something about that," Hailey replied, batting her eyes. She reached over and took the offered envelope. "So, I take it your chat with Mattie was at least helpful," she said as she opened the envelope and peered inside.

"Whoa, are you kidding me!" she blurted out as she removed the 25 hundreds. "Since when did we hit the big time?" she asked, giving me a look as if I had just handed her a million dollars.

"Big clients, big pay-offs," I answered, waiting for her to say more.

"I should say so! First you start bringing in A-list attorneys, then you tell me you and Eddy Milagre are new found friends. Now you're paying me 10 times the normal referral fee. If I didn't know better...," she replied, shaking her head. Sitting down at her desk she picked up her purse from the floor and placed the money into a zippered pocket. Then she opened a drawer and put the purse inside.

"Seriously, Robert, what the hell are you up to? Do I have to start worrying about you?"

Grabbing a *Hailey's Legal Services* cup I poured myself some coffee and then leaned against the service window, looking over at her as I stirred. "Hail, I'll admit it, it's the damndest thing. But you know me better than that; it's just that my client list seems to have jumped up a class or two."

"I guess so...but I just want you to be careful," she replied, giving me one of her worried mother looks. "Besides, you might actually start making real money and then where would I be? I'd have to find a new tenant while you move into the towers or somewhere."

"Never happen," I said, laughing. "You're stuck with me."

"Well, alright," she replied. "But remember to drop a few of my business cards. I could use some of those high class clients myself."

"I always do," I answered, and then I turned and headed into my office to see what kind of damage I could do to my inbox. Besides, I figured I'd better let her calm down for a few before I tell her I'm taking a couple of weeks off.

"We'll see when they start calling," I heard her yell from the front.

I sat at my desk and booted up the computer. Except for the latest few minor inquiries that needed a rush job done, most of what I had left wasn't urgent. Some of the other stuff I'd farm out to a few other P.I.'s that I frequently worked with, the rest could wait. Once the computer was up I went through my caseload and divvied a few things up and sent out some emails. A few phone calls, invoices, and hours later, I was done.

Business concluded, I had some time to think. I wanted a couple weeks to let all that had been happening play out; I couldn't believe nothing would change, hell, it already had. I also had to decide what to do.

I sat there for a moment. I would have thought that my trip with Meredith would have sent up a few flags. It seemed like everything else I had done had. But why hadn't Bernd shown up? Was that a good thing or a bad thing? Shit, I had no idea.

I guess I could have put all the good things on one side of a paper and the bad things on the other side, but that old trick never worked for me. So instead I thought about what I would do with any problem.

I know I had to deal with people, well, Fae anyway. But the concept was the same; I needed people I could trust in case things got out of control. Well, at least more out of control then they already were. I guess they didn't have to be people, either. Now that's just a weird thing to say, be it true or not.

But I was going to have to be careful; I didn't want to be noticed any more than I had to. Just a few friends would do. Obviously, I already had Siegfried and Diantha, and Chibeaux would surely help out. Was that enough? If I included Mal I'd at least have some folks with a variety of skills, assuming I could get him involved. Hell, I wasn't even sure if I should get him involved. Especially since Siegfried had said that Milagre probably wouldn't like bringing a human in.

But what the hell, it's good to be a king, or at least thought of as one, so it was something to consider. I shut down my computer and walked out of my office. I told Hailey that I was going to take some time off, explaining that I needed a break, she laughed at that one. Then I decided to go for a walk.

"I'm gonna walk down to Starbucks before I leave, you want anything?" I asked her as I stopped by the doorway.

"No, I'm good," she replied.

"Ok, see you when I get back," I called out as I walked out the door and into the street.

Without realizing it, I ended up walking northbound towards Fremont Street, totally forgetting about Starbucks. Before I knew it, I was standing across the street from the El Cortez, one of Las Vegas' downtown landmarks.

Actually, I was standing on the corner of 6th and Fremont next to what had once been the JC Penney building. Catty-corner across the street had been where Sears and Roebuck had once stood. Of course, that was in the early days of Vegas, before the corporations and massive building boom of the 70s, 80s and 90s. But I wasn't really thinking about department stores or Las Vegas' past as I stood here, I was thinking about mine.

Maybe it was the Fae thing, hell, maybe it was just a sign of getting older, but all I saw as I stood there was my past. There, by the side door of the El Cortez, I recalled a car stop of a big time pimp back in the early 80s.

I caught myself laughing. What was funny about it was that my partner and I had backed up a couple of the Organized Crime Unit guys when we made the stop. Out of the car with our guns drawn we watched as they pulled the pimp and two of his girls out of the Rolls Royce as probably a hundred tourists watched on. After ordering them to the ground and putting them in handcuffs we went to help them up.

I grabbed one gal and my partner, long since retired, grabbed the other. As if choreographed, we stood the two girls up and almost simultaneously their breasts popped out of their loose tops to the awe and enjoyment of the tourists watching. We wound up arresting them and putting them in our car to their applause. I had been just a rookie, but some calls you never forget.

I went west, past the new downtown bars toward the Fremont Street Experience. Here and there wisps of memories collided. On that corner I'd arrested a wanted murderer. The warrants had said he was armed and dangerous but he'd cried when I put the handcuffs on. Things aren't always what they seem. Something I was quickly being reminded of.

By the time I made it to Casino Center the canopy was playing Frank Sinatra's *Luck be a Lady*. I smiled as I remembered the Fremont Street of the 70s. In those days there was no canopy and the street was two way. This was where we'd drive up and down and meet girls. I'd met Kathy, my ex, here one night after a university toga party. Damn but wasn't I becoming nostalgic? I paused and looked around. Here, the casinos are all open to the street. Something was missing, and then I saw it.

Tendrils of magic started to appear. They were barely visible, but just as I'd seen at the Neptune, they were here. Once again I was seeing the magic that was Vegas. Wishes, dreams, whatever you want to call them, wafted through the air here. More than that, they fueled the magic within me. Like my Aunt had said, the bottle could be refilled. This was why the Fae had come here, Vegas really was magic.

I walked back up Fremont and noticed others as well. Fae...damned if I knew what kind they were, but they were there. A girl at the casino entrance, some kind of Faerie, and further inside, at the tables was another. I even felt what had to be a few roaming around with the other tourists, none of them noticing me. I guess that's a good thing, especially when you're trying to keep a low profile.

Suddenly, I stopped and looked around. Something wasn't right. It was just a wisp of something but...how do I describe it? It just didn't smell right. I tried to find it again but it was gone. I felt goose bumps down my spine.

My gun was on my back but I reached for the seax, its weight comforting me. What the hell had that been? I tried to reach out with my magic but nothing else jumped out at me so I started walking again. By the time I got back to the office I had almost convinced myself that I had imagined it. I took a last look around before I got into my car. Nothing, hell, maybe I had just imagined it.

Damn, I wish I knew for sure. That was the problem with this magic stuff, I didn't know enough to know what to do. I'd thought the connection to the Fae world I'd felt would be of more help, at least as far as my magic was concerned. I don't know what I had been thinking last night. How was I going to resolve all this if I still didn't really know what the hell I had gotten in to?

King of the Faeries, yeah right!

Once in in my car I started driving with no destination in mind. I've often done this when I need to think. Actually, it's one of the few times I talk to myself, and answer back. It's a technique I've used to work out problems, that or maybe I really am crazy. Werewolves, Faeries, Lil, Norse legends, how was someone supposed to deal with all this? I drove in silence for a while and then the answer came.

I am such an idiot. I was letting all this unknown get to me way too easy. I mean what would I do if I needed to know the answer to something. Duh! I've been doing investigations for thirty years for God's sake. Maybe it was time to do just that, but where to start?

Then I smiled as a snatch of a ditty I'd recently heard came to mind, "Little Lilly needs my willy." Well, you have to start somewhere, so I turned my car back toward downtown and headed for Danu's.

Chapter 22

I pulled around the corner from the old fire station and parked my car. Walking towards Danu's I once again felt goose bumps. I stopped and looked around but there was—nothing. Not satisfied, I closed my eyes and tried to reach out with my new found magic.

Still nothing. Ok, maybe there was something, but it was just the normal things you find at night in any downtown area. I didn't feel anything suspicious, but I still couldn't shake the feeling. I wasn't sure if there was nothing there or if I just wasn't doing something right. Hoping it was just the result of a rough day, I walked the rest of the way to Danu's and then went inside.

The place looked the same as it had the last two times I'd been here. It was quiet; there was only one table occupied with an older couple and one guy sat at the far end of the bar. As I walked in I saw Bart at the bar, Delia wasn't in sight. He didn't look happy to see me but I walked to the bar and sat down anyway. I waited as he spoke with the other patron at the bar who apparently was leaving.

As he got up and headed for the door, Bart walked over to me, stopping at the tap and pouring a beer. He placed it down in front of me. "Listen, I don't want any problems with the other Fae," he said as he set the beer down. "I don't know what you want but I have tried hard to make a place for her kind here." He gestured toward a door in the far end of the room.

I took a deep drink and placed the mug down. Interesting, from what Bernd had told me, and what he was projecting, I had a guess that Bart must be an Elf. "It's Bart, right?"

He didn't say anything.

"Ok, I'm not here to cause you, or her, any grief, and quite frankly, the disagreements between her kind and the Fae don't interest me." So I was being less than truthful. "I'm just here to have a beer." Ok, so I was a liar as well. So sue me

Bart gave me one of those 'yeah, right' looks. "As you wish, just so we don't have a repeat of last time."

"About that, since we're just talking here, I know what I did to piss him off, but what do you have against the Weres?" I asked as I took another drink.

Bart leaned over the bar towards me as he picked up some mugs and wiped them with a towel. "I have no quarrel with any of the races but that cannot be said for individuals. That one is evil."

I looked back at him, incredulously. "Evil, if he's so evil then why are you upset with me? Hell, I agree with you," I said as I took another swig from my mug.

"That one knew he was not welcome here. Your incident with Delia must have set him off. He is seldom so bold. Threatening his pup was not wise."

I started to laugh and then caught myself. "Yeah, well, as I recall he didn't fare so well."

He put down the mug he was wiping and looked at me like I was some kind of idiot. "Were's travel in packs, I would prefer not to have the local pack causing me, or her, problems. Make an enemy of one and you often make an enemy of them all," he explained.

I just held my mug up near my eyes, swirling what was left in the glass. "I don't think that will be a problem," I commented, putting down the almost empty mug. I was going to say more but Delia chose that moment to come out from the back.

She didn't seem to see me. Instead she walked toward the other couple who were still seated. Speaking to them for a moment I could see that they were settling their tab. As they got up she picked up their now empty glasses and began to walk toward the other side of the bar where the gate was. I watched them amble toward the doorway. Then, without warning, my magic kicked in.

Bart had started to pick up my mug when I reached out and grabbed his hand. "Hold on a moment," I said, sensing something. Then I almost gagged as the feeling washed over me. Looking over at the door I knew something was coming, and it was evil, pure evil. I looked up at Bart and asked, "Do either of you have a weapon?"

He was clearly startled, although if it was simply because of the question or if it was the fact that I was pulling out my gun, I wasn't sure. "What are you doing?" he asked, then his face twisted and he jumped up. "What the...Delia, behind the bar, MOVE!"

He ran around the bar area racing toward her and pulled her back. I saw them leap over the bar just as several figures burst through the front door.

I don't know who or what the two folk that just waved goodbye had been but they never made it to the doorway. There was a burst of light and they were down before I could take cover. The Mage who had taken them out was standing over them, a wand in his hand. I recognized him immediately. He was the one that got away. There were at least two others behind him near the doorway. Call it instinct, call it rage, but I owed this guy.

Reaching behind my back I came off the barstool firing. As he went down I started running to get to better cover around the bar. I heard a yell from one of them as he went down and before I could get off another shot I was hit with a burst of magic. Unfortunately, this one was much stronger than last time and I went tumbling across the room, my gun flying.

I wound up on the other side of the bar feeling like someone had taken a two by four to me. The parts that didn't hurt were numb. Magic was pouring through me and I wasn't seeing things as clearly as before. Was this some kind of spell?

I crawled closer to the bar and pulled the seax, shaking my head to clear it. I looked around it to see where the other attackers were and saw Bart and Delia engaged with the two of them. They were both holding swords. Bart was close in but didn't seem to be getting anywhere. Although the Mage had a knife, Bart's movements were preventing him from fully utilizing it or his wand.

As for Delia, whatever she was fighting had a sword as well. I couldn't seem to focus on her opponent but he was big. They were slashing and cutting at one another faster than I could keep track of.

Making sure my legs worked I tried to decide who to help first. I looked around but my gun was nowhere to be seen. Figuring Delia's opponent was bigger and his attack more ferocious, I ran her way.

Before I got two steps I saw Bart take a fall and the Mage had the advantage. Pivoting, I gave a yell and caught the mage's attention. Forgetting about Bart he turned his wand towards me. This time I was ready. Summoning every bit of power I could think of I raised my hand just as he fired.

Without even thinking about the how I managed it, I projected a wall of force that blocked his magic. Running toward him I saw the confusion on his face just as I tackled him. We went down and before he could get either his wand or the knife back up I buried the seax in his chest. I saw the surprise in his face as he realized what I'd done.

"You are no half breed..." he croaked, and then he was silent.

I expected to be assailed with information when his blood spilled over me like the last times but there was—nothing. His blood was like an empty jar. I could feel that it once held something but it was long gone. I wondered what that meant but within seconds I heard a terrific howl.

Rolling off him and pulling the seax out I turned to the noise and saw the thing that Delia had been fighting standing over her, its head staring up and growling. As I got to my feet it started to come into focus, now holding its sword pointed downward over Delia's still body. It looked like a man, a really big man.

I did a quick scan and saw Bart still on the floor. He was bleeding but at least he was breathing. Turning back to the now human looking creature I took an offensive stance and started to move toward it.

"Stop or this creature dies!" it said, holding the sword menacingly close to Delia's throat.

"Let her go!" I yelled back. Now that it was in focus I thought I knew what it was. It may be in human form but it was a Demon.

"I think not," the creature responded, bending lower and inching his sword closer to her neck.

"Your friends are dead," I said, angrily. "Let her go and maybe I'll let you live."

The Demon looked up at me and snarled. "So sayeth one of the mighty Fae," it replied.

I was weighing my options when I heard a noise behind me. I took a quick glance and saw that Bart was getting to his feet.

"Wait," the Elf said to the Demon, "he that bound you was killed by this Fae, you are now free. Let the girl live, she is nothing to you."

"I will not trade one master for another," he said, now raising and pointing its sword at me. "His kind cannot be trusted."

I may not know a lot about this whole Fae thing, but it didn't take a genius to figure out what had happened. The Mage I had killed had summoned this Demon. These Mages must have been working for another Fae. I needed to know who, and why, they were killing people. I decided to follow the Elf's lead.

"What is your name, Demon?" I asked as I lowered my seax.

"I am Usag, son of Asug, Prince," he answered, snarling.

"Well, Usag, son of Asug," I said, cleaning the blood off my seax as I wiped it on my pants. "I do not want to fight you. Free the girl and return to your home."

"Why do you care for this creature?" Usag asked, his blade still at Delia's throat. "Your kind has shown nothing but disdain for these outcasts."

Ok, now I was getting irritated. It's bad enough when you have to hear what elitists your people are from fancy lawyers, but from a Demon? Give me a break!

"Usag," I said, standing straight and sheathing my blade. I concentrated as Bernd had shown me and my appearance changed into the Fae version of myself. "My name is Robert Hoskins. Now I don't know what it's gonna take to convince you but I can tell you this. I am the son of the Dryad, Gabriele, daughter of Maria, eldest of her clan and a High Fae. I can't change the past but I tell you here and now. My quarrel is not with you but with those that would make us enemies."

Usag looked up and laughed. A sheet of flame poured over him and when it was gone he was no longer in the guise of a human. He was huge and looked like what you expect a Demon to be. He had an almost reptilian skin of some kind with a dark, leathery consistency. He turned his head towards me and unfurled his wings, his eyes burning like tiny flames. "Very good, Fae, as strange as you may be, you no longer hide, nor will I."

Damn, he was big!

"Let the girl go, Usag, and return to your home," I said again.

"Tell me first, High Fae," he asked, stringing out the words as if mocking me, his sword circling over Delia. "What is she to you? She is closer to my kind then yours. I was not aware that the Lilin were special to you, except perhaps to kill."

I wasn't sure what he wanted to hear. I mean, he looked as evil as they come and my first thought was that I had made a mistake in sheathing my seax. I could try to use magic but I was still new at this and was afraid he could harm her further before I could strike. Then I remembered what Siegfried had said about some Demons just wanting to be left alone. I didn't want to show any weakness but I figured it was worth a try.

"It is enough to know that she is special to me, Demon, and I would not have her harmed if I can prevent it," I answered, not using his name. "But I promise you this, if you hurt her, I will kill you."

Then he did something that surprised me.

"Well said," he replied, sheathing his blade and taking several steps back.

I just stood there and watched him for a moment in case it was a trap.

"Perhaps I will trust you, Robert of the High Fae, at least for now. I return her to you. I wish only to be gone from this realm. She fought well, but this battle was not mine to begin with."

He took a few more steps back and I ran over to her, kneeling and taking her head in my arms. She was badly injured and extremely pale. I saw there were several deep cuts on her chest and sides and she was bleeding heavily. At that moment, Bart appeared at my side.

"Watch the Demon; I will see what can be done," he said, and began checking her wounds.

I gently laid her head down and stood up and approached Usag, who eyed me warily. "Thank you, Usag," I said. "Do you have a way home?"

"Yes," he answered, "the portal calls to me even as we speak."

"Before you go, the one that summoned you," I inquired, pointing to the Mage I had killed. "Do you know his master?"

Usag looked over at the dead Mage and growled. "It was of the High, as you are, but I did not see him, only felt his presence as that one said the words," he answered as he pointed at the dead mage.

He closed his wings against his back and started to glow. "I thought the High gone, they will not trap me again. Now that I know the portal is still open I can protect my clan from it. But we are only one clan, others may still come."

"When I defeat him I will find a way to help," I replied. Then I stepped back as the glow intensified. I could see that he was saying something but I couldn't hear his words. Then, with a crackle in the air, he was gone.

I was left to ponder what that meant for me, another High Fae. This was bad, but as before, I didn't have time to think about it.

Bart was kneeling next to Delia and called out to me. "She is gravely wounded."

"What else can we do?" I asked, looking down at her still form.

"There is nothing that we can do. She must rest," he answered. "The Lilin inside will heal her if it can. She is too weak to feed and it may be days before we know if she will live. Your friend, Siegfried is on his way," he said as he stood up. He threw a cell phone on a nearby table. "These two will have friends. We must find a place to keep her safe."

"It's my fault this happened," I said, bending down next to her. "I'll take her to my place, she will be safe there."

"What of the pact? Demeter allowed the Lilin to live but is forbidden for your kind to comfort them. You cannot do this without violating the terms and their oath," he said, looking at me as if that mattered.

Screw that, I thought to myself. I started to say something, and then realized I still appeared as my Fae self. "Bart," I said, "take a good look at me."

In light of what we'd been through I don't think he ever really noticed that I'd changed. His eyes widened as he finally realized who, and possibly what, I was.

"Maybe you didn't hear what I said to the Demon. I am more than just another Fae. I am the heir of Demeter and since she's gone I figure I can do whatever the hell I please."

I thought he was going to argue with me, but he remained silent.

I picked Delia up gently and cradled her in my arms. Then I started towards the door. Shifting back to my mortal self I stopped and looked back at him.

"Bart, you need to trust me on this. I'll do what I can for her. Maybe I can do something for her people as well. Let Siegfried know that we're safe." Then, carrying her gently, I walked through the doorway and out into the night.

Chapter 23

I know I've said this before, but Bernd was right, Fate certainly is endowed with a sense of humor. More importantly than that, I couldn't seem to escape her—Fate that is. I pulled up to the gate waiting for it to open.

Delia, in the passenger seat, looked like shit. There was a lot of blood, but at least she was still breathing.

I pulled into the driveway and opened the garage door. Getting out I lifted up Delia and carried her into the house and laid her gently on the bed in the downstairs bedroom. She was still covered in blood and Charlie was frantic. I tried to calm him down as I called for Lucy.

She ran into the room and jumped on the bed. For a moment she looked like a black cat you'd see in a Halloween cartoon, her fur standing up and eyes wide open, then she hissed, "Danger."

Like, no shit, I thought to myself.

"Just find Bernd," I ordered. "Go, and don't come back without him," I yelled, pointing toward the rear of the house.

With a hiss she bounded out of the room.

I did the best I could to make her comfortable considering she was still unconscious. I stripped off her clothes and cleaned her wounds and body. I saw that the bleeding had slowed, but she was burning up and deathly pale, and there was blood pooled around her eyes. I put a makeshift bandage on the wounds.

Her blood had not been like the Mages nor did it affect me like the others. Her blood sang to me. Although I was trying to focus on her wounds her blood filled my senses with her lust for life. It also sang of a tragic past. Life had not been kind to this Lil. I didn't feel any evil inside her, certainly not any threat to me. Instead, I felt a sorrow for what had been and a feeling that things ahead were no better.

Well, perhaps I could change that. I'd have to see where this was all going to all lead.

Once I had gotten her as comfortable as I could I just sat there wondering how the hell I had gotten into this mess and just what a second High Fae meant. Of course, I knew it was bad. Hell, he'd killed several Fae already and I was certain I was gonna jump up a notch or two on his list.

The phone had rung several times as I was tending to Delia. Looking at the screen I saw that it had, as expected, been Siegfried. He was just going to have to wait for another minute.

I looked over at Charlie, standing in the doorway. "Charlie, come here, boy," I called. He ran over to me. "I need you to guard the place, Charlie. We could be in some deep shit here."

He stared into my eyes.

"We need to keep her safe."

He barked and then I heard him answer. "Guard, watch, protect," he said and then ran out towards his door into the yard.

I went into the kitchen and got out a large paper bag I had saved from my last take out from a local Italian joint. Taking that into the bedroom I placed Delia's bloody clothes into it to preserve them. Returning to the kitchen I started a pot of coffee. Then I picked up my cell phone and dialed Siegfried.

"Hey, everything handled over there?" I asked when he answered.

"It's being worked on. How is the girl?"

"She's still out," I answered. "One of the dead guys is the same one that got away at the Neptune. I think you better get someone to watch Milagre. I may have pissed someone off with this battle."

"Michael is flying out to meet him as we speak. He was scheduled to return later this week but I convinced him to come home early. I expect he will want to see you." There was a short pause. "He is close to Bjartr and has an interest in this place."

"I should of guessed that when he called you so fast," I said, feeling stupid for not putting that together.

"It might be best if you let us take the girl. This could cause some problems with a few of the other Fae."

"I don't think so," I replied. "It's my fault she got involved in this. I need to get a few of her things. Do you know where she lives?"

"I do, but she may need special care...," he started to say, but I interrupted him.

"I've got someone coming. How about swinging by her place when you're done there and getting some clothes for her? Maybe you can bring Diantha by to watch over her. I'd like to get a few hours sleep and I'd feel better if someone else was here."

"As you wish, I can do that when I'm finished here. I'm sure Diantha will be available. Give me a few hours."

I could tell he wasn't happy, but hey, sometimes it's good to be a king. "Call me when you get close. So much for a couple of days, huh?"

I heard a grunt in acknowledgement and he disconnected.

After checking on Delia one more time I grabbed a *Shit Happens* coffee cup with a big yellow happy face and poured myself a cup. Then I just sat down at the kitchen table to wait. I must have been asleep as it took me a second to recognize that it was the phone ringing. Still groggy, I answered.

"Yeah."

The voice of Siegfried came on the line. "We're down the street."

"I'll meet you outside," I said. I called Charlie and hit the keys to open the gate and then we went outside. Siegfried's black SUV pulled into the driveway and stopped in front of me.

"I hope that's not your blood," he asked as he and Diantha popped open the doors and walked towards me.

I had totally forgotten how I must look still wearing my blood-soaked clothes. "The other guy looks a lot worse," I answered, trying for a touch of humor.

"So I've seen," he replied as they both petted Charlie.

Diantha came over to me and gave me a peck on the cheek. "I see you have once again vanquished your foes, my Lord."

"Diantha, what did I say about the 'my Lord' crap?"

She just rolled her eyes. "As you wish. Then take me to this mysterious patient I am to watch over."

She took my arm and the three of us went into the house while Charlie bounded back into the yard. We checked on Delia and then moved back into the kitchen to talk. Siegfried looked concerned when he saw her condition but didn't say anything.

"You did not tell me she was a Lil," Diantha commented as she sat down at the table.

"Is that a problem?" I asked, looking back at her as I picked up my smiley face cup and filled it.

She almost looked like she was going to say something else and then changed her mind. "No," she replied.

"Diantha, what is it you want to say?"

"This is a dangerous action, my Lord," she said, looking concerned.

"Yes, it could be. So if you want out I'll have Siegfried take you back to the Neptune," I said, having decided to be straight with her and give her an out. "I won't hold it against you," I added.

Siegfried seemed amused but turned his head so she could not see the expression on his face.

Diantha sat quietly for a moment, gathering her composure, I guess, then answered. "That will not be necessary. I have given my oath."

"Fine," I said, the matter closed. "We have other problems to discuss as well." I gave them the dime version of what had happened.

"So, is it true?" Siegfried asked. "There is another?"

"So the Demon said," I answered. "But at least we know what's behind this, if not who."

"That does not exactly comfort me," he added.

"Me either. You saw the bodies?"

He nodded.

"The one by the door was one of those that went after Milagre. I'm sorry I wasn't able to save the other two customers, they were inside before I realized what they were."

"Such things happen; even you are not all-knowing, nor invincible, though you seem to be doing quite well against them."

"We may have gotten lucky there. The last one called me a half-breed; apparently they aren't sure of what I am." I got up and refilled my coffee. "If nothing else that gives us the advantage."

"For now," Siegfried replied.

"For now," I agreed, leaning back against the counter. "Anyway, that doesn't get us any closer to finding out who is behind this or even why it's happening. Have either of you heard of any other High Fae or Gods still around since *The Fall*?"

They both shook their heads.

"None of the Gods have been seen in thousands of years, that I can attest to." Diantha said, pushing back her chair and standing up. "Believe me; I have searched for them, both in the Aether as well as on foot. After Apollo abandoned me I searched everywhere but their presence was gone from this world. I thought they had simply left but now I am not so sure. Perhaps they truly are all dead."

"Well, according to the Demon there's at least one more," I said.

"If that is so than he is not like you, he is evil," she replied.

"That's what I'm afraid of..." I started to add but at that moment Siegfried's cellphone rang. I couldn't hear what was being said but by the look he gave me, he was surprised. I wasn't sure if that was good or bad.

"Keep me informed," I heard him say as he disconnected a short time later. "Well, I think you will find this interesting. A body has been discovered around the corner from Danu's. The local police are already on the scene.

"Oh, oh," I thought to myself.

He must have seen the concern on my face. "Don't worry, there is nothing to tie it to Danu's and besides, there is nothing to find."

"Then what is it?" I asked, sitting back down at the table.

Siegfried continued. "That was one of our sources on the local PD. The body is that of Ben Turner."

One of their sources on the local PD? That was the second time he'd mentioned sources like that. Only Homicide would know who the body was this soon. Suddenly, that comment about the Dullahan by O'Malley didn't seem so unusual. Had he been feeling me out? Jesus, I'd known him most of my life. Then again I'd never known any of this before now. I would have to find out more when I got the chance. I got back to the issues at hand.

"Turner, why doesn't that surprise me? That explains how they tracked me. He has plenty of reason to hate me and knew about my ties to Danu's as well as what I looked like. But what's his tie to the Mages?"

"That I do not know. Whatever it was, it was not enough to save his life."

"How did he die?" I asked, wondering if he was killed before the attack, or after.

"His skull was crushed, not a simple thing to do to a Were," he answered.

"The Demon could have done it. We'll have to be extra careful until we know who else is involved." I turned to Diantha. "Would you be able to, what's the word for it, divine something?"

"I am sorry, that I cannot do?" she answered with a sigh.

"Oh well, I had to ask. Anything else I'm missing?"

"Not for now. We may have more to go on after the Mage's bodies are examined," Siegfried said, shaking his head.

"Ok, look, I'm tired and we're not going to solve anything else tonight. Let's continue this later." I turned to Diantha. "You're good staying here tonight, or at least what's left of it, right? I'd like you here in case she wakes up and I don't hear her."

"Of course, my Lord, that's why I'm here," she answered with a smile.

I ignored the "my Lord" comment. I seemed to be doing that a lot tonight. I got up to go check on Delia. They both did the same and followed me into the bedroom. She didn't look any different but at least she didn't look any worse. I heard a sound and turned towards the door.

"Bernd is here," I heard him say.

"About time you showed up," I said in a not so pleasant voice.

"I came when I was needed as you should have known I would," he remarked, giving me a disapproving look. Then he walked into the room and took in the scene.

Oh shit, another Fae Faux Pas on my part, I guess. Not that he didn't deserve it.

There was sudden hush and both Siegfried and Diantha fell to their knees. I heard Siegfried say "Einn Dvergar" with astonishment as Bernd walked over to him.

"Please Siegfried, son of Olafr, rise. Your deeds are well known to my kind," Bernd said as he and helped the tall man to his feet.

Siegfried seemed in awe that the Dwarf knew who he was.

Then Bernd turned to Diantha.

"Rise priestess," he said. "There is no need for ceremony here. Long past are the days of old when such reverence was necessary, or expected. Come, let me pass and inspect your injured comrade."

Diantha didn't say anything but she stood up and backed away. I noticed that her eyes remain downward as if she was reluctant to look upon him.

"Fader," Siegfried replied as he stepped back as well.

Bernd turned and walked into the bedroom where Delia was. His head barely reached the top of the pillow-top mattress, but with a single leap he was on the bed and examining Delia. When he was finished he jumped off.

"Well?" I asked when he didn't say anything right away.

"The wound is deep."

"That much I know but I was hoping it was starting to heal," I said.

"On the surface, that is true, but this is the mark of a Demon's blade. Such blades are deadly in this realm and their wounds not easily cured, and," he added, "her Lilin is weak." He just stood there, when I didn't say anything he continued. "Tell me first of the battle and what else has transpired."

I gave him the short version, including learning of the High Fae and the Demon's claim that another was involved.

"Much has happened, I see, but of this Demon I have heard," Bernd said. "If he was bound with the assistance of a High Fae then things are indeed dark, and there is still the other matter."

"What other matter," I asked, not sure where he was leading me.

"She is of the Lilin and to heal her would go against the terms of surrender decreed by Demeter."

"But I'm asking you to, and besides, I thought you said I could change that," I countered.

"Indeed I did. However, I told you it was not our place to interfere. I also mentioned a reckoning, and although I did not expect one from you so soon, it appears that you have hastened such time as a decision must be made."

Oh, oh. Why did I have the feeling I was being manipulated again. "So where are we going with this?" I asked.

"Only you can decide that, Robert," he said, walking out of the bedroom. Then he stopped by the kitchen table, a pipe appearing in his hand. Raising it to his lips he blew a smoke ring and continued. "Yes, I can save her, possibly. But only the true High Fae of the Dryad can ask that of me and you have not yet declared your title."

Following him into the kitchen I walked over to the refrigerator and grabbed a beer. Taking a drink I watched as he blew smoke rings for a moment. Siegfried and Diantha stood near the doorway to the bedroom, neither one appearing to want to join in the conversation.

"So, to keep it simple, either I choose a Fae life or she dies," I said, angrily. "So what do I have to do, go live in the Fae world and play the good king, or what? I'm gonna be honest here, Bernd, I just can't see myself hanging out at Fae night clubs and eating grapes, not to mention that I'm still pissed that I had to learn this High Fae thing from an outsider." I glanced over at Diantha, "No offence," I added.

His pipe came out of his mouth and he froze. "No, no, you misunderstand," he said in a shocked tone. "For that I will apologize, at least for not telling you the possibility after your success with the scepter. But while it is true that Maria and I believed that it was possible that you could be a High Fae, even I was not certain until now.

"As to the Lilin, I am not asking you to give up this life. Robert, you must understand, I can guide you, but even I cannot violate the terms of that accord. In this case to take such action as necessary to heal her wounds would break the terms set by Demeter. Only a High Fae or her heir can properly release them from their bond."

I took another swig of my beer. Yep; it sure felt like I was being manipulated. "Fine, so what happens if I say yes?"

"You have already declared yourself in battle. But if you truly wish to release the Lilin from their oath you must formerly acknowledge what you are and claim your birthright." His pipe disappeared and he looked me right in the eyes. "Robert, I would never deceive you."

Here it comes.

"Although you need not take the throne in your lands many will seek you out. You will be their Lord and you will be expected to aid them if they are threatened."

"What about Cacilia? What is she going to do if I do this?" I asked, already worrying about internal politics.

"Cacilia knows what she must do," he answered simply, whatever that meant.

Oh, well, what the hell. I'd already forged an alliance with Meredith and the Nereid after all. Rushed or not it seemed like I was already so far into this that I wasn't getting out anytime soon.

"I suppose there's more," I said, cracking a smile, there always was.

"Of course," he answered, taking my hands in his, "and I will tell you as much as I am able once you decide. Do not fear, I will be by your side to guide you'" He let go of me and took a seat as Lucy jumped up on the table next to him.

"But before you decide, there is one thing I must tell you. Not everyone will be happy if you free the Lilin from their oath. High Fae and King you may have become but the Fae and Lilin were foes for a very long time before they were defeated. You will make enemies."

I thought about that for a minute and then remembered my earlier conversation with Diantha. "Then I'd better work at making them my allies since it seems like I might need a few." I said as I stood up, "let's do this."

Bernd slid off the chair and Lucy jumped to the floor.

She looked up at me, her tail twitching. "So it begins," I heard her say. Then she ran out into the backyard and was gone.

Chapter 24

"So what do I need to do?" I asked as the Dwarf walked toward Siegfried and Diantha.

"First we must wait for Lucinda to return with a healer and then we will travel to the Fae lands," he answered.

"The Fae lands? What about Delia? I'm not sure she can last that long."

"Tell me in your own words what you plan to do."

What had he said? Oh yeah. "I acknowledge my, what'd you call it? Heritage? Does that sound right? Then I claim my birthright as, oh hell, King of the Faeries, or Dryads, whatever, right?" I answered, feeling kind of silly.

"It will do." He turned back to Siegfried and Diantha. "You have witnessed his declaration?" he asked them.

They both looked over at me and nodded.

"Speak out loud," Bernd ordered.

"I have witnessed it, Fader," Siegfried said, looking back at the Dwarf.

"As have I," answered Diantha.

"Then I will do what I can for her. Come," he said, motioning me into the bedroom.

He jumped back on the bed and knelt beside her head. "Give me your arm," he said.

"What?" I asked, not sure what he meant.

"If you really want to save her she will need your blood. Kneel down here," he pointed to a spot next to her head by the bed. "Drape your arm over her neck. It will take me a moment to get her ready."

"My blood?" I said, as I knelt and moved my arm over her chest. "Is she really some kind of vampire? Siegfried said the Lilin were the stuff behind the legend."

"Not exactly," he said as he opened her mouth and began to manipulate her tongue. "But he is correct, the Vampire are only a legend." He made it sound like vampeer. Then he pulled on something underneath her tongue. As he massaged it, a needle like object, which reminded me of a proboscis on an insect, started to emerge from the base.

"What is that?" I asked, as he grabbed my arm with his other hand. We all watched as he inserted the object into my arm on the inside of my elbow and pushed it closer to her mouth. "What the …?" I said, flinching. I was expecting it to hurt, but there was no pain.

"Do not move," he said. "She is weak, even with your blood it will take a moment for her to ingest a sufficient quantity."

"I thought you said she wasn't a vampire," I replied, watching the bizarre transfusion.

Bernd just shook his head. "She is not, but as Siegfried has told you, even legends have to arise from somewhere. What did you think the Lilin were?"

"I don't know," I replied. "I only know what he told me."

He watched her face for a few minutes and then removed my arm from her mouth and I watched as the proboscis slid back under her tongue.

"That should be sufficient," he said, jumping down off the bed.

I pulled back my arm and looked at it. There was very little blood. There was the barest trace of what looked like a needle stick and it disappeared as I watched.

"I have done what I can. She must rest now, the Lilin inside must heal itself so that she can recover. Diantha, stay with her for a moment, if she starts to thrash you must calm her."

Diantha nodded her head and sat down next to her.

"So what exactly are they, anyway? The Lilin, I mean," I asked as I followed him back to the kitchen.

"I will tell you what you want to know, but first, let me congratulate you for your actions tonight. I am very proud of you. Perhaps, just perhaps, you have begun to mend some old wounds."

"I thought you said I was going to make enemies."

"That you will, but you will also make friends. Perhaps even the alliances you spoke of."

I grabbed a few beers from the fridge. I handed one to Siegfried who had not said a word yet but took the beer. I tossed one to Diantha as well. Then we sat down at the table.

"Ok, who am I forging alliances with?" I asked as I took a deep drink.

"Why, between the High Fae and the others, of course, Demon kind and the Lilin, not to mention the Elves. Much respect was lost for the High Fae during the wars. And Bjartr is a powerful Elf in his own right, although you may not have known it," he said, stroking his beard. "Light Elves are not warriors. They are builders and lovers of all living things. It must have been difficult for him to take up the sword. Nonetheless, he may feel beholden to you after this. A very good start if I do say so myself."

"What, did the High Fae piss everybody off?" I asked, rather sarcastically.

"The more they fought one another the more the other races were affected. Of course the Lilin are a different story, as I have already explained."

"What's the deal about them being Demons? I'd like to hear to hear more about that," I added. "Even the Demon mentioned that they were closer to his kind than ours."

"As would I," Siegfried commented, finally saying something.

"As you wish," he answered. "There is still some time before Lucinda returns." His pipe appeared again, as did a mug. After taking a deep drink he began.

"Much has happened since this world was born. I will tell you more of the tale of the Lilin. This is a long tale and I have told you some of it but I will be brief. When I am finished, you will understand more.

"First, you must know that the Earth we stand on is only one part, or plane, of this world. Think of the various planes as layers. One layer contains mortal kind, another, the Fae, and yet another is the home of the Demons. Between these layers live others as well, such as the Light Elves, and that place that the High Fae once dwelt. All these layers intersect with the plane we now stand on.

"Since the beginning of time many creatures have called this plane home, but few can call this their natural home. One that can is the Lilin. The mother of the Lilin was a mortal turned Demon named Lilith, who was cursed by the true God for her disobedience. Her curse prevented her from having living children. Instead she spawned demon-like creatures who could not survive for long out of the womb. Lilith soon discovered, however, that by blending her spawn with those of mortal men, that both could live, thus the Lilin were able to survive."

"So you're saying she has some demon-like parasite in her?" I asked, stopping him before he could continue.

"Not exactly a parasite, think of it instead as a symbiote. It grants its companion long life and great strength, as well as other powers. The host, in return, locates and supplies blood that it needs to survive," he answered. "You must remember that the first generations of Lilin were spawned directly by Lilith but subsequent generations are the result of a mating of the symbiotes, with the help of a willing, or unwilling, human host."

"A willing host? What would cause someone to freely accept such a creature?" I asked, getting goose bumps at the thought.

"Hmm, a variety of reasons, perhaps most obvious is to escape death. Were you offered such a choice on your deathbed are you sure you know how you would answer? Do not be so quick to judge," he replied. "The end result of the union is of course, a powerful being. Yes, the Lilin are predators but they seldom kill their victims in these times, and as you yourself have witnessed, their feeding results in little pain."

"I guess that's true," I said as I rubbed the spot on my arm.

I had read some of the Lilith mythology. How her children, the Lilin, supposedly waylaid travellers and drank their blood. There was, of course, a lot more to the legend, but knowing what I just heard, and felt, I could understood how the vampire legends had come to be.

Who knew why Delia had chosen such a path. Had she done so willingly, to escape death, or had she been forced to become such a creature? In the end it didn't really matter. I had been close to her and seen no evil there. To be truthful, after thinking about it, it didn't really change how I felt about her, either.

"To continue," Bernd said, snapping me back to the conversation at hand. "The first generation was much more bloodthirsty than their children, true Demons they still were, as well as true predators. When they came into contact with the Fae they found that Fae blood gave them a power hereto not seen from mere mortal blood. Fae blood can be like a narcotic to a Lilin. In some cases it caused fits of madness.

"Needless to say the High Fae did not take kindly to the Lilin feeding on their kind. Bloody battles followed with the High Fae hunting the Lilin to the brink of extinction. Eventually, the children of the original Lilin were able to sue for peace and an agreement was made."

"I remember you mentioning something about Elves, but why didn't they just wipe them out?" I asked, wondering what could have caused them to back down.

"Well," he answered, "in truth, the High Fae were more like true Gods in those times. Remember, it was not until the Fae themselves were targeted that they began their war of genocide."

"But why did they stop?" I asked as I sat down.

"Each subsequent generation of Lilin became less savage. Apparently the blending with mortals had that effect. So they did what most mortals would do in such a situation," he said, once again pausing as he stroked his beard. "They prayed to their gods and Demeter answered, although, in truth, it was only after the Elves intervened. Even then, the Fae were not kind"

"You're kidding," I said, not expecting the power of prayer to be the answer. Without thinking I rubbed the spot on my arm that Delia had fed from. "Ok, so you just gave her my Fae blood. What's that going to do to her?"

"That remains to be seen," he answered, sliding off the chair. He walked into the bedroom and Siegfried and I followed. "Any change?" he asked, looking up at Diantha.

"Her color is returning," she said, getting up from the bed. "She still shows no other signs, my Lord."

Ok, fine, so everyone's a Lord these days, I thought as Bernd jumped on the bed and put his hands over her chest.

"Ahh, it stirs. I believe your blood is healing her. She must rest," he said, getting off from the bed.

"How long is it going to take?" I asked, bending over her. They were right, there was color returning to her cheeks. I put my hand on her head, it was cool, it had been so hot before.

"Who can say?" he answered. "As I have told you, Demon blades are deadly. In her condition even Fae blood is not always a cure. But as I have said, the Lilin appears to be healing her, and your blood is much stronger than regular Fae. As soon as her Lilin recovers she will heal quickly." Bernd turned to Diantha. "You need not watch her anymore. The most dangerous time is when she first feeds. By now she has accepted his blood."

She nodded and then picked up the beer I had tossed her earlier and handed to me. "Thank you, my Lord," she said, leaning over and kissing my cheek. Then she put her lips to my ear. "But I really do prefer wine."

"I'll get you some," I replied. I couldn't help but laugh, she was good. I couldn't tell if there had been a hint of jealousy in her voice or just displeasure at having to watch over Delia as we talked. Either way she'd been careful not to do, or say, anything rash. She also, very subtly, had made her point.

I went back into the kitchen and pulled a bottle of wine from the hallway rack. I opened it and poured her a glass. Bernd was still with Delia, but she and Siegfried had sat down at the table. Siegfried, I knew, was in awe of Bernd, but Diantha, I wasn't sure if she was afraid of him or if he just made her uncomfortable. I had just given Diantha the glass when I heard a commotion in the backyard. Apparently Lucy was back and she wasn't alone.

Chapter 25

I opened the sliding glass door and looked out into the yard. Charlie and Lucy were there with another Dwarf and what could only be a Faerie. She appeared to be the size of a bird and casting a golden light. I could feel their presence but I couldn't tell much else because they were still in the grass next to the trees and even with her light, they remained mostly in shadow.

Charlie separated and ran up to me broadcasting that they were friends. Of course I didn't have to be a Fae to figure that out but, it never hurt to hear it from him. He was, after all, a watchdog, and as Bernd had confirmed, guardian of my lands.

As she set down onto the patio—I could tell it was a she now—I watched as she grew to normal size. Her wings seemed to shrink back into her body as she stepped closer. She was, of course, totally naked. Instantly I stepped onto the patio and pulled a pool towel from a cabinet, wrapping it around her to cover her.

"Thank you, my Lord. I am Elithia," she said as she wrapped the towel around her shoulders.

Even with that she still revealed way too much. I guess I should be getting used to that by now, but at least it was less distracting with the towel. She was, as was all too common with the Fae, drop dead gorgeous. She stepped through the patio doorway and I turned to see who else was here.

He had to be the oldest looking creature I had ever seen, real or imagined. A Dwarf, like Bernd, but shorter, his face like carved stone, weathered and aged, but like Bernd, his eyes sparkled. Dressed in hues of brown and gray he stepped onto the patio and stopped, watching me for a moment. Lucy appeared at his leg. He looked down at her.

"So this is the one, is it?" he asked the cat. He must have been powerful or at least had different magic because I couldn't hear her response. "Hmm, that remains to be seen," he said and then walked past me thru the doorway into the house.

"What was that about?" I asked, but she didn't reply. Cats, go figure.

Charlie was the last one through the door but I still did a quick scan of the yard just to make sure. Seeing, and sensing, no one else, I closed the patio door and stepped back into the kitchen.

I stifled a laugh. Siegfried was, once again, shocked, or I guess I should say awed, as a second Dwarf now stood before him. As for Diantha, she covered it well, but I caught her look before she had a chance to avert her face. Like I had said, she was good, but it didn't take a Fae to smell the whiff of discomfort about her. I wondered what that was about.

"Motgnir," Bernd said, walking up as I came back in. "We welcome you."

The other Dwarf nodded and removed the pack from his shoulders, placing it next to him on the floor. Lucy immediately walked over to it and sat down.

I was a little surprised to see Charlie, who was actually taller than Motgnir, walk over and nudge him in the chest. He seemed to already know him and when the Dwarf reached up and petted him, I knew that, once again, I didn't have the complete picture. Hell, I'd gotten Charlie as a pup and he seemed to know more Fae than I did. Bernd must have noticed my confusion.

"Do not be surprised," he said. "You are not the only descendent of highborn. Artemis herself received her hunting dogs from Pan. This one is of a noble line.

Ok, so now he tells me that Charlie is descended from Fae breeders. Who knew?

"You are sure of this?" Motgnir asked Bernd.

"Indeed, Maria's spell hid him from us but he has acknowledged his lineage," Bernd answered.

"These are the witnesses?" he asked, pointing to Siegfried and Diantha.

Bernd nodded in agreement.

He turned to them. "You have heard his declaration?"

"Yes, Fader," Siegfried replied as he stood up. Diantha just bowed her head.

"Then we will begin." Motgnir said as he picked up his pack. Then he turned to me. "Your claim is recognized," he said as he motioned to Elithia who immediately walked into the bedroom.

"What's going on?" I asked.

"Elithia is a healer, she will see to your charge," he replied. He walked over to Bernd and then the two of them relocated to the living room, I assume, to talk.

I left Siegfried and Diantha still seated at the table and went into the bedroom to see what was going on. As I stepped into the doorway I saw the Faerie leaning over, her back toward me, her hands clasping Delia's face. She turned and looked up at me as I stepped into the room and removed them, stepping back. Seeing that she was still only wearing the towel I had given her I pulled open the closet and removed an old robe and handed it to her.

"Is it your blood she has been given?" she asked as she put it on and then sat back down.

"Yes," I replied, nodding my head. "How is she?"

"See for yourself"

I could now see that Delia's eyes were opening.

"What happened? Where am I?" she asked, groggily. She started to sit up but couldn't quite make it.

"Sorry, dizzy, what's wrong with me?"

Elithia placed her hand on Delia's arm. "You have received the blood of a Fae Lord. It has quickened your healing. No Lilin has received such a gift in millennia, it is very potent and its affect can be overwhelming. Care must be taken. Rest a while and the feeling will pass."

Delia pushed her head up. "A Fae Lord? What kind of a trick is this?"

"There is no trick," Elithia said, placing a pillow under her head. "Please rest now."

Delia threw her head back and laughed. "A Fae Lord's blood would be a death sentence, if any still lived. And you, are we not enemies? Why does a Fae healer tend to me, does not her oath forbid it?" she asked with a mocking tone.

Elithia looked up at me and then returned her gaze to Delia. "It is not my place to question the will of my Lord. Is it not enough to know that you were injured in battle with his enemies and have been healed at his direction?"

"I have never known the Fae to be so compassionate," she answered, curtly.

So I guess saving someone from Mages and Demons doesn't count much these days, I thought to myself. It was going to be tough to erase the sins of the past. I decided to go back into the kitchen and ask Siegfried about her clothes.

He stood up and headed out to his SUV to retrieve them as I sat down next to Diantha.

"Are you alright?" I asked. "You don't seem too thrilled with the company."

She stifled a grin. "I do not trust the Dwarves," she said. "And you should be not either." She glanced over at the two and placed a finger to her lips.

I peered over at Bernd and Motgnir, now speaking in hushed voices in the other room.

"We can discuss it later," I said, "but for now I'm kinda committed."

"As you say, my Lord, but take care," she replied, a look of concern on her face.

I thought about saying more but Siegfried returned with the clothes he had secured for Delia. He held the bag out to me and I squeezed Diantha's hand before taking it and returning to the bedroom.

This time, Delia was sitting up and talking loudly. Elithia looked frustrated. "...I don't care! Do you realize the position I've been put in? ...and Fae blood? Just who is this Fae Lord?"

Elithia looked up as I entered the room. "Perhaps it would be better to hear it from him," she answered as she stepped away from the bed.

Delia turned to see who she was talking about. "You!" she cried out. "Bjartr was right. I would have healed fine on my own! What game are you playing?"

"I'll take it from here," I said to Elithia. "Oh, look upstairs in the middle bedroom, you should find some of my daughter's clothes there, they might be more comfortable than just a robe."

She bowed her head and left the room.

"Just a thought," I said as I walked up to Delia and placed the bag of clothes on the bed. "I figured you could use these. I didn't think anything here would fit so I had Siegfried bring some clothes from your place."

She looked even more shocked. "What have you dragged me into? I should have fled and left you to fend for yourself." Her head drooped and I saw tears well up in her eyes.

"But you didn't," I replied, "and that's got to count for something."

"At what cost, you fool. Do you not remember the words? I do and they burn in my mind.

"Lay down your arms, life I will grant you, but expect not kindness. Where Fae be you must flee and to taste of ichor is forbidden. Where three or more gather, except to hear my words, I will call down my wrath. One in ten may bear life. This I offer, but no more, and death to any that violate this decree. Bound by the blood of your tears it shall be.

"I know them, Fae, and by saving me you have sentenced me to death and place my kind in jeopardy."

Ouch, Bernd hadn't mentioned that part. Before I could say anything in response she grabbed the bag I had brought in and looked inside.

"I am well enough to get dressed," she said and I turned away to give her some privacy. A moment later I heard her behind me. "So, who's this supposed Fae Lord that you work for?"

"That would be me," I said, turning around to face her.

This time she was actually speechless for a moment. "You? What kind of Fae Lord are you?" she finally inquired.

I was just about to answer when I heard Bernd's voice instead.

"He would be the Fae Lord that saved your life," Bernd said as he entered the room.

Like the others had, she fell to her knees. "Father Swart Elf, I meant no disrespect. It was just that..."

He interrupted her. "It was just that you believed him to be as the other Fae you have met, or at least many of them. There is no shame in this," Bernd said, taking her hands and helping her up. "Particularly in light of past experience."

"Then why, father? I admit I thought he meant to trick me. But what has changed? Why does this Fae act as he does?" she asked, looking over at me, the confusion still evident on her face. "He violates his own God's words with such deeds. It would be better I die than the war begin again. Surely you know this."

Bernd walked back over to me. "That would be true," he replied, "if before you stood any other." He grabbed my arm. "Allow me to introduce you to Robert, High Fae and Demeter's heir." Then Bernd winked at me and left the room.

Oops, she was speechless again, but I knew that wouldn't last, just wonderful.

"It was said that the High Fae were no more. Why all the deception?" she asked, recovering. She stood there with her arms crossed, not in a defiant posture, more like a *what the hell is going on?*' kind. "Tell, me please, what is this about? Why does a High Fae go against his own kind's words? What do you want of the Lilin? I ask you again, what has changed?"

I walked over to the bed and sat down. How to answer? "Well, it's kind of complicated," I finally said, "and that's a lot of questions."

"Everything with the Fae is complicated," she stated in response.

Screw it, maybe I better keep it simple. "Look, it's like this. As far as I am concerned, the Lilin are free. I guess I've got to make it official, but your people are no longer bound by, what did you call them, Demeter's words?"

Well, at least I hope that's true, I thought.

"I'd hope we'd become allies rather than enemies, but there's no strings attached, ok?"

She just stared at me for a moment before responding. "Just like that?"

"Pretty much," I answered. "Yep."

"Then why the deception, and why me? Why didn't you just go to the Elder?"

"The Lilin have an Elder that's in charge?" I asked.

"Yes, why don't you know this? Just what kind of High Fae are you that you know so little about us yet say you will set us free?"

Damn, a "what are you" question again. I hate those.

This was getting too complicated, I shook my head. "Look, that's too much to get into right now, so here's the deal, I don't think you or your people, Lilin, or whatever you call yourselves, should be slaves or treated like that anymore. Hell, I think that's true for everyone if you must know. Why I feel that way doesn't really matter. Besides, you jumped in when the Mages attacked. I appreciate that, so I'm responding in kind. As to your Council, never heard of them and I'd prefer to deal with you. Fair?"

Once again she didn't answer right away. "You are the strangest Fae I have ever met," she finally said in an astonished voice.

"I get that a lot," I murmured. "So do we have a deal?"

"Were it not for the Swart Elf I would think this a Fae trick. But if you speak true then I do not know how to thank you. And yes, I will convey your words to my Elder and my people."

"We must go," Bernd interrupted. He motioned to Delia. "You are well enough? It would be best if you came with us."

"As you wish, Father. This one's blood has healed my wounds. Where are we going?" she asked, bowing to the dwarf.

Bernd let out a laugh. "Why to witness the return of the High Fae, of course. Come, come, you are needed." With that said, he waved with his hands and Delia and I followed him into the kitchen where the others were waiting.

Chapter 26

"This is your wish then?" Motgnir asked me as Delia and I entered the room.

I assumed he meant my position on the Lilin.

"It is," I answered.

He turned to Delia. "And what say you, Lilin?"

She paused as she looked at the second Dwarf. "If this is true then I will gladly bring him to the Elder," she answered.

"You must speak for your kind. Do you accept this Fae's words?" Motgnir asked, his hands on his hips.

As he spoke, Bernd walked up to her and took her hand. "Fate has placed you here, Delia. Do not be afraid to seize an opportunity when it presents itself. Besides, were it not for you, none of this would have occurred," he said.

I could tell she was surprised at that and wanted to ask more, but Motgnir interrupted. "You must decide," he said.

I saw Bernd squeeze her hand.

Delia looked over at the other Dwarf and shrugged. "Agreed, then," she replied.

The Dwarf then raised his hand. "Then we will begin," he declared and walked into the backyard.

"We must go with Motgnir," Bernd said as he motioned for us to follow the other Dwarf.

Siegfried, Diantha and Elithia headed for the doorway with Charlie and Lucy right behind them.

"What are we doing?" I asked Bernd as they headed for the backyard.

"To do what must be done," he answered.

That sounded ominous but then he laughed and I saw a twinkle in his eyes. What the hell, I thought to myself and then followed him into the yard, Delia at my side.

I caught up with Siegfried and gave him a nudge. "You ok?"

"It is much to take in. The Dwarves are sacred to my line, and to meet two..." he said, stumbling over his words.

Diantha just rolled her eyes.

"Don't worry about it. I kinda know how you feel," I said to him as we reached the oak tree in the yard.

Motgnir stood in front of it, watching me and waiting. Elithia, now in Faerie form, flitted around the tree. The rest of us stopped in front of him. He took a moment and looked at us, then he raised his arm and touched the tree, and then we were somewhere else.

This was nothing like my first trip with Meredith. Bolts of electricity were shooting through my body. I felt weak at the knees and had to bend over. It passed quickly but if I ever had any doubt as to what, or who, I had become, I certainly didn't anymore. Every fiber in my body sang. What a rush that had been!

I looked down and saw that I was once again in my Fae persona. Relieved, I also saw that I was still wearing clothes. What was different about this trip? Still bent over I looked around the room we had appeared in.

I'm not sure what I expected but it wasn't this. Maybe it was the dust, or the gloom, but wherever we were it was old and smelled like it, too. It took a moment for my eyes to adjust. We were in some kind of amphitheater, no, that's not quite right, maybe a temple then.

Funny, I didn't sense anyone besides the eight of us. Then I saw something that caused me to do a double take. I could see Charlie next to Bernd and next to him was what had to be a panther. Was that Lucy? Damn, maybe I should start calling her Lucinda again.

The floor was littered with stones as if the place was slowly falling apart. In the center looked like what may have once been a raised pool, now empty. Just off that to one side stood what must have been a dais. I looked around to see more, the sides were raised and the open ceiling was supported by columns. There were seats carved into the stone between them. I counted twelve, with one more ornate than the rest.

The ceiling was open to the sky and I could see it was cloudy. Although to be truthful, I'd never seen clouds like that before. They swirled around like a maelstrom. I turned back toward the larger seat. Was that a throne? No, it couldn't be. Wait, was this Olympus?

It must be, or at least had been. There was something else, the magic, it was different here. More powerful, yes, but almost as if it was distant, muted. I could barely sense our group. I knew they were here but it was if there was a veil between us. Strange, it reminded me of some kind of privacy curtain out of a sci-fi story.

"Are you alright?" Siegfried asked.

I straightened up, and then did another double take; Siegfried had changed as well. "Yeah, fine, caught me off guard for a moment," I replied. It was the same Siegfried, of course. He just looked a little younger, and stronger for that matter.

He tapped my shoulder and then pointed at Motgnir, who with Bernd had moved next to the dais. "They appear to have forgotten us for the moment."

I looked over at where he was pointing; the two Dwarves deep in discussion.

Diantha and Delia were still next to me, looking confused. I turned to them. "You ok?" I asked.

"I have never been to any of the Fae lands before but this is not what I expected," Delia replied. "This is...disconcerting. I am not sure what to think. Where are we?"

Shaking her head, Diantha answered for me. "Olympus, this was Olympus," she said with a hint of sadness in her voice.

Out of the corner of my eye I spotted movement and noticed that Elithia, back in her Faerie form, was flitting about near the top of the temple. I watched as she went out through an opening, and since we appeared to have been forgotten for the moment, decided to follow her.

"Let's take a look around," I said, cutting between two of the stone chairs to follow her. When I reached the top I saw that the opening led outdoors.

As I started to step through, Diantha grabbed my arm. "Be careful, my Lord, there is something strange about this place," she whispered.

"We'll be ok," I replied and stepped out into the open.

I would have thought the temple would have been the tallest thing here, but it wasn't. We appeared to be on a mountain and the temple itself rested on the side of a peak. Although it was now only a trickle, a waterfall fell to a pool below me, a meadow with grass and trees surrounding it. Nothing was in bloom and the temperature was brisk. It was if winter had clothed itself upon the mountaintop and just settled in.

Elithia had stopped at the far edge of the meadow. I couldn't tell if there was anything past her as it seemed like the peak we were on was in the clouds. Which, I guess, if this was indeed Olympus, made sense.

It must have been beautiful once, I thought to myself as I walked down toward the pool and meadow, stopping on an overhang just above them. Maybe it could be so once again if these weird clouds would get burned away by the sun.

"What has happened here?" Delia asked as she and Siegfried walked up behind me.

"Age, disorder, it doesn't seem like anyone has been here for years," I answered. "The place seems stuck in winter."

"Chaos," I heard Bernd say from behind us. "Not winter, we are surrounded by Chaos, the great void beckons and the magic has fled this place."

I hadn't even heard him approach. "I thought the universe was supposed to have been sprung from Chaos, not return," I commented, wondering if I remembered my Greek mythology correctly

"From whence they came all things return," he answered in typical Bernd form.

"So what are we doing now?" I asked.

"I must apologize," he said. "It has been millennia since this place was last inhabited and much of its power has been lost, or at best, hidden. It will take us time to get things in order."

"What are you trying to get in order?" I asked.

"You will see shortly," Bernd replied and then turned and went back towards the temple.

"Dwarves," I muttered. What the hell had I gotten myself into, I asked myself for the thousandth time?

"Do not worry," Siegfried said as he said as he clasped my shoulder.

Oh well, I was committed anyway.

"Come on," I said to the rest, "let's go see what Elithia is doing." I stepped down and walked around the front of the pool fed by the waterfall. Well, at least this still looked nice, if not cold from the feel of the mist off of the falls.

Crossing the meadow, I approached the diminutive Faerie, who by now had landed on a berm and was looking down at something. As I stepped up to get a better look she heard me and flipped around. Seeing it was me she popped back up to human size and ran towards me. I barely had time to be surprised when I felt her quivering arms around me. Then I felt her tears. She was crying.

Any other time, I suppose having a gorgeous naked woman throw herself at you, Faerie or not, would have to a good thing, but this wasn't one of those times. To say she was upset didn't come close. I tried to comfort her as best I could while still inching forward to see why she was so distraught. She let go of me and slowly turned as what was in front of us came into view.

I heard a gasp from either Diantha or Delia and it took me a moment to understand what I was seeing. At first the field of rocks and unknown artifacts I was looking down at seemed like something out of a twisted artist's idea of a field that needed some serious plowing. Then what I was seeing came into focus and I understood her distress. I'd heard of the wars between the Fae but never thought I'd witness them.

Displayed before us were fields of the dead. Fae and other creatures still laying where they fallen so long ago. There were no victor's here, just withered skin and old bones, calcified and weathered, many still in armor and holding their weapons where they fell. They should have turned to dust by now. Why this place had frozen them in time for us to find I cannot even begin to understand, yet here they were.

I'm not an archeologist, but I was a cop, so there's no surprise in how they died. They died fighting to the man, or Faerie, or Beast. What I couldn't explain was the condition they were in. This had to have happened thousands of years ago and yet they had been preserved in some bizarre way. Must be the magic, I thought to myself as I bent down to examine one such mound.

"Incredible," Siegfried commented as we stared down at the remains. "They should be dust by now."

"That they should," I replied, looking closer.

"What happened here?" Delia asked.

"This was where Loki's armies battled Zeus for control of Olympus," answered Elithia. "It is said that here was the final battle before the Gods faded."

"Faded?" Delia enquired.

"It was *The Fall*," Siegfried added. "The Gods battled one another for dominion and in the end faded from the Earth. Some say that it was Gaea's punishment for squandering their power."

Delia shook her head and looked at me, "Fae," she said with a tone of disgust.

"This was a long time ago, don't judge me by what happened here," I said, trying to look closer. "Besides, Lil history is savage as well.

"Perhaps," she said, "but at least we didn't battle one another to such a large scale." Her point made, she turned and walked away from the field.

I went back to my examination. I could tell this one had been some kind of Fae warrior. Although his skin was shrunken and clung to the bone, it had obviously been a human-shaped individual. There was a helmet the color of dull gold on his head and he wore armor of the same metal. His sword was still in what was left of his hand, and I could tell that the blade had seen much use even in its worn and weather-beaten condition.

Next to him was a fossilized horse-shaped creature, and upon closer examination, I saw the remains of a horn type protuberance on its head. This must have been a unicorn. I couldn't believe it—they were real.

Something drew me back to the warrior. As I wondered who he had been, it almost felt like I could feel the rush of battle. The air seemed to get thicker as I stared at him and wondered who or what had killed him. I don't know what came over me, but I reached out towards him and placed my hand on what was left of his face.

There was a sound of thunder. For a moment, I thought I was losing it as images and scenes of battle rushed through my head. It lasted only for an instant but then it felt like someone had pulled all the energy out of me.

I saw a flash and the next thing I knew both Siegfried and I were thrown onto our backs. I looked to where the warrior had been and was almost blinded by lightning flashing down on the spot. The clouds above swirled faster as the ground blazed with the strikes. Suddenly there was a flash of pure flame and with a loud crack the clouds cleared and the maelstrom dissipated.

"What the..." was all I could say. I glanced over at the others.

"Unbelievable," Siegfried commented as he brushed dust off his shirt.

"Well that should convince them," Diantha said with a laugh as she got up from the ground a few feet from me. "Look at what your magic has done."

I started to say something when everything began to change. There was a rumble and the earth moved. I watched as what was once the dead Fae warrior began to crumble and sink into the ground. Then the process continued outward, touching each mound as it progressed. It was like what had happened to Diantha. Whatever had frozen this place in time was receding. Olympus was being reborn.

We watched in wonder as the effect spread outward and the mounds disappeared and grass returned. Trees and shrubs appeared as if seen through a time lapse video and I felt the sun on my skin. Within moments the mounds were gone as far as the eye could see. Surprisingly, a few weapons remained, including the sword of the Fae I had touched.

"What just happened?" Delia asked as she stood up.

"I believe he just did," answered Siegfried, pointing at me.

"Do you see now, my Lord?" Diantha pronounced as she swept her arms around. "Who but a God could do such a thing?"

"Let's not jump to conclusions," I answered, thinking she was going to be the death of me. I was going to reply when it hit me. The air was no longer as heavy and my senses less muted, but what I felt most was evil. It was the same feeling I'd had before the battle at Danu's.

"Find a weapon!" I yelled, turning to see where the danger would come from. There was nothing in sight.

"What is it?" Siegfried asked, pulling his seax.

"Something's wrong." I walked over and grabbed the sword the fallen Fae had carried. It was no longer worn and dull, its luster had been restored and it looked as if it had just been forged. "Diantha, can you use a weapon?" I didn't bother asking Delia, I'd seen her swordplay. She was already running toward something lying in the field and I saw her reach down and pick up what looked like a bow.

"I am no warrior," Diantha answered.

"Then look for arrows."

She didn't hesitate this time but started searching through the grass.

By now Siegfried had found a sword as well. He walked over to me. "Where is the danger?"

"Back toward the temple," I answered.

"Can you tell what we are up against?"

"No, it's like something, or maybe someone, is blocking it, same as last time. I only know it's here."

Delia had come back with the bow and a sword as well. "Danger seems to follow you, Fae," she said.

"So it appears."

Diantha chose that moment to come back. She was carrying a dozen or so undamaged arrows. "Will these do?" she asked.

Delia took them from her and examined them. "They will suffice," she said as she placed them in a leather holster she had also found.

I turned back to Diantha. "You ever fire a gun?"

"A few times, my Lord."

I knelt down and took my Walther from its holster. "Here," I said as I handed her the gun. I pointed to the safety and toggled it. "Just make sure this is switched up before you use it."

I watched as she took it. I was a little worried. She didn't look that confident. "Listen," I added, "stay behind us and find a place to hide when we get closer. And be careful with that thing, you only have seven shots."

Well, we were as ready as we would ever be. Wait, where was Elithia? "Anybody seen the Faerie?" I asked.

The others shook their heads. I knew I hadn't seen her after I touched the ancient Fae but I had no clue to where she'd gone. I also knew we weren't safe where we were.

"We'll just have to keep an eye out for her then." I said as I started back towards the temple.

Siegfried took the lead and headed up the rise to where Elithia had first stopped. As he approached the berm he fell to his knees and signaled that something was in front of him. Damn, why didn't my magic come into focus?

I told Delia and Diantha to stay put and crawled up to his position. He signaled me that there were three somebodies ahead of us. I took a quick peek. Shit, Mages again. They weren't coming our way, but they were at the now rushing waterfall, blocking our way back to the temple. Damn, where were the Dwarves, where were the animals? I couldn't believe they'd just give up. No, I was missing something, again. I motioned to Siegfried and we slid back down to the others.

I turned to Delia who was fingering the bow.

"You any good with that thing?" I asked. I figured she must know a little as she had already nocked an arrow.

"I can hold my own, Fae," she answered.

"Good, I hope you feel like some payback because there's three Mages over the hill and I'm guessing we've met their type before."

"If these arrows will hurt them then I can take one or two out."

"These are High Fae weapons or they wouldn't have survived. They will defeat most magic as well as kill," he answered. "If you can take two I can put down the third, if I can get close enough. If we are skillful, the others may not know what is happening," Siegfried said, leaning in

"Whoa, what about me, I'm supposed to be the High Fae here, remember?" That was assuming, of course, that my magic started working better than my senses had been doing.

"It is you they will be after, besides, there will be more...no, better to keep them in the dark for as long as possible. Once we eliminate these three we can make for the temple."

"Fine, we'll go with your plan. Once these three are down we'll rally just this side of the waterfall, out of view from the temple. I don't know about the Dwarves, but Charlie and Lucinda wouldn't just sit back while these guys ambush us, so watch for them as well. Diantha, you stay behind me and keep an eye out for Elithia." I wasn't happy, but it made sense. I just hoped my magic would kick in gear when I needed it.

She nodded her assent as Siegfried and Delia started moving up the hill. Then she moved closer. "Remember, my Lord, if need be, I cannot die," she whispered.

I considered what she said. "I hope you're right, but there's a lot of strange magic here and I'd rather not test that again just yet," I whispered, remembering her bout with the Were-creature.

"I knew you cared," she whispered in my ear, adding a kiss as we followed Siegfried and Delia up the hill.

I stopped a few feet down from the two of them. I watched as Delia placed two extra arrows at her side and then, with bow ready, waited for Siegfried.

He looked down at me and I nodded. Looking over at Delia he nodded again and with a quick look she loosed two arrows as Siegfried jumped up and went over the berm, seax and sword in hand. Damn they were quick.

Delia hadn't been boasting about her prowess with a bow, either. Two Mages were down with arrows in their chests and Siegfried was already pulling the Seax from the third when I caught movement out of the corner of my eye. A fourth Mage had come from around the waterfall, but before he could raise his wand or call out, a black shape pounced on him. It was Lucinda. We didn't need to worry about him revealing us to anyone. She had ripped his throat out.

Siegfried and Delia started moving bodies out of view and I watched as Lucinda dragged hers to their position. I caught up with them behind the waterfall with Diantha not far behind me.

Lucinda turned to me, tail twitching from side to side. "Five more," I heard her say in a slightly deeper whisper than I was used to. "Charlie watches," she added a moment later.

"What about the Dwarves?"

"They cannot interfere," she replied.

"Dwarves, did I not warn you?" Diantha muttered behind me.

This time I agreed with her.

"Can't interfere, why not?" I asked, incredulously. What the hell was going on? I mean besides me discussing strategy in the middle of a battle with a panther? Her large head looked directly at me, her eyes wide and glinting in the new found sunlight.

"It is forbidden. I believe the other one is like you. We must do this alone," she growled lowly so the others couldn't hear and then moved to the pool to take a drink.

Like me? Shit! I wasn't sure if I was ready for this confrontation, not that I had a choice. If the other one like me was another High Fae I could only hope that his powers were as muted as mine in this place. We needed a plan, fast. With the dead Mages safely tucked out of view for the moment we huddled behind the rock wall next to the waterfall to discuss our next move.

Chapter 27

"Ok, things just got complicated," I said. "Lucinda, do they know you're here?"

"I do not believe so. Charlie was with the Dwarves when they appeared but I was behind the thrones and came to warn you." she answered, her tail swishing back and forth.

I turned back to the others.

"We defeated these four easy enough," Delia boasted. "What is different?"

"The other one may be a High Fae," I answered.

"What of it, you are here as well. We are at worst evenly matched," Delia snickered.

"I agree," Siegfried chimed in. "We are indeed evenly matched. While not of our choosing, this may be our best chance to defeat him."

"Maybe, but even with the clearing of the skies something about this place is still obscuring my magic. I can't sense much and that worries me."

"Well," he said, "there has been no counter attack so perhaps their magic will also be obscured."

"We can only hope," I answered. I turned to Delia. "Come here a minute," I said, leading her around the rock wall until we were out of sight of the others. "How are you doing?"

"I can hold my own."

"I'm sure you can, and while and I'm sure Fae blood works wonders it can't last forever, not as badly wounded as you were. I need you at your best." I started rolling up my sleeve. I watched as her eyes widened and then she backed away.

"No, I will be fine. I don't need your blood, Fae."

"Don't be an idiot," I said. "I got you into this mess so the least I can do is try to help you survive." I pulled her closer to me and held out my arm. "Take it."

Her green eyes stared into mine as she moved her mouth to my arm. The look she got as she took in my blood was almost erotic. After a minute or so I pulled my arm away. Hesitantly, she let go.

"Mmm...," she purred. "I see now why this was forbidden, Fae."

Oh, great, and I was setting them free.

She looked up at me and smiled. "Fortunately, we are not the same Lil as those your ancestors fought against."

"I'd love to discuss this later," I said, pulling down my sleeves, "but we've got a battle to win. You ready?"

"Oh, yes," she answered, glowing with the strength the Fae blood had given her. Still fingering her bow, we rejoined the others.

"How do you wish to proceed?" Siegfried asked as we approached.

Wait a minute, wasn't he the warrior? Another disadvantage to being the King, you have to make all the decisions. I was just about to come up with a brilliant plan when Charlie appeared, almost knocking me over as he ran up to greet me. My face wet, I pushed him away.

"Charlie, down. What's happened?"

He stayed close and once again I heard him in my head as he spoke. "Danger, she waits, Bernd says must come."

Wow, that's the most I'd ever heard him speak. Wait, did he say *she*?

"Charlie, did you say, she?"

"She," he repeated. "Bad, danger, Bernd says must come."

I heard a guttural growl from Lucinda and then looked at the others.

"It matters not," Siegfried commented. "God or Goddess, we are committed to battle."

"True," I noted. "Ok, she knows we're here and she's gotta know we already took out a few of her Mages. If Bernd sent Charlie to get us I don't see any reason to use stealth, we're just going in. Siegfried, how many entrances to that temple do you remember?"

"At least twelve, one between each throne. What are you thinking?"

"Well, I'm hoping her powers are as muted as mine. Maybe she can't tell how many of us there are. I wanna go in the same way we came out while you and Delia take the entrances to each side. Charlie will be with me. Lucinda, you pick a spot halfway around. Diantha, can you lay back on the other end and just keep an eye on us? You've got my gun and I'd prefer to keep you two a secret for as long as I can."

She nodded and then gave me a wink. Good.

"I may need a diversion so find a good place but try and keep out of sight."

"You wish to challenge her then?" Siegfried asked, checking the sharpness of the sword he was carrying with his thumb.

"Not necessarily, but I will if I have to. There's a lot going on that we don't know about. I'm hoping to get a few answers before we go to war."

"You cannot trust one as this. We should go in fighting."

Maybe he was right. But I had to think there was more going on here than just another battle. Hell, the dead didn't sink into the earth and the skies clear in this place for nothing.

"No, I don't think so. But that doesn't mean we won't be ready."

I removed my seax and then picked up the Fae sword, Charlie was already at my side. "Ok, let's do it," I said.

Delia had an arrow nocked and Siegfried was armed as I was. Lucinda was already out of sight but as we started around the pool and back to the temple Diantha ran up to me.

"Be careful," she said as she hugged me, "and remember what I said, I will be there when you need me."

"Just don't do anything foolish," I sighed.

"Only if I have to," she countered before sprinting off to the other side of the temple with Lucinda. That girl was gonna be the death of me, I mused.

We halted a few feet from the entrance to the temple. This wouldn't be the first time I'd walked into an unknown situation. Since it was clear I was going to be at a disadvantage, four dead Mages down or not, I took a cue from some past experiences and decided to play it unconventional. I was hoping I could at least keep her off guard long enough to know what I was up against.

"You guys ready?" I asked.

Both Siegfried and Delia nodded.

"Ok, come in after me and just follow my lead. Let me do the talking but be ready for anything. If it comes to force we'll let them make the first move."

With that said, they took off toward their respective entrances and as they reached them, with Charlie at my side, I went in.

The moment I went through the arch I felt something. It reminded me of when I put the jewel on Diantha. There were no tendrils of green magic coming at me but it was almost as if the temple itself was trying to talk to me. I glanced at the stone column, it looked the same. Whatever had happened outside had not made it into here, but yet there was something. It almost seemed like it was waiting for me to wake it up but that didn't make sense, did it?

I'll have to admit I was nervous. Other than another High Fae I had no idea who, or what, we'd be facing. But something had passed between the temple and me, and although I wasn't sure what it was, it gave me comfort. Then the magic kicked in. It wasn't quite like before, less intense, and although it was muted, at least I felt like it was part of me again.

As I passed through the arch I sensed her presence but I also sensed something more. There were six others with her, two Mages and, damn, the other four were Fae. They weren't High Fae of course, but they were still an unknown I'd have to deal with.

I had a second to see our adversaries as I stepped fully into the temple. The two Mages were like the others we'd encountered outside, maybe a little stronger looking, and they carried bows. The Fae reminded me of Siegfried, they were probably warriors as well...and then I saw her on the main floor in front of the Dwarves.

She didn't look like some High Fae Goddess but then again I wasn't the spitting image of Zeus either. She was dressed in leather like and I couldn't see a weapon. Of course that didn't mean she didn't have one or make her any less dangerous, for that matter. She had long dark hair woven into a single braid that reached to her waist. I wouldn't guess her age, but she had to be younger than Meredith. I suppose you could say she was beautiful, as most Fae are, especially with those pointed Elfin ears. But the beauty faded when she turned to face me. Her blue eyes were cold and I could almost feel the hatred as she stared up at me.

"You," she whispered and then turned to the Dwarves. "Surely this is a jest, Motgnir; you cannot have chosen this one over me," she said, gesturing widely.

Interesting, she hadn't known it would be me.

"What'd I miss?" I asked as I took a few more steps.

Like I said, unconventional.

"Sorry I was delayed. I hope you aren't waiting for those other guys, because if you are...well, I don't think they're gonna make it." I may have overdone it a bit.

"I have had enough!" she exclaimed, pointing at Motgnir. "This half-breed is nothing, I claim what is mine."

"He has bested everyone you have thrown against him, Marissa. Besides, he has the stronger claim and is no half-breed, as you should well know," he replied, angrily.

So now I knew her name but what did the rest mean? I watched as she threw her arms up in frustration.

"I have had enough of false rivals and of Dwarves," she said and then she paused. A half smirk came to her face. "Kill him, and then kill them all."

I dodged as two arrows came my way from the Mages. Damn they were fast. One missed me but with my still diminished magic the second one should have hit me. Instead there had been a blur and I heard a yelp. Charlie and taken the arrow, that damn lovable mutt! He was down but at least he was still alive. I didn't have time to check on him any further as I expected more arrows to be coming my way.

I shouldn't have worried. Not seconds had passed and both Mages were down as Delia strung a third arrow in her bow. I watched her start to aim but the two Fae were moving too fast. She dropped it and pulled her sword as Siegfried showed up beside her.

Then I had problems of my own as the other two Fae warriors came towards me. The first one swung at me running and I ducked and stabbed, he was down but the other caught himself and we traded blows for a few seconds. He seemed clumsy and I found an opening, it took a moment but he was no match for my Fae sword.

I didn't think about it at the time but it had to be that whatever had muted the magic had given me an advantage. I think they were surprised that their magic wasn't stronger whereas it was all new to me and I didn't depend on it as they apparently had. That was something to remember for the future. Then again, it could have just been that I was pissed off that Charlie had been hurt. ·

Seeing Siegfried and Delia holding their own I left the other warriors to them and started down the stairs towards Marissa. She pulled a sword from behind her back. Damn, I hadn't even seen it. But her next move was worse. She reached down and grabbed something.

"That's close enough or this one dies," she uttered as I realized that the tiny form she had picked up was actually the Faerie healer, Elithia. "Drop your weapons."

Then Elithia screamed as Marissa held her by the neck and drew her sword closer.

The problem was that I knew that Marissa was serious, which meant that Elithia was already as good as dead and there was nothing I could do about it. On TV, the good guy always puts down his weapon and a moment later miraculously saves the day.

Unfortunately, the real world is somewhat different. I knew that if I dropped my sword or ordered Siegfried and Delia to drop theirs, Marissa would not only have Elithia as a hostage, but us, too. Judging from what I had seen so far, she'd kill us all when she got the chance. Sometimes the real world just sucks. I took a few steps closer. Her sword point moved closer to the Faeries neck.

"Marissa, stop this foolishness," I heard Bernd say.

"I have had enough of you, Dwarf," she jeered, "I tire of your kind and their ways." She cut the Faerie's neck and threw her broken body to the ground. Stepping toward him she raised her sword at both Bernd and Motgnir as she closed the distance.

I started to run towards them but knew I was still too far away to get there in time. Suddenly I heard a shout and then shots rang out; it was Diantha with Lucinda close behind. She had stopped halfway down the steps and fired, the gun still smoking in her hand. Marissa stared down as her leather shirt became stained with blood.

"Whore of Apollo, you shot me," she said with disbelief and then collapsed to the floor. Whatever power she had given to aid the Fae warriors failed at the same instant because, as I watched, Siegfried and Delia incapacitated both their opponents.

I stopped for a second to see if Marissa would heal as I had when fighting the Weres but she didn't move so I immediately ran to Charlie's side. The arrow had pierced his left rear leg in the upper muscle and continued on and grazed the other. He was breathing but didn't seem able to move his legs.

"This is a Fae arrow," I heard Bernd say as he bent down to examine the wound. "Its spell prevents him from moving. Have no fear. As I have said, this one is no ordinary hound."

"Steady boy, it must come out," he said as he reached for the arrow. He placed his other hand on Charlie's chest.

Charlie gave a short bark which I knew meant that he understood and I told Bernd to do it. Grabbing the arrow gently he used both hands to break it on each end and then slid the shaft out of the wound. Blood gushed as Charlie immediately tried to stand. Bernd placed his hand on the wound and it slowed but did not stop completely.

Holding him down I pulled my seax and cut a few long strips from my shirt, binding the wound to stem the bleeding. It wasn't perfect but it'd do until I could get him to a vet or a Fae healer. Then I hugged the big dog and told him thanks. I heard him say "safe" and he began licking my face. Between him and the others there was no one I'd rather be in a battle with. Then the earth began to shake.

I turned to see what was happening and I saw the temple vibrating. No, that wasn't right. It was more like it parts of it had turned molten. The floor on the other side of the pool from Motgnir began to rise and before long a giant figure began to come into focus. It was like watching a mold pour upward and form from the floor. It took a few moments but it slowly coalesced and then the shaking stopped. The giant form had become a huge nude figure of a man some 20 or so feet tall.

Bearded, it reminded me of a statue of a Greek God, although I had no idea which one it could be. Turning its head as its eyes rested on us it began to laugh. Like THX in a movie theater, the walls seemed to reverberate to the sound and the giant's arms came to rest on its hips as it turned its attention in my direction.

"Well played, well played indeed," the creature declared. Then it turned to Motgnir. "You have chosen well, Dwarf."

Not knowing exactly what the hell was going on I started to say something but Bernd put his hand on my shoulder. "Wait," he whispered.

The creature bent down and placed its hand over Marissa. I heard a gasp as she took in breath and her eyes opened. She looked aghast as the creature picked her up.

I watched as she struggled against it but the creature just seemed to examine her.

"Let me down!" she exclaimed, beating at his giant hand.

"I think not, little one. Too much like my other offspring are you." he said, shaking his head. She continued to struggle as he spoke. "You chose the dark path and have been beaten by the light." Then he laughed again and walked a few steps, holding her up as he continued to examine her. "Perhaps you can learn from your opponent. His allies fought for him out of loyalty, not fear.

"But I believe what you need most is time to think about your failure. I will give you that which made me stronger. To Tartarus I will send you," he said in a commanding voice and I saw a look of terror come over her face. "If you escape, you may fight again. If not, well, then perhaps you were not meant to have come this far."

Then a shimmering light surrounded her and with a bright flash she was gone.

"That's it?" I said out loud as she disappeared.

The creature turned its attention back to me. "Disappointed? Today was not her day to die young Fae. I would have done the same for you if it is any consolation"

"Then what was this all about?" I asked.

"A test," he answered, "and you have triumphed. Olympus is awake and I have witnessed your return. Be content with that."

"Content!" I yelled back as I stood up. "My dog just got shot with an arrow. And what about Elithia, the Faerie?" I yelled, pointing down at her broken body still lying on the floor. "Are you gonna bring her back to life as well?"

"She is not my concern," he answered and waved his hand as a throne rose from the floor. Sitting down upon it he looked back at me. "There are as many ways to die as jewels in my crown." He pointed upwards and the sky darkened as the clouds parted and the stars appeared. I watched as several brightened and then faded to be replaced by blackness. "Can you save them all?"

"I can try," I replied. I would have said more but once again Bernd stopped me. I guess that was wise since the giant was three times my size, but still.

"Then perhaps next time it will be you who fails," he commented as he then turned to Motgnir. "Is it not enough that I have thwarted Gaea and given him a godsend? Why must all my children's children be so ungrateful?"

"He is still young and does not understand his role, great Ouranos," Motgnir replied with quick bow of the head. "He still has much to learn."

Oh shit, I thought to myself, Ouranos, also known as Uranus, had been father of the Titans and husband of Gaea. This guy was as close to a real God as they came. That's who I had been arguing with!

Motgnir then removed what looked like a short scepter from beneath the Dais he had been standing behind. He held it outward toward Ouranos with both hands. "He has triumphed, has he not?"

"Indeed he has," he answered, and then with a nod laughed and turned his head towards me. "You have indeed triumphed today, my young Fae Lord. As you have proven yourself, I welcome your return. You have earned the right to fulfill the prophecy, if you can, and I have gifted you some time. Light you may be but the darkness will not be chained forever, even in Tartarus."

He stood and bowed his head at Motgnir. With a nod to me and a wave of his hand the temple vanished and the eight of us now stood where we had started, back in my own backyard.

Chapter 28

"What the hell just happened?" I asked.

Motgnir ignored my question. He held up what I thought had been a scepter but I now saw was the hilt of a sword. He pushed it into my hand.

"Light has triumphed over dark and here is the prize, the sword of Cronus, most powerful of the Titans. This is the same sword that was carried by Zeus and prized by all the Gods. Wield it wisely. The prophecy has been fulfilled. The High Fae have returned and the light is now a beacon against the coming darkness," he answered.

"Well ain't that just dandy," I replied sarcastically. Sorry, but I was pissed. "You don't think maybe a word or two about what was going on might not have been prudent? Maybe Elithia wouldn't be dead and Charlie wouldn't have taken an arrow if we'd have known what we were getting into."

I waved the sword hilt; suddenly the sword itself emerged like some magic metal version of a light saber. Startled, I almost dropped it. "And this...maybe a warning about what the damn thing does would have been nice!" I put my arm down and watched as the sword retracted into the hilt. I guess I should be more grateful, I mean, we had won and all, or at least I think we did.

"You have been among the humans for far too long," he said. "Elithia died a noble death and will shine among the stars. As for your hound," he continued, walking over to Charlie, "this I do in answer."

He bent down and grabbed the big dog's leg between both hands. Charlie's leg began to glow and when Motgnir stood back up, the leg was healed. "Not since the Gods last walked this earth have I done such a thing. I will not do so again. I have done what I must; the rest is up to you.

"As for you Robert, you have earned the sword, but the war is not yet over. You have allies and weapons but there is still much that you must overcome." He walked back to the oak tree and turned to Bernd. "I leave it to you to teach them further, I have fulfilled my pledge."

There was a flash and he was gone.

Siegfried and Diantha just stood there but Delia threw down her sword. "Fae, you have too many Gods and too many problems," she said with a note of disgust as she looked over at Bernd. "Tell me the truth, Dwarf, does his promise of freedom still stand?"

"Robert has pledged it," he replied with a nod.

"What if the other had triumphed?" she asked as she fingered the string of her bow, her arrows still sheathed.

"Then it would have been short lived," he answered.

"I thought as much," she commented and then slung the bow across her back. "I wish to take my leave for now. Siegfried, can you return me to Danu's?"

"I can," he answered. "We have had enough excitement for one evening. There is still much to discuss but tomorrow is another day." He bent down and patted Charlie and Lucinda, who was by now back in cat form. "You both fought well."

Charlie gave him a few licks and Lucinda purred as he straightened back up.

"Diantha, will you ride back with us?"

"I'll give her a ride," I answered before she could respond.

"That will be fine," she said.

"Before you go," Bernd chimed in. "You are all owed an explanation. There is still much to explain, but this I will tell you now: You have fought bravely, and because of your actions the light has prevailed. Although I had not foreseen Ouranos' additional gift of time by his imprisonment of Marissa, there is still danger. She may be imprisoned but the darkness has not been defeated. Her allies will not take kindly to her confinement, temporary or not."

He walked up to each of us and took our hands (or paws) in his, nodding in thanks as he did so. Then he turned to me.

"Prior to Apollo seizing the temple at Delphi, it belonged to the Titans. These were the daughters of Gaea and Ouranos." He looked over at Diantha for a moment before continuing. "When he slew the dragon that guarded it, the Oracle at Dodona foretold that as punishment for his heresy, Gaea had decreed that the Gods, whom she already saw had become petty and corrupt, would consume themselves in darkness. This much you can see has come true.

"As the story goes, one Fae, a Dryad, prayed to Gaea for forgiveness as the battles between the Gods threatened not just hers, but all the races. Gaea is said to have appeared before her in a grove of oak, and this particular Fae offered her life if Gaea would only spare her people.

"Gaea, moved by this gesture, told this Dryad that, in time, she would see that the High Fae return. But, when such time arose, she warned, the Fae would have to make a choice—light or dark. Whichever triumphed would decide their future."

"Why would she do that?" I asked. It didn't seem to make sense.

"Who can know her mind?" he shrugged. "Gods are fickle and their desires do not always coincide with those of their creations. But I believe she offers us a choice, a chance to restore the honor of the Fae, or, if we fail and the darkness prevails, then the dark Fae's thirst for power will set fire to the human world as sure as it burns those of the Fae. Remember, she is a God and can always start over."

"Heaven or hell. Just dandy," I sighed.

"A human concept, but in this case it may describe the situation accurately. But enough for one night, we will talk more of this tomorrow. Know that you have proven yourself and that the return of the High Fae has stemmed the darkness, if even for only a short time. You should all get some rest, you have earned it."

"Fine, I've had enough for today," I said in reply. "Delia, will you join us tomorrow to discuss this further?"

"I will," she answered, "if you will still meet with the Elder as well as proclaim our freedom to the rest of the Fae."

I nodded in the affirmative and then we stood up and walked out to Siegfried's SUV to say our goodbyes. Siegfried stopped in front of the driver's door and clasped my hands.

"Thank you for everything, my friend," I said, and then hugged him.

"Thank you," he answered, removing his Fae sword and putting it into the SUV. "Until tomorrow, then."

"Until tomorrow," I repeated and then walked around the vehicle.

"Delia, thank you as well. I am sorry to have dragged you into this but I'm glad you were there. We wouldn't have made it without your help."

"Then we are even," she replied as she got into the passenger side. "We will talk again soon," she said as she pulled the door closed.

She hadn't sounded happy but I probably wouldn't have been either had the roles been reversed. At least she had agreed to come back. Siegfried started the Escalade and Diantha and I watched as he drove out towards the street.

Charlie and Lucinda had disappeared so we walked back into the house alone. Diantha sat down at the table and I started a pot of coffee.

"There is one more thing," Bernd said as he walked over and placed a crystal bottle on the table in front of me. It was cloudy in color but I could tell it held 4 or 5 ounces of a thick, red liquid. The stopper was sealed with what appeared to be wax. "You will need this if you truly plan to free the Lilin."

"What is it?" I asked.

"When the Lilin surrendered to the Fae, Demeter collected their tears." He picked up the bottle and swirled the contents as he held them up in front of me.

"The Lilin cry tears of blood. This vessel contains one tear from every Lilin that survived that day, their oath to the Fae bound by the tears in this bottle. When opened by you, they will be released from their bond." He handed me the bottle.

"Keep it safe, and tell no one until you are ready to use it. We will talk more of this," he said as he walked towards the back door. Then he just vanished.

I stared at the bottle for a moment and then glanced at Diantha. She didn't say anything so I went into my office and put the bottle into the safe and then ran upstairs to put on a clean shirt.

Returning to the kitchen I saw that the coffee was done. I reached into the cabinet and pulled out a *Hitchhiker's Guide to the Galaxy* mug with an emblazoned number 42 on it and filled it. Taking a sip I leaned back against the counter and just looked at her. There was one more thing that I had to do.

"Anything you want to add?" I asked, not forgetting that Marissa had called her Apollo's whore.

"Well," she began, "he grew his balls back."

I would have spilled my coffee if I wasn't so angry.

"She knew you," I countered, ignoring her reference to Cronus cutting off Ouranos' testicles and scattering the bits in the ocean.

She looked to one side as if she was embarrassed. "I didn't recognize her at first, but when I saw her face it startled me. You're right, I had met her before. But it's not what you think."

I didn't say a word for a moment or two. I just stood there, sipping my coffee. "Convince me," I finally said.

She stood up and began to pace in front of the table, pausing every now and then to see my reaction. "It was 40 or 50 years ago, before I found the job in Pahrump. I was in Vegas working as a masseuse. Times were different then, and it was still a small town, nobody asked too many questions. She showed up one day and confronted me in the parking lot of my apartment. She knew who I was."

"What did she want?" I asked as I reached out with my magic to look for deception.

"She was looking for Fae," she said, and then her tone changed. "Fine, I knew she was evil and, no, it didn't matter, but that doesn't mean I trusted her. She offered to return my beauty but I could tell it was a lie. Anyway, I convinced her I was hiding and the last thing I wanted to find was a Fae.

"She acted like she might believe me but I didn't stick around to find out. I'm not supposed to be able to die, but she frightened me. I am no coward but there are things worse than death. So I disappeared for a while and then wound up where you found me. I never saw her again until today."

"For what it's worth, my Lord, I'd hear rumors now and then, people disappearing, most likely Fae from their descriptions. That's why I was so nervous when you showed up." She sat back down. "That's all I know. I stayed away from everyone until you came along. I hope that helps."

I pulled out the chair next to her and sat down. Diantha's information was disturbing. As best I could tell she was being truthful. I knew Diantha had her own agenda, but I think Marissa had frightened her. And she was right; there were things worse than death. Besides, she saved our ass back there and had proven herself. No, something else was bothering me.

What had Marissa been doing in Vegas 40 or so years ago? Was she looking for Fae in general or was she searching for a particular Fae? Had she possibly been searching for me, or maybe my parents? Once again I didn't have enough information. But if she had had anything to do with my parent's death, even Tartarus wasn't safe for her. I banged my cup on the table, spilling coffee.

I didn't move as Diantha stood and fetched a towel and then cleaned the spill without a word. Then I felt her warm hand caress my cheek.

"I am sorry to have disturbed you so, my Lord."

That got my attention. "No, I'm the one that should be sorry, for doubting you," I said as I reached up and clasped her hand. "You really came through tonight. If you hadn't shot her when you did it could have been a lot different, I owe you one."

"Well then," she replied in a mischievous tone. "In that case I know just what you can do to thank me." She began to unbutton her blouse. After a few buttons were loose she wrapped her arms around my neck again.

"There is so much that we can do before tomorrow," she whispered as she kissed me.

To hell with it, I thought. It'd been a long day, and worrying about things wasn't going to change the past, or the future.

"You're right," I said with a smile as I returned her kiss.

Let's face it, what good is being with an Oracle if you're not going to heed her advice?

The End

About the Author

A former computer forensics expert and web site designer, Tom Keller is a retired police sergeant now working as a defense investigator. He lives in Las Vegas, Nevada with his family, two dogs, and a cat. This is his first novel; he is currently working on the second book in the Vegas Fae series.

Social Media:

http://www.facebook.com/tomsbooks

http://twitter.com/dryadsgarden

Email:

tom@tomsbooks.com

Made in the USA
Charleston, SC
05 August 2012